The Rejected Writers' Book Club

Center Point
Large Print

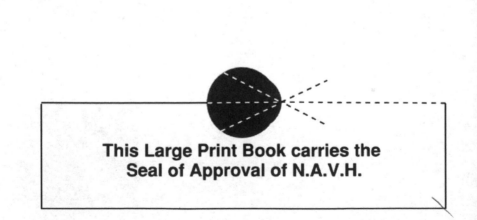

**This Large Print Book carries the
Seal of Approval of N.A.V.H.**

The Rejected Writers' Book Club

A SOUTHLEA BAY NOVEL

Suzanne Kelman

CENTER POINT LARGE PRINT
THORNDIKE, MAINE

This Center Point Large Print edition
is published in the year 2016 by arrangement with
Amazon Publishing, www.apub.com.

Originally published in the United States
by Amazon Publishing, 2014.

This is a work of fiction.
Names, characters, organizations, places, events,
and incidents are either products of the author's
imagination or are used fictitiously.

The text of this Large Print edition is unabridged.
In other aspects, this book may vary
from the original edition.
Printed in the United States of America
on permanent paper.
Set in 16-point Times New Roman type.

ISBN: 978-1-68324-037-2

Publisher's Cataloging-In-Publication Data
(Prepared by The Donohue Group, Inc.)

Names: Kelman, Suzanne.
Title: The Rejected Writers' Book Club / Suzanne Kelman.
Description: Center Point Large Print edition. | Thorndike, Maine :
Center Point Large Print, 2016.
Identifiers: LCCN 2016018534 | ISBN 9781683240372
    (hardcover : alk. paper)
Subjects: LCSH: Women librarians—Washington (State)—Fiction. |
Book clubs (Discussion groups)—Fiction. | Female friendship—Fiction.
| Self-actualization (Psychology)—Fiction. | Large type books. | San
Francisco (Calif.)—Description and travel—Fiction.
Classification: LCC PS3611.E464 R45 2016 | DDC 813/.6—dc23

Dedicated to Matthew & Christopher,
my soul supporters.

No man is a failure who has friends.

—*It's a Wonderful Life*

Chapter One

TYRANTS & TRASH CANS

"Come and live in the country; you won't regret it!" The advertisement in a glossy real estate periodical implored us. The glowing photo that accompanied the ad brazenly flaunted a charming timber-framed blue cottage adorned with whimsical white shutters and stunning window boxes brimming with gorgeous pink geraniums.

"Amazing beaches, rolling farmlands, and the enchanting village of Southlea Bay, voted 'Best of the Northwest,' are just minutes from your doorstep . . ." Then, to keep us firmly on the hook, the ads on the opposite page displayed a splashy chocolate-box vista of this dream property, complete with a velvety-eyed deer nibbling clover from a dew-kissed English country garden.

As the advertisement freely extolled the property's other wondrous virtues, all that was missing was a photo of a double rainbow and a host of heralding angels.

We had drooled over this spectacular sight as giddy empty nesters from California, and we went barreling over to view the house the minute our feet had left the local ferry. We were itching to snatch up this "hard to believe it's still on the market" three-bedroom wonder with its adjoining rustic five acres.

To clinch the deal, the real estate agent, wearing a flowery apron, enthusiastically opened the quaint Dutch doors as the aroma of freshly baked apple pie wafted out from the limed oak kitchen.

We were toast.

What I never realized as we practically fell over each other to put an offer in on our fantasy abode was that to live in the country also meant the country lived with you.

It didn't take long to experience the less-mentioned joys of "country living" at its finest.

We have successfully fought off a plague of termites, a swarm of hornets, a gang of carpenter ants, and an attack of crazed moths. We encountered rats in the basement, bats in the attic, and mice in the pantry. We've saved nests of baby bunnies, countless injured birds that seemed to want to fly kamikaze-like at our windows, and one dazed, wayward turkey that limped into our yard. We keep pest control on our speed dial because, as we have found, taking care of the "country" is practically a full-time job.

On a balmy evening in the fall five years later, I opened the back door and sighed deeply. It was clear that once again we had received a visit from one of Mother Nature's rascally rodents. Mangled mounds of leftovers and sloppy piles of food scraps, all remnants of dinners gone by, were heaped haphazardly across my once perfectly manicured lawn. It was now barely recognizable as the carefully coiffed backyard that I'd watered daily to keep as green as the picture on the lawn seed box—the place I'd tottered around precariously in special spiked shoes to aerate in the fall. The pampered yard I'd trimmed, preened, and revived as it recovered from an attack of moles was now a food-fight war zone.

I squelched out onto the grass, weaving around remains of last week's Irish stew and a soggy Caesar salad. A flattened Swedish meatball box, a hard lump of moldy cheese, half a pork chop that had been nibbled on and then discarded, and a slew of rotting fruit littered the landscape. A sprinkling of eggshell was scattered about like rice at a wedding, and I spotted something unrecognizable that my husband must have emptied out of his own fridge. (Some people have separate beds. Now that we're both in our late forties, we'd lived twenty-five glorious years together as long as we kept separate refrigerators. Fish bait, guts, and elk in his; hummus, strawberries, and froufrou French chocolate pastries in mine.) As I continued to survey Hurricane Rice-A-Roni, it was abundantly clear that a creature with four paws had devoured the contents of our trash can. Just then, my husband, Martin, arrived back from closing up our chicken coop.

"Raccoons!" he said with that assured tone that had managed to lure me into all sorts of foolhardy schemes in our years together.

I suspect men were given that intense, unwavering conviction to lull you into believing they always know exactly what they are talking about. It takes about six months into a marriage to figure out that you've been fooled.

Men seem to be fluent in an assortment of magisterial statements, such as, "It's not going to rain today, trust me," or "The tires on the car are fine. You could drive to Albuquerque and back on that tread," and my all-time favorite, "Go ahead and use the check card. There's loads of money in our joint account!"

"Yep," said the king of his domain. "We've got raccoons, alright."

"What shall we do? Call pest control?" I asked the knower of all wisdom.

"Too expensive. I'm going to trap it," he said with that male assurance. "Then I'll throw it in a sack and take it to the woods!"

Ding. The spell was broken.

"Trap it? And throw it in a sack?" I emphasized the last sentence in mock horror. "We can't just trap it. It's not a mouse. Raccoons are the size of a small mountain lion or something."

You see, I like to exaggerate a little, just enough to expose his ideas as a little ridiculous. Verbal tennis is about the most exercise we get.

"No they're not," he volleyed back. "They're not much bigger than, say . . . a cat."

"A cat?" I served high. "What kind of cat do you know that can tip over a full metal garbage can? Why don't I just call pest control for their advice?"

Point to me.

He squinted and said, "Hmmm," which translated from "male" means, "I don't actually agree with that idea, but I don't have a comeback line to common sense." Instead, he answered with, "I think I'll talk to Dwayne about it."

Set point.

Dwayne was just like Ask.com, except he was a large, beefy tank of a man with a reddened, rugged appearance and a long gray beard. His hygiene wasn't quite up to par, but according to my husband, there wasn't much Dwayne didn't know about living on the land.

Back in the kitchen, I typed "how to trap a raccoon" into my Web browser as Martin reached for the phone. As I scanned through the online pages and all the cute pictures of raccoons, some of the ideas of how to catch them verged on the ridiculous.

There was an odd assortment of "Heath Robinson" cobbled-together projects with even odder people describing them, my favorite being, "How to build a raccoon trap using nothing but duct tape and birdseed."

Martin had barely hung up with Dwayne before the phone rang again.

"Hello, Doris," he said with emphasis so that I could hear him.

I shook my head at him furiously; he smirked mischievously.

"Sorry, you just missed her," Martin said. "She's just gone to, umm . . . choir practice."

I threw up my hands in mock horror and mouthed, "What!" I couldn't carry a tune in a bucket and wouldn't be caught dead singing in front of people. In fact, I would rather be caught dead.

He paced away from me to make sure he stayed out of my reach.

"No, she didn't know she could sing either. It was when she hit menopause that she discovered this amazing new singing voice. We're hoping the pastor at Holy Souls might ask her to sing a solo in the Christmas pageant this year."

I slumped my head down onto my desk.

"Yes, yes, it *is* good that you know about this now, especially when you need to organize one of your Christmas carol services at the Senior Center." He moved rapidly farther away to a position where I couldn't hurt him. "Oh yes, I'm sure she'd be fine with a microphone."

Slamming my hand down on the desk, I lifted my head and mouthed, "Stop." He turned his back to me, but I could tell he was giggling.

"Yes, I will let her know . . . very important . . . yes, I'm writing it down."

He pulled out a Post-it note, drew a face with its tongue sticking out, and showed it to me.

"Okay, Doris, as soon as she gets in . . . Bye."

He put the phone down and raced quickly toward the back door as I picked up a pillow and prepared to attack.

"That was Doris," he said as he bolted out, shouting back over his shoulder, "You need to call her. It's urgent." He slammed the door and the pillow ricocheted off the back of it.

I sighed deeply as I contemplated Doris Newberry. She was a fascinating character, a pioneer and instigator of many weird and wooly projects who liked to "instigate" you right along with her. Every village has one, and Doris was ours: a lively individual always throwing herself into some harebrained scheme or other, taking no prisoners as she pulled you into her wild world of wackiness. Doris's "urgent" could mean anything from the need to raise money for lame goats to singing at the top of a living Christmas tree. About an hour later, curiosity got the better of me.

"Hi, Doris. It's Janet."

"Janet Johnson from the library?" she barked. "Good. I've been trying to get hold of you. I need you to come to my house tomorrow afternoon. There is a meeting of my rejected ladies here, and you'll fit right in."

I furrowed my brow. "A meeting of your rejected ladies?" I was not sure if I should be offended that I would "fit right in."

"You'll see," said Doris enthusiastically. "But it's invitation only, so don't bring hordes of people with you."

I sighed; my mind had moved from goats to camel races to choreographing male strippers. I wondered whether I should wear a riding hat or take a wad of dollar bills.

The next morning, I slept right through the alarm I'd set for work. Skipping a shower, I threw on some clothes, grabbed a cup of coffee, and raced out the door.

Dashing toward the car, I tripped and almost fell over an object obstructing my path. My trash can had been emptied again, even though Martin had tied it shut.

I sighed. The raccoons had enjoyed another party, and my trash can had been the piñata! They'd obviously indulged in a great evening of feasting on our wares and then staggered off the property, loaded up with our birdseed as a little take-home gift!

I jumped into my car. Over the years, I'd become quite skilled at steering with my knees while applying makeup and drinking coffee and could've driven myself to the library with my eyes closed. Our cottage was on the outskirts of

Southlea Bay Village, only a quick five-minute drive into the hub of our little town. Southlea Bay was everything you would expect from a small town on an island in the corner of the Pacific Northwest, the sort of place where people still stopped on the street to talk while children chained together daisies and created chalk art on the sidewalk. Bake sales, farmers' markets, street dances, and pancake breakfasts at the firehouse were all regular occurrences.

The village sat in a low rise surrounded by three large hills. My drive to work took me down Main Street, which afforded a stunning view of the water that surrounded Southlea Bay on three sides. It was an ever-changing outlook depending on the time of year. In the winter, the water was choppy and gray as it mirrored the overcast sky and accordingly reflected a cool undertone across the village. During the summer, the water playfully danced beneath cobalt heavens and, when the sun caught it, shimmered like diamonds, bouncing refractive light across the whole town. A stunning vista of the Cascade mountains, frosted with snow year-round, made for the perfect backdrop.

This particular morning was dark and gloomy, and the first thing to greet me as I made my way down Main Street hill was the skunky aroma of roasting coffee. The rich, pungent fragrance hung on the air like a veil, emanating from our one and only diner, the Crabapple. It was tucked in the middle of the square and named after a gnarly old tree that used to dominate the parking lot. The Crab, as it was affectionately known locally, had been owned and run by the same family for generations. We had a pub with a bar menu at the bottom of Main Street and a pizza place at the far end, but the Crab was the only place where a family could sit down and eat a Sunday brunch or dinner together.

Across the street from the Crab was our local florist, All Stems from Here. With its black, swooping-lettered sign and bold, Parisian-style pink-and-black awnings, I always thought it looked a little out of place. But the owner, Carol Bickerstaff, had a passion for anything French, so who was I to argue? Next door to that, and in direct contrast, was a rainbow-colored, hippie-artsy store very majestically named Ruby-Skye's Knitting Emporium.

I passed the florist and climbed the Main Street hill, heading toward the oldest building in our town. Built in 1896, this impressive redbrick building housed our post office and stood at the brow of the hill, watching over us like a somber old gentleman. Directly across the street was the Southlea Bay library, where I worked.

The library, with its white shutters and over-flowing hanging baskets, was painted a rich barn-red and looked more like a charming farmhouse. I believe that's why it was always a hive of activity; people felt more like they were visiting a favorite elderly aunt rather than coming to a public building. In front, on a bench in the midst of a little rock garden planted by a group of children from Southlea Bay Primary School, sat a honey-colored carved wooden bear reading a book. On a small brass plaque at his feet were the words of Jorge Luis Borges: "I have always imagined that paradise will be a kind of library."

"The paradise" greeting me was overshadowed by dark, looming rain clouds. I reached the library parking lot, and the heavens opened. Jumping out of my car, I was instantly soaked, and my hastily chosen pink blouse and crepe pants clung to me like a second skin. I snatched at my purse, but I only got hold of one strap, and the contents scattered across the asphalt. With rain hovering on the tips of my lashes, I stared down at the mangled pile as "Mount Janet" had erupted in a hundred different directions. There were soggy tissues, Q-tips, a rolling lipstick, my change purse, a pack of antacids, and a herd of assorted pens, all skittering away. It was shaping up to be a pretty sucky morning.

Heaping the soggy mass back into my bag, I raced toward the library. Squelching inside, I dripped an unavoidable trail to the bathroom. I locked the door, tipped my head forward, and dried my hair under the hand dryer, and then I stood up and studied myself in the mirror. Once mistaken for Jaclyn Smith by a drunk when I was in my twenties, I had long since cut my long, bouncing, seventies-style tresses into a sensible bob. My chestnut-brown eyes now had more than their share of wrinkles around them.

But nothing could prepare me for the reflection that greeted me. I gasped. The hand dryer had dried my hair straight up, like an ever-spouting geyser. I was wearing the majority of my mascara on my nose and chin. My pants sagged in a wet crease, and I could see the black bra I'd thrown on in my haste through my damp blouse. This was not a good look. It certainly didn't say small-town librarian. To top it off, the heat in the bathroom had given me a hot flash. As I fanned my blouse to try to cool down, I remembered the meeting with Doris Newberry later. I just hoped her "closed meeting" didn't include any members of the royal family.

Someone tapped lightly on the bathroom door. It was my boss, Karen Shore. "Are you okay, Janet? You've been in there for quite a while." The concern was evident in her tone.

"Coming," I responded breezily as I licked a piece of toilet paper and rubbed furiously at my face. "Just had a minor emergency."

When she opened the door, Karen had difficulty concealing her surprise. "I see what you mean," she said.

"Got caught in that downpour." I stated the

obvious as I straightened up my sodden blouse and attempted to move with a professional air into the main library. Squelching to my usual spot behind the counter, I was relieved to turn to the task of checking in the never-ending pile of library books.

I soon forgot about my bedraggled appearance—until an old man shuffled in and propped himself, hunched and wheezing, over the check-in desk. Right in the middle of checking the database for him, my computer crashed, so I moved to another one. Karen came to the counter and asked him if he needed assistance.

"No," he grunted, sucking on his teeth. "Your wet-T-shirt librarian with the punk-rock hair is helping me out just fine."

Deciding to avoid the public, I buried myself in the back office. I was sorting the mail when I suddenly noticed Ruby-Skye, one of our story-time readers, glaring at me from the children's area. Ruby, as we called her for short, was a typical example of the assortment of characters that make up our little town. A genuine hippie with heart, she left her knitting emporium twice a week to read stories to the young folk in our community. She was a notorious local character and was always dressed in a very eclectic style. Today was no exception. She was wearing an ankle-length orange wool poodle coat with large green pompoms that dangled from it like branches. On her head sat a green knitted hat embellished with

21

an enormous emerald-colored peacock feather that came to a dramatic point on her forehead and wouldn't have looked out of place on Robin Hood. She was adorned in a number of glistening and clattering accessories that she was well known for. In fact, not unlike the silver-belled ponies at the circus, she was often heard coming well before she arrived. I'm not sure if the children came to listen to stories or just to stare at Ruby's outfits as she jingled, glistened, and bobbled in the sunlit windows. As I caught her eye again, she was smiling and nodding from behind a display of Disney bears that she was building into a pile. She looked around covertly, then urgently beckoned a multi-gold-bangled arm toward me.

I moved across the library, and she pulled me in quickly, close to her. She handed me an open book of *Goodnight Moon*, pretending to point to something in it as she whispered, "I heard you were invited. You're coming, aren't you?"

Her peacock feather spiraled balletically as her head started a long, slow nod, and, mesmerized, my head started to bob too, even though I'd no idea what she was talking about.

"Coming?" I eventually inquired.

"Shhh," she responded, quickly looking over her shoulder and circling me around into a display of Winnie-the-Pooh bears as the pompoms on her coat bounced wildly. "We never know who's listening. Keep your voice down. Today's meeting is going to be very special, and Doris told me you were coming."

Suddenly, the penny dropped.

"Oh, Doris's rejection group."

She put a finger to her lips. "Right on," she whispered, smiling. "We have to be careful," she warned in her hushed, mysterious way. "Not everyone can be rejected. If we just shout about it, everyone will come running to join." She emphasized "rejected" as if she were talking about being crowned homecoming queen. Her face broke out into a benevolent smile as she tapped my arm and added, "*You* are one of the lucky ones, man."

Smiling and nodding, I feigned understanding, even though, once again, I was completely stumped by the curious intrigues that I encountered while navigating my way through small-town life.

Chapter Two

LEMON CAKE & LOONIES

Sitting in the car before venturing to Doris's, I tried in vain to spruce up my appearance. Reapplying "Shimmering Pink Ice" to my lips in the rearview mirror, I noticed my hair still looked a real fright. My clothes had decided to dry in creases that lay in accordion pleats around my body. Sighing, I conceded that this was as good as it got.

When I stepped out, I was immediately greeted by Doris's four overexcited dogs. They jumped up and covered me with mud and sloppy kisses.

Doris had a pleasant country-style home and yard with little whimsical wooden doodads smiling up at you from every corner of her garden, each of them wishing you a pleasant day in one form or another.

I rang the doorbell and the dogs disappeared, distracted by a brave rabbit that had appeared in the garden. I took a deep breath and tried ineffectively to brush off my now dog-muddied clothes.

As the door opened, a hand-painted angel with the words "Welcome Friends" swung back and forth. The face that greeted me, however, was definitely not friendly or welcoming. It belonged to a miniature stick insect of a woman with wiry white hair and enormous glasses that emphasized her heavily wrinkled face. She blinked twice and looked me up and down. By the look on her face, I could tell she wasn't that impressed with what she saw. I smiled pleasantly, but before I had a chance to speak, I heard Doris shout from somewhere in the house.

"Who is it, Ethel?"

"It's some homeless woman," the bespectacled scarecrow responded. "She looks like she needs money and a good wash."

And I thought I'd already reached the lowest point of my day.

Doris bustled up to the door with a change purse and a concerned look. When she realized it was me, I could tell she was more than a little bemused by my appearance.

"Hello, Doris," I said in as airy a fashion as I could muster, trying to shake off the homeless comment.

"Why, this isn't a homeless woman, Ethel," said Doris, with just a hint of disappointment. "It's only Mrs. Johnson from the library. I invited her today." Doris looked me up and down again and inquired with obvious concern, "Are you okay?"

"I'm fine," I said overly enthusiastically.

"Come on in and have some tea and cake. You

look as if you need it." She pushed open the door and waddled away.

Following her up the hallway, I was flanked all the way by Ethel, who warily eyed me in a sort of "guard the silver" mode.

The front room was stuffed to the brim with ladies all chatting excitedly while seated in a circle on an odd assortment of chairs. Each one juggled a dainty teacup and a large slab of cake on a little rosebud-patterned tea plate. Doris's décor was . . . eclectic, to say the least. Some seventies pieces, a green sofa covered in clear plastic, and furry orange bucket chairs, for example, mixed with white wicker furniture and country florals. It was as if two completely different styles were in the process of fighting to the death.

I finally caught up with Doris as she was starting to cut me a very large slice of lemon cake. "Are you sure you want me here today?" I felt acutely self-conscious of my appearance. "I got caught in a downpour this morning before work. I could always come back another time, maybe later when I've had a chance to change—"

She cut me off. "Nonsense. You look . . . fine," she retorted, though I noticed she sounded far from convinced as she forced me down into a flowery bedroom chair and handed me the hunk of cake and a brimming teacup. As she unfolded one of her dainty lace napkins and placed it on my knee, she scrutinized me, as if considering if it was worth paying the asking price for a battered bunch of bruised bananas. Then, standing back to view me from a distance, she muttered to herself, "No, that will never do."

She pulled a large tablecloth from her tea table drawer, unfurled it, and tucked it firmly into the top of my blouse. "That should help. After all, it's only my rejected ladies," she pointed out offhandedly as she carried on dressing me.

Once she'd wobbled away, I looked down at myself. The tablecloth now shrouded me like a poncho and was obviously in keeping with the seventies ensemble. It was lime-green and decorated with hideous orange and brown flowers. In one hand, I held high the teacup, and in the other I balanced the huge slab of cake. I looked like a psychedelic Lady Justice, except right then, I actually envied the fact she was blind.

Looking around the group of ladies as they nibbled on their slabs of cake, sharing and savoring nuggets of village gossip, I found I knew most of them, at least by sight.

Ruby was also there. It was rumored she'd lived a very wild life in her twenties being a part of the sixties music scene. It was also rumored her name was really Brenda, but she had changed it to Ruby-Skye during that time. She liked to brag she'd once dated Bob Dylan and insisted she helped him write the lyrics for "Blowing in the Wind." She also claimed she'd been on a crazy road of drugs and rock 'n' roll until she'd discovered knitting in her thirty-second year, professing that yarn had been her savior and the only way to channel her wayward energy into something productive. She may have been a knitted hippie at heart, but if you were looking for someone to lead a revolution, she was your gal. She'd never married, and when people asked her about it, she would say, "Why would I do something like that?!" as if you had just asked her to eat dirt. When she'd claimed this year on her seventieth birthday that it was time for her to start slowing down, no one had much believed her, especially as she'd celebrated it by dancing naked on the beach at midnight and then skinny-dipping in the bone-chilling Sound. I could hear her talking about patterns to a woman next to her. I didn't know that woman, but she was knitting a blue matinee coat using sparkly purple needles.

Across the room was Flora, who worked at the florist and was painfully shy. Gangly and awkward, she stared at the ground and sipped delicately from her teacup. She'd been a teenager the first time I'd met her when her family had moved to the island from a large city on the East Coast. Floating into the library, she'd been not unlike an uncomfortable waif out of a Dickens novel; with a pair of oversized spectacles perched on her nose, she'd given the appearance of a scared owl. She had the palest hair that hung long and limp down her back and rice-paper skin to match. I remembered thinking if I could hold her up to the light, I would be able to see right through her. That first day she'd drifted up to my desk looking for *Anne of Green Gables*. That was five years ago, and even though her body had grown into that of a woman, she still looked exactly the same: a shy, gentle creature, uncomfortable in her own skin. You couldn't help but adore her.

As I tried to get her attention, the door burst open. The Labette twins had arrived, identically dressed, as usual. Always impeccable, they wore midnight-blue suits trimmed in shell-pink with matching blue hats, white silk blouses, and pumps. They arrived accompanied by Doris's mother, whom everyone lovingly referred to as Gracie. The three of them entered carrying a pile of colorful packages, creating a flurry of activity as they juggled them to administer heartfelt hugs.

"Darlinnngs, so sorry we kept y'all waiting," said Lavinia in her strong Southern drawl. And as twins often do, Charlotte, whom everyone called Lottie, picked up her sister's sentence.

"I told her, I told Lavinia, I said, 'Lavinia, we are going to be late unless you get your patootie into gear.' I prayed all the way from town, 'Lord, please don't let us be late and have us keep those dear ladies waiting. That would never be part of God's plan.'"

"I'm so sorry, y'all," interjected Lavinia, picking

up Lottie's thread. "I just needed to poke my head into Claudette's for one tiny minute. She's having a sale, and her new season's stock is just too divine. Besides, Lottie, we would never have met up with Doris's momma if we had been here on time. Have you thought that might have been God's real plan?"

Lavinia and Lottie were about as different as two people who just happen to look identical could be. Lottie was a deeply spiritual woman while Lavinia had three husbands before her twenty-fifth birthday. I knew them both as library regulars. We never had to try to figure out which twin had ordered what; it was always pretty obvious to us. If it was entitled *A Day Close to God*, it was for Lottie; if it was called *A Night Close to a God*, it was for Lavinia.

It was widely known they had moved to our sleepy little town in the mid-1970s, running from some scandal of Lavinia's, who, on arriving here, had run right into another one. Within two weeks of moving to the village, she'd started a notorious affair with the mayor of Southlea Bay that steamrolled him right out of office and back to his family home in Georgia. The last thing he'd promised Lavinia before leaving was that he would divorce his wife and then return to marry her. That had been the last time anyone had ever heard from him. The embarrassment of being jilted so publicly had been the final straw. Lavinia had vowed never to marry again, and Lottie had vowed to help her keep that promise. They used their father's money to buy an elegant house with a stunning view of the Sound on the edge of town. Though Lottie had entertained a couple of suitors over the years, she'd remained single in order to keep her eye on her troublesome twin. And apparently, if the rumors were true, Lavinia had given her sister a run for her money over the years. The poor woman had probably never gotten off her knees.

Pulling a stunning periwinkle-blue silk scarf from black-and-white tissue paper, Lavinia wrapped it around her neck with a flurry and then posed like a twenties movie star, saying, "Look what we got for a steal at Claudette's."

I chuckled to myself. Claudette's was an exclusive ladies' dress shop with a door that had to be unlocked to let customers in, and what Lavinia was calling a steal was probably what the rest of us used to buy a week of groceries.

"Never mind your purchases, Lavinia," Lottie admonished her. "We should get Doris's momma settled. Where would you like to sit, Gracie, dear?"

The room fell silent.

"Ohh," Gracie squealed. She seemed to be enjoying all the attention. "I'll take my usual seat." She pointed and then floated over to a wicker chair with delicate peach cushions and gently settled herself down.

You couldn't have gotten much different than Gracie and her daughter, Doris. Doris was a large, rotund woman with a brusque manner. Gracie was gentle with lively blue eyes and delicate, porcelain features. She traveled softly through the world with a childlike awe. She'd moved into her daughter's house ten years before, when Doris's father had passed away. Insisting on moving all of her furniture in with her, the country florals were hers.

"At last," said Doris as she bustled in from the kitchen. "I thought you ladies were never going to get here. We do start at five o'clock, you know."

Lavinia melted like butter and laid on the Southern charm. She took Doris's hand and looked directly into her eyes. "Doris, darling, it's all my fault, and I'm so sorry. You're a wonderful woman and a sweetheart for waiting for us. But we did find your momma off on one of her little walks, and we decided to stop and bring her home."

Doris's face softened.

"Okay," she said, a little less surly. "Thank you for that. Now we need to get going."

She cut two slices of lemon cake for the sisters, who thanked her with the same glassy smile, placed them directly on a side table, and never touched a morsel.

Doris started the meeting by banging a gavel on her wooden tea table. "Let's get started. First, the promise."

Each woman responded instinctively by joining hands and reciting together a pledge.

"Selected for rejection
We reach for true connection
Choosing a path of celebration
As we bond with true affection."

Finishing, they burst into spontaneous applause and hugged each other. As bizarre as this whole thing seemed to me, I envied their obvious care for one another.

Doris brought them back to order with her gavel again, placed her hand on the top of my head, and announced in a tone that sounded as if she were about to auction me off to the highest bidder, "I want to introduce you all to our special guest today. She's going to help us with our little plan. Mrs. Johnson, from the library." Everybody started to clap again, and Doris leaned into me and whispered, "I wouldn't stand up if I were you, dear." Then she readjusted my tablecloth to cover the rest of my blouse and stood back to study her work with a hesitant smile.

Not knowing what else to do, I lifted my hand in a pathetic little wave.

"Janet, let me introduce you to the ladies of the Rejected Writers' Book Club. I'm sure you know Ruby-Skye, as she volunteers at the library." I nodded in her direction, as Doris went on, "Ruby writes horror." I had to take a minute to let that digest. So, the woman who read stories to our under-fives . . . wrote . . . horror.

"They're awful"—Ruby grinned ruefully, then sipped her herbal tea—"but oh, so much fun to write."

"Next to her is Lavinia—I'm guessing it wouldn't take much to guess what she writes."

Lavinia laughed. "Romance with a good dose of spice, that's what I like to call them. They're the kind of books Lottie wouldn't be caught dead reading. It's my own little wicked pleasure."

Lottie tapped her sister on the hand, saying, "Lavinia," with the tone of mock horror. Lottie jumped in, saying, "I've written a lovely piece about the Psalms and how they can help us find peace in a troubled world. I think it's perfect, but nobody seems to want it. But I don't care; now I'm part of this group. We're just so happy sharing our work with each other, who'd want to be published?"

Doris continued. "Then there is Momma. She's writing her memoirs—and a beautiful job she is doing of them too."

Gracie's face lit up. "All about the work I did during World War II. I was living in England when I met Doris's father. He was this handsome American GI that swept into our small town with his bubblegum and Hershey bars." She lifted her shoulders and giggled like a schoolgirl before adding, "And swept me right off my feet."

She was enchanting.

"Apparently the market is just flooded with World War II memoirs, and my story just isn't . . . interesting enough." Her voice trailed off, and there was an intense sadness in her blue eyes.

Lottie, who was seated close in one of the furry orange bucket chairs, patted her hand and reassured her. "But you get to share your stories with us, and we love them."

Gracie seemed to brighten and lightly covered Lottie's hand with her own.

"Next to Momma is Flora," announced Doris. "She's the poet of our group."

Flora flushed a deep crimson. "I've written one hundred and twenty-three of them. I like to write poetry," Flora squeaked out in a tiny voice.

Lavinia jumped in to help Flora, who had started to squirm with the attention. "But poetry is hard to sell, so we get to hear her poems here. And we love them."

The woman with the sparkly knitting needles piped up, "I'm Annie." A bright, warm smile spread across her ruddy cheeks. She had round, soft features, and her head was a mass of tight white curls. She wore bright-white sneakers and a plum velour lounge suit. She hooked a stitch. "I'm not as talented as the rest of them, but—"

There was an outcry in the room. Doris brought them all to order saying, "Annie, remember the rule: There are no bad writers here, only rejected ones. If you were published, you couldn't be a part of our group." Doris turned to me. "That's the only rule here. We want a feeling of solidarity. Having someone get published would just not work. We've lost a few over the years due to success," noted Doris grimly, "but fortunately, as it is very hard to get published, we keep more than we lose."

Annie brightened. "I like to write dog stories. I love dogs, so I write about them."

"Janet is going to help us take our stories out to the world," Doris announced with wild exuberance.

I was going to do what? I wondered if maybe I'd passed out at some point and missed something, but before I could comment, Doris continued without taking a breath.

"But first, before we have Janet talk to us, I hear we have another Fabulous Female Failure."

Ruby started rooting around in a knitted bag with a purple peace sign adorning the front and pulled out an envelope.

All the women clapped enthusiastically. I clapped absently as well; I was still contemplating what Doris had just said about me.

"Wonderful," said Doris, taking it from her and holding it high with all the gusto of a circus ring-leader announcing its star performer. "Get the book, Ethel."

Ethel disappeared, and Doris handed a large mason jar around the circle. Everybody except Ruby threw in some change.

Ruby said, "It's so good when I'm bad."

I leaned toward Ruby and asked her, "What's the jar for?"

"Everyone without a letter this month has to throw in some money. We're collecting for a big celebration when we hit five hundred letters."

I then asked a question that I'd been wondering about. "Does Ethel write?"

Ruby shook her head. "She's just a friend of Doris's. She's more of a helper to the group." Then she added with pride, "As I said before, not everybody can be a rejected lady."

A few minutes later, Ethel paraded back into the center of the room, holding aloft "the book" as if it were a much-anticipated birthday cake. It was a large black leather-bound affair bulging at the seams. She handed it to Doris, who received it reverently before opening it.

Doris cleared her throat and spoke. "As you all know, the Rejected Writers' Book Club has been meeting for five years now, and apart from that unfortunate bout of dysentery two years ago, we have met every single month, upholding our motto, Connection with Rejection. In my hands is our fabulous file of failure, of which I am proud to announce we now have four hundred and seventy-five rejection letters. As is the custom at the beginning of each session, I would like to take a moment to recognize one of them.

"Here's one of my favorites.

Dear Mrs. Newberry,
Thank you for sending us your manuscript, *Love in the Forest*, but at the moment we are only looking for manuscripts that have a plot, a setting, interesting characters, understandable dialogue, a conflict, a main character, and . . . a point. As your manuscript meets none of the criteria, we will have to pass on this project.
   Yours sincerely,
   Myrtle Williams
   Slivers, Ronald, and Co. Books."

The whole group clapped and roared with laughter.

"Isn't that marvelous?" howled Doris as her whole body wobbled like jelly.

As the guffawing continued, I nibbled nervously on the remnants of my lemon cake, deciding I must be in some sort of island episode of the *Twilight Zone*. They were all thoroughly batty.

As soon as the laughter subsided, Doris turned to a blank page and placed Ruby's letter on it.

"Thank you, Ruby. Only twenty-five now to our goal."

Doris placed the book down on a table.

"Now, for the real reason for this special meeting."

She paused for effect.

"We have been reading our books to one another

for many years, and we have enjoyed them so much. But I think it's time that other people in our community had the benefit of our work. So I've asked Janet here today to help us organize an event as part of our weeklong rejection celebration. I believe now is the right time to unveil our group to the extended community and connect with other rejected people in Southlea Bay. Our festivities will culminate in an event at the library I am calling Reflection and Connection for Those Who Know Rejection."

Sipping my tea, I was in an odd kind of awe; only Doris could create a successful event out of other people's utter failures.

"During the week leading up to the celebration, we'll hold a number of fun special events, such as the burnt cake tea party and a demonstration of how to kill your houseplants with style."

All the ladies in the group talked at once.

Doris waited, her domineering silence quickly taking command.

"This will build to our special library event. Available to all walks of the community, it will allow them to bring all their rejected gifts together at one event to share. Tone-deaf singers, dancers with two left feet, musicians that are all thumbs, and nurses that make their patients worse are all welcome. We'll be there to support them with our rejected letters and books; the only criteria would be they have to love what they do. Anyone sharing his or her gift will have to add some money to our rejection jar. All the money we raise will go to the charity we support, the Rejected Children's Fund of Island County. It would be like a mighty Rejectathon. What do you all think?"

They clapped enthusiastically, their mutual excitement bubbling in the air as Doris nudged me, saying, "What do you think, Janet?"

What did I think? That I should get out of here before it was too late, that's what I thought. It was a very noble sentiment, but I couldn't imagine anyone actually turning up. I just grinned and said, "Well . . . that . . . sounds . . . interesting. Let me talk to Karen and get back to you." I jumped to my feet then, handed my empty cake plate to Doris, and added, "But I really should be going now."

"Already?" said Ruby. "This month we're reading my newest book, *Blood and Gore in Hell Town*."

"And I was going to read a snippet of *Carnal Love in the Land of Spices*, if Lottie ever went to the bathroom," piped up Lavinia.

And there it was again.

"Lavinia!" exclaimed her sister.

I just kept moving down the hall; I was on a roll.

"Oh, they all sound so amazing and maybe another time, but I really need to go." I handed the tablecloth I was wearing to Doris and made my way to the door. Ethel was already waiting for me there, making sure I didn't leave with the candlesticks, no doubt.

As I started the car, my cell phone rang. It was my daughter, Stacy. I picked it up, but the reception was terrible.

"Mom," she said. Her tone was odd, frantic. "Mom, I need you . . ." Then she was cut off.

I started to panic. Something was wrong; she didn't sound like herself. I tried to call her back, but there was no reception. I considered going back into Doris's and calling from there but thought better of it. I would just get home as fast as I could.

Chapter Three

MYSTERIES OF PREGNANCY, BY WARE-DID-MA-FEET-GO

Driving home, I mulled over my relationship with my one and only daughter. I had mixed feelings. We did not have an easy relationship. I love and adore my offspring, and I would throw myself in front of a train to save her life. But I have wondered more than once if she'd actually come out of my body.

It should have been a red flag for me when she'd presented as a breech birth, because from the first day, it had been a character-clashing, white-knuckle roller-coaster ride. We seem to knock heads at every turn, like a couple of frenzied bells on a turbulent ship during a hurricane.

When I arrived back at the cottage, there was a note from Martin. Stacy had also called home. Now I was really worried. She never just called me to chat; the last time she called, her kitchen had been on fire. I paced my own blue-and-white, Laura Ashley–decorated kitchen as I redialed. She lived in San Francisco, and at times like this, I hated being so far away from her. She picked up on the second ring.

"Hi, darling," I said, trying to keep it airy. "Is everything alright?"

"Mom?" She sounded desperate.

"Yes, darling." A viselike grip was taking hold of my chest.

"No! Everything's not alright," she said as she burst into tears.

Oh no. Not cancer or an accident or a death or a—before I could make it all the way through my top ten list of doom, gloom, and dismemberment, she blurted out, "I'm pregnant!"

It took a couple of seconds for my brain to register what she'd just said.

"Sorry, darling? Did you say you were pregnant?"

"Yes."

She started to cry again. The vise released its grip from my chest, and I let out the breath I didn't realize I'd been holding.

"That's wonderful," I said, relieved. "You must be very happy. After all, you and Chris have been—"

She cut me off.

"How can you do that?" she wailed, as if I'd just slapped her in the face with a wet kipper.

"Do what?"

"Do that happy Pollyanna thing you always do. This is the worst day of my life!"

She was starting to get hysterical. My concern returned. This was really out of character for my ice child, who was usually calm and collected, with never a hair out of place. Outbursts were just not her style. But her voice was undeniably starting to escalate. I needed damage control, fast, or I would lose her.

"Are you sure, sweetheart?" I asked, coaxing her down off her emotional ledge. "You could be mistaken?"

Suddenly, the crying stopped. Ah, a glimmer of hope. Maybe she hadn't taken a test or seen a doctor and just suspected pregnancy. I was just about to pat myself on the back for my superior parenting skills when I heard her retch—a loud, grumbling, and gut-wrenching retch at that. What followed was the unmistakable sound of someone throwing up in all the acoustic resonance that a modern telephone can produce.

Oh dear, I thought. She wasn't going to need to pee on a stick to confirm this pregnancy. By the sounds of it, her hormones were already doing a full West Coast swing.

Between the third or fourth heave, I suggested that I call her back later.

"Congratulations!" I shouted into the phone, but she'd already hung up. I fought the urge to call her right back, reminding myself not to push it when dealing with Stacy. We had moved to Southlea Bay in an attempt to give her the space she seemed to need in California.

Making myself a cup of tea, I mulled over the situation. I had mixed feelings. Excited to be a grandma, of course, but was I ready? I had only just come up for air from raising my own child and wasn't sure I was prepared to take on a responsible role with someone else's. Stacy was only twenty-four, and we had only just finished paying for her wedding the year before. Sitting down in my favorite armchair and slowly sipping my tea, I allowed this new realization to sink in. Outside the kitchen window, the sun was just starting to set.

Enjoying its rosy descent, I started to focus on all those Hallmark moments that would come with this new experience, reminiscing about all the lovely times we had enjoyed as Stacy grew up. Trips to see Santa and the Easter Bunny, butterfly kisses, and sloppily painted fridge pictures. Fun-filled days at the zoo and cool evenings warming ourselves, watching marshmallows melt in hot chocolates around a campfire. I remembered fondly the Christmas we had bought her very first two-wheel bike. Martin had stayed up till four in the morning putting it together and then wheeled it under a Christmas tree that was twinkling with tinsel. It had remained there in all its glory for exactly forty-five minutes before an excited six-year-old had bounded down the stairs to greet it. It had been a sparkly purple, princess affair, her favorite color at the time, with white handlebars and silver tassels. I remember the joy on her upturned little freckled face, a broad smile shining through gapped-tooth wonderment, caught in the glow of the tree lights. The joy had lasted for exactly three hours, until her chain had come off and clattered to the floor. She, grief-stricken, had thrown the bike to the ground. Martin had quietly replaced the chain while she sobbed in my lap, elevating him to her instant hero when he was done. If only it was that easy now, I thought.

Just about to add corny music to my inner thoughts, I heard the back door open. It was the hero. He was still grumpy about the raccoons, which were still treating our property as their own private holiday resort, complete with bed-and-breakfast services.

"Do I have some news for you!" I said, greeting him in the hallway as he sat to take off his boots.

He looked up at me wearily.

"Can you guess?" I asked, trying to sound mysterious.

"You made meatloaf for dinner?" he asked halfheartedly.

It was obvious he didn't want to play. But I wasn't giving up that easily.

"Let me give you a clue. If you listen closely, you might start to hear the faint pitter-patter of tiny feet running up our hallway."

He let go of a long, slow breath and slumped forward.

"Don't tell me that those darn raccoons have made it into the house now."

. . .

I recounted the rest of the conversation with Stacy to him over dinner, but he only seemed to be half-listening as he peered at a book propped up against the saltshaker entitled *How to Catch a Critter*. He smirked when I mentioned our daughter's feelings toward her pregnancy.

"She'd be disappointed if the angel Gabriel popped down from heaven to tell her the meaning of life, this week's lottery numbers, and where the treasure is buried," he quipped. I could tell he was secretly delighted.

"I think it's because she's such a perfectionist," I said protectively. "She likes to feel she's in control of everything, and pregnancy is a classic situation that is completely out of her control."

Martin raised his eyebrows over his book suggestively.

"And don't you go and blame me for her attitude," I added defensively. "She takes after your mother!"

Martin shook his head in bewilderment. He had long since stopped trying to figure out our daughter, who as an adult had quietly removed his superhero cape and in return offered him a cape of indifference.

Later that evening I wandered outside to find Martin whistling to himself as he lashed yet another thick rope around the top of our trash can.

On the deck was a large roll of duct tape and a huge bag of newly purchased birdseed.

"I'm building the perfect trap!" said the Wizard of Oz.

Smiling to myself, I surveyed his equipment, which looked suspiciously like materials needed for the shoddy affair I'd seen on the Internet.

When I asked him if he been surfing the Web, he screwed up his face and shook his head with disgust. "I prefer to consult with people who know what they're talking about," he stated with indignation. "Dwayne was over earlier. This is a special trap that he told me about."

I couldn't help smiling as I went in the house to make a cup of tea. Maybe Dwayne wasn't everything he was cracked up to be; maybe he was just the Grizzly Adams of the World Wide Web.

Martin's hopes were dashed the very next morning, when not only had our trash can mysteriously disappeared but also half the chicken feed that had been locked in an outside shed.

He shook his head and muttered something about not understanding why the birdseed and duct tape trap wasn't working. Standing in mutual commiseration with him for about five seconds, I left him staring at the empty space where our trash can used to be. I informed him that though I would love to go on a wild trash can hunt with him, I really needed to get ready for work. Then I realized my purse was missing.

Now, if I lived in a big city, I might have rushed to call in the police, SWAT team, and K-9 patrol, screaming about burglaries. But I lived in a town where everybody left their keys in the car so they could find them, and we all still left our front doors open in case someone wanted to drop off a bunch of flowers or an extra helping of stew. In fact, when we went on holiday to Hawaii a few years ago, Martin had decided that we should probably lock our front door just to be on the safe side. When we got home, it took us an hour to find the key.

Wandering back outside, I called to Martin, who was still staring at the empty spot. I shook my head. He was thinking; I'd observed it many times before in our long marriage. I could think while sitting on the toilet, talking on the phone, reviewing the to-do list balanced on my knee as I planned the evening meal, rubbing at a spot on the bathroom floor with my big toe, and putting on mascara. In order for my husband to think, he had to stop perfectly still, like one of those street performers who pretends to be a statue. Then he could just allow his brain to work, without any other bodily movements to distract him. I was always amazed he remembered to breathe.

Breaking his spell, I asked, "Have you seen my purse anywhere?"

"You're kidding," he said as he turned to me, a worried look on his face. "Don't tell me the raccoons got that as well?"

I was going to say something clever and witty about the color of my purse not matching their shoes when the phone rang. I dashed to answer it, hoping it might be Stacy.

"Is that you, Janet?" shouted a gruff female voice. I held the phone away from my ear.

"Yes. Who is this?" I answered.

"It's me," boomed the voice. "Doris Newberry. You wouldn't be missing your purse by any chance, would you?"

I arranged to stop by Doris's and pick up my purse later that afternoon and left for work.

On the way there, I decided to stop at the vet's in case he had any ideas of what to do about our raccoons. Happy Paws Animal Clinic was tucked right behind the library. As I got out of the car, I noticed a handwritten sign pinned to the inside of the door: "Off on a call, wounded bald eagle, back in 30 minutes."

I decided to walk over and pick up my mail from the post office while waiting for the vet to return.

I explained our problem with the furry inter-lopers to Mrs. Barber, the woman who ran Southlea Bay Post Office. She was a beloved, soccer-ball-shaped woman with wild, bird's nest hair that always hid more than one pair of sparkly reading glasses. She loved to dish out her daily wisdom as she hung her enormous bosoms, disjointedly, over the post office counter.

She contemplated my plight as she nibbled on a plate of snickerdoodles she'd received from a group of first graders. Next to the plate was a tremendous crayon portrait of her waving, a roll of stamps in one hand and a letter in the other. A speech bubble in green crayon above her head read, "Welcum to the post ofice." It was, in fact, a perfect resemblance of her, complete with "Mount Bosoms."

She stopped chewing, and her eyes grew wide. "What you need to catch those critters is a trail of breadcrumbs."

"Breadcrumbs? Well, I'm no expert on a raccoon's dietary habits, but they seemed to be more interested in my Swedish meatballs than my moldy rye!"

"No, not real breadcrumbs. I was speaking figurativcly. You need to create a food trail that leads right out to the Spinney Woods, and hopefully they'll follow it."

"But the Spinney Woods is five miles away. I would need to hold up the food bank to create a trail out to there."

"See what you mean," muttered Mrs. Barber, spraying a shower of cookie crumbs all over the countertop. "I'll think of something else." She stared, zombielike, out over the counter as she chewed on her snickerdoodle, not unlike a cow working on its cud.

I went to check my mailbox. Inside there was a large envelope reminding me that interest rates could go up at any minute, with bold black letters indicating the contents were "TIME SENSITIVE." What exactly does that mean? Is it like being skin sensitive? Or light sensitive? Quick, take this envelope away from "time." It might break out in a rash.

I threw it in the trash. As I did, I noticed a card that had become affixed to the envelope by a gold "Act Now" sticker gone awry. Unpeeling the card, I recognized the writing straightaway. It was from my best friend in California, and I felt a pang, missing her. We had met when we had lived in California. We were both middle school teacher assistants, my job for many years.

I loved Southlea Bay and would never want to move back to California, but I hadn't really found a friend or a group of friends I truly felt a part of. A "tribe," my husband called them.

I opened the card and found a picture of two old ladies doing splits and the words, "There's life in the old birds yet." She'd scribbled a short note about her family and that the card had reminded her of us. She also updated me on all the members of our little Classical Books and Walking Club we had formed when our children had been young. All harassed moms at the time, we had welcomed the company and a weekly walking break to Long Beach. We would walk the shores, looking out over the water, discussing with vigor our latest Jane Austen or Emily Brontë classic, after which we would settle to share a picnic together while rosy-faced children slept soundly in their strollers. I smiled as I looked at a recent snapshot of our little group that she'd slipped into the envelope. Older, happy, squinting faces smiled back at me from the picture with their own rosy-faced grandchildren now in tow. It made we wonder if Stacy and I would get to a place where I could trundle off with her children for the day.

I placed it in my bag.

Just as I was about to leave, Mrs. Barber came to life again.

"What you need is a big net. Dennis has one he uses for his trout fishing. I could get him to catch 'em for you. He could do with the exercise."

The Dennis she was referring to happened to be her sweet, barely-able-to-stand, seventy-year-old husband, a long string of bones and sinew. He looked like he weighed about fifty pounds dripping wet. In fact, against our black-eyed bandits, I would have given the odds about 70/30 in the raccoons' favor.

"Let me think about it," I said, secretly knowing there was no way I would be responsible for poor, sweet Dennis riding rogue around my property as he played animal bounty hunter.

Leaving to head back toward the vet's, I was just rounding the far corner of the post office building when suddenly one of the post office windows flew open, and Mrs. Barber called after me. Her mangled bird's nest popped out, followed by her swaddle of bosoms. They plopped right down on the windowsill, like two tightly gift-wrapped melons.

"You know," she said excitedly, "I just remembered. You should ask Doris Newberry. She got rid of a whole family of them from her barn last year."

I grinned and waved; Doris Newberry was stalking me, even through other people.

At the vet's, a rather odd-looking woman wearing a green tweed suit and a buttoned-up white starched blouse was unlocking the door. Her hair was coiffed into a big swoop, and she appeared to be wearing enough hair spray to keep her hair frozen in time from a sixties Aqua Net commercial.

She fixed me with an admonishing glare over the rim of her cat-eye glasses as I told her about my raccoons. She cut me off midsentence with a sniff and informed me in no uncertain terms that the vet "didn't do vermin."

Defeated, I walked on to work. No sooner had I arrived than Ruby rushed past me, all flaying arms and jumbled jangles. She looked angry and determined. Shaking her head, she grabbed and squeezed my arm as she passed, saying forcefully,

"It's so awful, Janet. About the club, just so awful, isn't it? We are going to have to do something about it."

But before I could ask her what it was, she was gone, a sweeping blur of bright-colored fabric and jingling jewelry, gliding and clanking down the library steps.

As I drove back toward Doris's house that afternoon, I was grateful that at least I wasn't heading into another rejects meeting. But my mood changed to bewilderment as I turned into her driveway, noting the same haphazard gathering of cars that had greeted me there yesterday. I felt like I was stuck in the movie *Groundhog Day*. Surely this couldn't be the same group of women two days in a row. My fears were realized when a disgruntled Ethel opened the front door. She clicked her tongue against her teeth in obvious disgust it was me. "That homeless woman's here again," she shouted up the hallway, without even trying to mask her unhappiness. "I told you not to feed her!"

What was I, a stray cat?

Doris arrived at the door, and in comparison to her demeanor the day before, she was positively depressed. The atmosphere didn't get any warmer as I followed her into her living room. There was the same circle of chairs, the same group of people with their tea and cake, except this time it was as if I'd entered a wake. The entire group sat in silence, and the sadness was palpable. Leaning forward, I whispered into Doris's ear as she absently sliced cake and slapped it onto plates, "Is this a bad time?"

She seemed distant. "We've had some bad news. I'll go and get your purse. Here, you may as well have a cup of tea and a piece of cake while you're waiting."

She handed me a teacup and cake wedge, pushed me down into the same flowery chair, and went to retrieve my bag. It was so quiet in that room I could practically hear the plants growing. Leaning forward, I whispered to Lottie, "I thought your group met just once a month?"

"We normally do, but this is an emergency meeting."

Lottie sighed and so did Lavinia, who finished her sentence. "I just can't believe it, can you? It's all so sad."

Before I could ask what was sad, Doris came back and practically thrust my bag into my lap. I got up and was about to excuse myself when she grabbed me by the arm. "Have you got a minute? So we could get an objective opinion?"

Caught in her desperate, clawlike grip, I felt like the blood was draining from my arm by the second. Hoping she would let go, I squeaked out, "Of course. Anything I can do to help."

Doris let go and cleared her throat. "Do you

remember when you were here yesterday?"

I nearly quipped, "How could I forget?" Instead, I nodded with mock enthusiasm and nervously stuffed a large bite of cake into my mouth.

Doris became misty-eyed. "That was a good day. That was one of our rejection letter days. Special and meaningful!" She paused to let her words take full effect. From the corner of the room, the woman with the tight poodle perm—Annie, I thought her name was—blew her nose quietly. Then Doris sneered with obvious disgust. "Then, today I got this."

She picked up a letter as if it contained something poisonous and flung it down on the coffee table in front of me, like a gauntlet.

It looked harmless enough.

"As you can imagine," she said with a hard sniff, "there was nothing else to be done but to call an emergency meeting of our club."

A quick glance around the room confirmed that every eye was lowered, staring at the despicable thing on the table.

I swallowed another rather large lump of cake. "Who's it from?" I asked meekly, not taking my eyes from it. I was too frightened to pick it up in case it self-destructed.

Doris was lost for a minute, and then she grunted, "Well, why don't you read it?"

Carefully, I picked up the envelope, took out one sheet of crisp white paper, and read:

"Dear Mrs. Newberry,

Thank you for sending us your manuscript, *Love in the Forest*. We enjoyed reading it very much and would like to talk to you about representation for your book. We feel it has a large audience and hope you will be willing to discuss further development of your manuscript. Congratulations, and we look forward to hearing from you soon.

Yours sincerely,
Mark Gilbert
Gaverston and Shrewsbury Books
MG/Andrea Stockbridge"

When I finished the letter, every eye had moved from staring at it to staring at me, apparently waiting in anticipation for some sort of inspired words of wisdom. But frankly, I was confused.

"I don't understand. What's wrong with this?"

"Well," said Doris, as if she were explaining it to a small child, "it's an *acceptance* letter. This publisher, Shewsbunny and someone I have never even heard of, wants to publish my book. I can't believe it."

"And isn't that a good thing? It means they like it." I wound my way down the rabbit hole. "Doesn't it mean they liked the book you wrote?" I added, trying to make myself clear.

Doris looked at me as if I'd gone mad. Then she

said in a monotone, "What it means is there will be No. More. Rejection. Letters. I'm being published, and I will have to step down from the club. What it means is there will be no more rejection parties here at my house." She was working herself up into a lather. "What it means is the end of our group as we know it! It is a very sad day indeed. We're all devastated."

I looked around the room. Every solemn face echoed her sentiment. I was still confused.

"But don't you want to be successful? Aren't you interested in getting your book published?" I asked. Because I didn't know what else to say, I added, delicately, "They will pay you."

Doris looked directly at me. "But it means no more rejection letters!"

"You don't have to accept them. Then you could keep collecting your letters."

"That is not the point," scoffed Doris. "Everyone will know. I can't just go on being a rejected writer if I've been accepted. It's the rules. Once you're accepted, you're out. It's not fair for everyone else. Now I have to go and buy myself a hat!"

A hat! Where did that come from?

"A hat?" I asked, genuinely thrown off balance.

It was then that I realized Doris was close to tears.

"Yes. A hat, and a funky scarf and snazzy glasses. All good authors wear snazzy glasses. Well, I won't do it. I look ridiculous in a hat!"

And with those words, she picked up a couple of empty teacups and hightailed it to the kitchen, Ethel at her heels like an obedient whippet.

Knocking back the last dregs of my tea, I decided this was a good time to make my excuses to leave.

Walking past the kitchen on my way to the front door, I caught a glimpse of Doris's hefty bulk hanging over the kitchen sink, washing up a cup. That's when I remembered the raccoons.

"Hey, I have raccoons," I blurted out before my brain had actually engaged.

Wow! That was a doozy. You could have cut the frost with an icepick. She stopped washing her cup and looked for a long hard moment out through her kitchen window as she digested my words. Words that now hung in midair like iced marbles, then fell crashing to the floor. I regretted saying them the minute they'd rolled under the kitchen table. She took a deep breath and turned to look at me, her hands still dripping with dish soap.

"Raccoons!" she spat out with all the distaste she could muster.

"Uh-huh," I said, not wanting to kick any more ice rocks around the kitchen floor.

She stared at me, and her chin started to wobble. I wasn't sure if she was going to hit me or cry.

And that was that. She turned back to the sink, and nothing more was said. As I turned to leave the kitchen, Lottie came running in.

"Doris, stop worrying. It has to be a huge mistake. We've all been talking. These things happen all the time at those big companies. Things get all mixed up. And I bet you a pretty penny that's what's happened here."

Creeping back into the hallway, I intended to try to leave during this new turn of events.

But on reaching the front door, I realized that my bag was still on my chair and that I would have to go back in to retrieve it. As I stepped gingerly into the living room, it was a completely different scene. It was Narnia after the snow had melted, Dorothy as she arrived in Oz. It was as if someone had used a Happy-Vac to suck all the happiness back into the room. It reminded me of an ad for plug-in air fresheners that started out all black-and-white with sullen people sitting around. Then some genius had the bright idea to plug in just the right scent, and suddenly, the room erupted into vibrant colors, with everyone dancing the cha-cha around the room, wearing fiesta clothes and flowers in their hair. I must admit there had never been much dancing in my house when I plugged in one of those. Normally we were just glad it had covered up the stink. But back here at Planet Craziness, all that was missing was a sombrero-wearing mariachi band to provide the accompaniment. Everyone was talking at once about how this was all a mistake, and Lottie ran about, topping off teacups and adding cake slabs to plates.

"It's the only thing that makes sense!" added Lavinia over the clatter. "Everyone knows your stories stink, Doris!"

With those words, everyone clapped and cheered. It was during their second whirlwind of tea and cake wedges that I managed to make my exit. Nobody cared or even saw me go.

Chapter Four

PORK RIBS & GREEN ALIENS

The days of fall were always pleasant in Southlea Bay, and this year was no exception. Boasting one of the warmest Octobers on record, the long, sun-filled days of October had allowed us to really appreciate the changing colors of the season. Now in their final flourish, the trees outside the library windows were a spectacular sight of gold and burnished red as they stood proud in their autumnal finery.

Halloween was a big deal in Southlea Bay. You couldn't even buy a stick of gum for miles around the day before. We stayed open late at the library, served hot cocoa or cider, and placed bowls of candy at our checkout desk. Then, in the evening, we dimmed the lights and illuminated the building with dozens of tea lights in mason jars. It was always a welcome stop for parents on their trick-or-treat routes, a place to get a much-needed warm drink and to catch up with friends and neighbors.

That morning I was on my knees, shelving in the fiction section and wearing my "Witch Book" costume. A perfect Halloween ensemble, I felt, with its stringy black wig, warty nose, tall crooked hat, and flowing black cloak. The words "Witch

Book" were painted in fluorescent-green lettering on my front, and on my back was "What can I help you find today?"

But what was hanging from my costume caused the children to squeal with delight whenever they entered the library. Dangling from thirty spidery strings were miniature handmade books, all with silly names painted on them, titles such as *Falling off a Cliff* by Ilene Dover and *Very Long Author Names* by Bob. During this time of the year, the children made a beeline for me to giggle at all the tiny books as the books swung back and forth from my cloak.

When two large shoes appeared in front of me, with Doris squished into them, I was pretty nonchalant about it. I hadn't seen her since I had made the mistake of stumbling into the rejected ladies meeting two weeks before. I scrambled to my feet.

"Hey there, Doris. Happy Halloweeeeeen."

I addressed her with my perfected Halloween greeting, the one that made the kids shriek with glee. No such luck with Doris. Looking at me like I had suddenly sprouted horns, it became quickly obvious she wasn't here to celebrate the season.

Removing my warty nose, I started again. "Can I help you with something, Doris? Are you looking for a book?"

Doris appeared confused, as if that were the last thing she would be doing in a library. "No," she said curtly. "I was looking for you. Can you stop by the house sometime today? There's something urgent I need to discuss with you."

My inner chambers started to shudder. I wasn't really in the mood for another *Twilight Zone* episode.

"Is it something we can talk about here?" I asked hopefully.

Doris paused, seemingly mesmerized by a tiny copy of *A Fascinating Read* by Paige Turner as it swung back and forth precariously from my cape.

"No," she said after careful consideration, and then, grabbing hold of the swinging book, she pulled me closer to emphasize her point. "This is something that has to be handled . . . delicately."

She made it sound as if she were planning to give me the launch codes for a nuclear bomb.

Reluctantly, I gave in. "I have a little time to spare between three and four, when I usually grab something to eat. But I need to be back in plenty of time to get the library ready for the kids. They'll start arriving as early as five o'clock."

"Perfect. And don't worry, I can feed you."

"Oh no, don't trouble yourself. I can just grab a sandwich at the store or something."

The thought of eating at Doris's again caused my insides to scream for mercy. It felt as if my blood sugar was only just returning to normal after my last visit.

"Nonsense," she said sternly as she waved a

hand dismissively at my costume. "You can't do all this . . . this . . . whatever it is on a store sandwich!"

She said "store" with such fervent disapproval in her tone that I couldn't stop myself from bursting out laughing, even though I could see she was deadly serious. Covering it up by coughing, I put my false nose back on.

"I will expect you at three o'clock sharp," she said.

I tried to protest one last time, but before I could get another word out, she was already out the library door. I thought she'd gone when her head popped back in and she shouted back to me, "I'll make pork ribs and beans. That ought to give you enough stamina for all this foolishness."

Then she was gone. Pork ribs and beans, God help me! I stood there, bereft and pretty sure I could hear my cardiovascular system starting to cry. Slumping back down onto the floor to finish shelving, I felt totally disheartened. Somehow, Doris had managed to take all the steam out of my day.

As I sat, pouting and stacking, an elf popped up over the top of the shelf. It was actually my boss, Karen, wearing a three-point green felt hat with miniature silver bells hanging from the points and jangling as she bobbed her head. She was dressed in a green felt tunic with a sparkly zigzag collar, red-ribbed woolen tights, and pointy shoes.

On her face, she had painted rosy red cheeks and dotted her nose with dainty brown freckles. She looked as cute as a button. But her tiny elf face appeared concerned.

"You have a phone call from someone called Christopher?"

Thoughtful for a moment, I followed her back toward her office.

I'd forgotten my cell phone that morning, but no one usually ever called me at the library. Martin worked locally as a production consultant at a local engineering company. This was a break from his years in California working with the big aircraft companies that were based there. During those years, he had spent the majority of his time crawling inside aircraft to make sure their equipment was up to FAA standards. Now, on the island, he had a more flexible and easy schedule and always just dropped by if he needed something.

Karen politely excused herself and closed the door as I picked up the telephone.

"Hello, this is Janet Johnson."

The voice that came back was tense, and there was a lot of background noise, as if the person were calling from a busy street. A strained voice filtered through. "Janet, it's Christopher."

I sat down hard and caught my breath. It was Stacy's husband. He'd never ever called me at work before and calling himself Christopher instead of Chris had thrown me. Something was wrong.

"Oh, hello, Chris. Is everything okay?"

"Not really. I'm here at the hospital with Stacy."

"What is it? What's wrong?" My throat tightened. I could barely get the words out.

"She started bleeding this morning. At first she was just spotting, and her doctor said not to worry and to just rest. But then as the morning went on, it got worse. So, we came here."

"I see," I said weakly. I really wanted to say something motherly and wise but was unable to as my heart tried to thump itself out of my chest. I tried to absorb this information.

"Are you still there?" he asked anxiously.

"Yes. Yes, I'm here. What is her doctor saying now?"

"She's reassuring but also concerned. The hospital did some preliminary tests, and now she's in with a specialist. Stacy just thought I should let you know."

"Of course. Call me when you know anything. I'll be here until just after eight and then home after that."

"Okay, I'll call you when I have an update."

Putting the phone down, I sat there feeling helpless and wanting to hold my daughter as I had when she'd been a little girl. It was times like this I hated being so far away from her, but Stacy had never liked the island and insisted on staying in California when we moved.

Karen tapped gently on the door.

"Everything alright?"

I told her the news, and she made all the right sympathetic noises. Though I wouldn't call us close, she was a wonderful boss, and we had gotten to know each other quite well over the years.

"Do you mind if I call my husband?"

"No, of course not." She shook her head, causing all her little bells to jingle. Despite how I was feeling, it delighted me.

"I won't be long; then I'll get on with shelving the DVDs."

"Take as long as you need," she replied.

I called Martin, and he listened intently, then commented in his levelheaded way. "Let's wait to see what the doctors say. She's in good hands. No point worrying about a storm until we smell rain."

"Maybe one of us should go?" I thought aloud.

"Let's see how things look in the morning first, shall we? Things always change so quickly with Stacy." Then, without a pause, he asked, "What's for dinner?"

Only my husband could change topics like that. He had that male way of thinking. In his mind, the problem of Stacy was now solved, so he could move on to his own culinary needs. He divided his whole world into little boxes on shelves. We had finished talking about the family box, so he'd put that one back. Now he'd taken down the dinner box. I, on the other hand, only had one large box that I juggled in the air, and random things bounced and spilled in and out of it all day long.

"I'll be having pork ribs, beans, and candy!"

"What?" he asked incredulously.

"There's spaghetti sauce in the slow cooker for you. I'm on Halloween haunting duty, remember?"

"Oh right, yes. Have fun." He was ready to wind up the conversation now that he knew his culinary needs were met. He was very predictable, and I did love him. Hanging up the phone, I got to work.

It was surprising how fast the time went with all the Halloween excitement. It was 2:45 p.m. before I knew it. My head was down, checking in books, when Karen reminded me to take my break before it got kid-crazy. I stopped and remembered I now had to face Doris and her urgent matter.

When I arrived at Doris's, I was grateful to see there were only two cars in the driveway. I was also pleasantly surprised to observe that even though Doris didn't appear to have an exceptionally high opinion of Halloween, she'd decorated her house in preparation for the event. Wiry black spiderwebs hung in shrouds from her front porch, eerie candlelit jack-o'-lanterns decorated her steps, and her welcome angel sign had been exchanged for a witch riding on a broomstick.

About to knock, I noticed the door was already ajar. Pushing it open slowly, I spied Ethel, seated like the Queen of Sheba in the middle of the hallway, dressed as an alien. At least I think that was what she was. Her face was painted green, and she had two silver pipe cleaners sticking out of her head. She wore a silver-and-green tunic, green tights, and an expression on her face as if she were chewing a bumblebee. The moment she saw me at the door, she grabbed the large bowl of candy balanced on her knees and protectively pulled it close to her chest.

"Hello, Ethel," I said, wondering if I would ever win this woman over. "Is Doris around?"

Doris bellowed from the kitchen, "Have your food all ready. Come on down, follow your nose!"

Entering her kitchen, I took in the heavenly smell. The table was already laid with a festive harvest-themed tablecloth and a vase brimming with golden chrysanthemums. In the center was a large pot of something that smelled wonderful. I beamed. It had been a long time since someone had cooked a hot meal for me, and it reminded me of my childhood.

"Did you know you have an alien in your

hallway?" I quipped, removing my nose and hat.

"Oh, yes," said Doris dismissively. "I always have to get Ethel to sit there to stop all those young rodents from trampling over my chrysanthemums. I hate this silly time of the year!"

She pulled a loaf of freshly baked bread out of the oven and turned around to face me—a fake knife was sticking out the side of her head. Starting to laugh, I covered it up with a fake cough as Doris just stared at me. Despite hints to the contrary, Doris didn't seem to have any overt sense of humor that I could find.

"If you don't like them coming up your driveway, you should turn off your lights. They wouldn't bother you then."

She glared at me with a look of disdain, and her fake knife trembled comically as she answered me. "Not do a holiday?" she said indignantly. "I don't think that's even American, is it? I might hate it! But I'm an American, and there's been Halloween candy at my door for forty years. I have to support this community in all its foolishness, whatever it is. I am, after all, patriotic!"

I had to stop myself from laughing again, realizing Doris's act of patriotism consisted of sticking a fake knife on her head and putting a disgruntled alien on garden guard duty.

Doris turned back toward the stove. She wrapped the hot, homemade bread in a green-and-white-checked napkin and placed it in a wicker basket. Her fake knife wobbled ominously as she bustled over and placed it on the table.

"Can I help?"

She brushed me off and pushed me down into a seat. She always seemed to be pushing me down into chairs. I felt as if I were five years old.

She moved around the kitchen and added a pitcher of iced tea, butter, and cutlery to the table. Then she fetched napkins and seated herself.

I poured myself some tea while she heaped piping-hot pork and beans from the pot into a bowl. It didn't take long for her to come straight to the point.

"I'm glad you could come," she said, cutting a whopping slab of the steaming bread and plopping it on my side plate. "I wanted to talk to you alone about all this publishing business." She said the word "publishing" as if it were a new epidemic. "This new turn of events is very hard, and I need some advice from a book person!"

Carefully, I tasted a small spoonful and was going to say that I wasn't actually a "book person" but a librarian. I was struck dumb by the taste of the food. It was just too delicious. I'd been eating gluten-free, fat-free, and sugar-free for so long, I'd forgotten what cholesterol on a plate tasted like. And it tasted so good, it was hard for me to concentrate on what she was saying.

"This has to be a mistake. I can't go getting published when no one else is. They're counting on me to be the worst of the bunch! I was hoping you could help me find a way to change the mind of this publisher so we can get the rejection letter we need."

I just listened and tried not to think about what this wondrous-tasting food was doing to my insides.

Doris searched my face as if she were sizing me up, as if she wanted to say something more. Then, taking a deep breath, she walked to the kitchen door and closed it quietly.

"There is something else too," she said, sitting back down, "and I don't know how to talk about it." She became quiet, even vulnerable, staring at the tablecloth as if she were hoping it would give her some inspiration.

"What is it?" I paused from the meal.

"I have something to confess, something that I can't tell the group because it would be too devastating."

My interest was really piqued.

"It's about the manuscript, the one I sent off to this publisher."

She became agitated, got up, and walked back to the kitchen door, opened it, looked down the hallway, and then closed it again. Sitting back down, she took a gulp of her iced tea, and I noticed her hand was shaking.

"What about it?"

She lowered her voice to a hushed tone. "It's

about the story itself. You see, I always have the core story I send out to each publisher. But I often add in little scenes here and there, just to amuse myself, just to keep up my writing skills. Adaptions of stories I read or snippets of news I hear. Anyway, I came across this scandalous story quite by accident. It was perfect, and I thought it would be a fun scene to add to my book."

She paused and took another swig of her tea. These words seemed really hard for her to say.

"Then yesterday I heard something, something very disturbing, and I realized there is a chance that the story I put in my manuscript, well, it might be true. And the worst thing about it is"—she was almost whispering—"it's about someone in this community, and if it were to become public knowledge, it would no doubt ruin that person's life . . ." Her voice trailed off, and she looked utterly bereft.

I took her hand and was about to say something wise and wonderful, I'm sure, but the door burst open, and Gracie danced in, dressed as a fairy. She had on a blue tutu, white tights, sparkly blue wings, a crown, and streaks of blue sparkles across her porcelain cheeks.

Doris pulled her hand from mine, and her shutters came down as she became "practical Doris" again. Bustling to her feet, she started to clear the table.

"Oh look, a witch," said Gracie confrontationally

as she balled up her fists on her hips. "I'm glad I have my wand to protect me." From her glittery belt, she pulled out a sparkly wand that had obviously been a feather duster in a previous life.

Doris went to the sink and started washing up. Feeling torn, I checked the time.

"Doris, I'm so sorry I have to leave. We can talk more later, if you want. I'll do anything I can to help."

Doris shook her head dismissively, and I realized how difficult it had been for her to open up to me.

She walked to the table then, and there was a thud, and there it was . . . an enormous slab of chocolate cake. "You can't go off without having dessert. It's Momma's favorite," she said encouragingly.

Gracie clapped her hands and tucked her wand away. I thanked her weakly, thinking I would need to run halfway to California to work off all these calories.

As I was getting in my car, all at once, I remembered the raccoons. Doris stood at her front door, next to her disgruntled alien.

"Hey, Doris, I hear you once managed to get rid of a whole family of raccoons from your barn. How did you do that?"

"Poisoned them," she shouted back matter-of-factly.

Poison. I tried not to show my horror. I wasn't even sure that was legal.

Driving back to work, I thought about what I had just learned, having encountered a whole different side of Doris Newberry.

The warm, cozy library was bustling with festiveness. Karen was behind the counter, refilling the large orange bowl with candy, and nodded as she saw me enter the library. "Did you manage to get something to eat?" she inquired.

"Did I!" I bragged, beaming at her broadly.

Our Halloween event went off without a hitch, and apart from one overstuffed fairy princess who managed to throw up on the carpet, there was no serious drama. I helped clear up the debris at the end of the night but was eager to get home to see if there was any word about Stacy. I was still pretty worried. I wanted to call her but didn't want to push her buttons; she was always telling me I was way too overprotective. Navigating my relationship with my offspring was akin to running through a minefield of live ammunition, I thought as I drove. I was never quite sure if this could be the phone call to trigger the explosion. In preparation for dealing with Stacy, I kept myself well and truly kitted out in my flak jacket and blast helmet at all times.

It was just after eight o'clock before I finally pulled into our driveway. Noticing that Martin's workshop light was still on, I tiptoed to his door.

Pulling open the door, I cackled, doing my own impression of the witch from *The Wizard of Oz*, hoping to make him jump.

"Good evening, Witch Book!" he said unflinchingly. He was impossible to scare; I blamed it on his happy childhood, darn it. "How was your day?" he asked, going back to looking intently at the plans he was studying.

"Good." Pulling up a stool next to his bench, I asked, "Did Chris call?"

"Not yet, and don't worry. I'm sure if there had been more complications he would have called already."

"Trick or treat!" I sang out, holding out a hand containing his favorite candy that I'd saved from the library bowl.

He sat back in his chair to open it. I surveyed the odd bits of wood, nails, and chicken wire that were spread out haphazardly over his workbench.

"What are you making?"

He suddenly became as excited as a ten-year-old with a model airplane. "You're going to love it."

As he showed me the rough plans he'd sketched on a piece of paper, I tried to follow. There were dimensions and calculations scribbled on it, but it looked like a big box with a wire frame to me.

"Where do I put my saucepans?" I asked in mock seriousness, teasing him. I'd been asking him to build me a kitchen island for six months, and even though I wasn't an engineering type, the chicken wire was a significant clue this wasn't going to be it.

"Huh? Oh, yes, well," he stuttered, "I thought this was much more of a priority. Don't you like it?"

"I might, if I knew what it was."

"I would've thought that was obvious," he said, appearing a little hurt that I hadn't recognized his emerging masterpiece. "It's a raccoon trap, of course!"

"Oh! What a good idea," I lied, trying to show some enthusiasm. Though, to be honest, nothing about this new plan sounded good to me.

Wild animals were called wild for a reason.

Just as I was about to get into that with him, the phone rang. I ran down the path, grabbing it on the last ring before the answering machine kicked in. It was Chris. He sounded tired, but calm.

"Hi there."

"Chris? How is she?"

"She's much better." The relief in his voice was obvious. "They've managed to stop the bleeding, and she's sleeping now. They're keeping her in overnight for observation, and they've booked her in for another scan tomorrow, just to be on the safe side."

"That's terrific news," I gushed, pulling off my

witch hat and slipping off my pointy witch shoes.

"Oh, and by the way, there's also some other news. Stacy is having twins."

"Twins!" I shrieked at the phone. "How on earth does she feel about that?"

"She's getting used to it," he said tactfully. "I'm sure it will be a handful, but I know she'll be a wonderful mother."

There it was: love in its entire rose-colored splendor. He was certain my ice child would be a wonderful mother. And who knows, I thought to myself. Motherhood could do the most remarkable things to a woman.

"I'll call you in the morning after the doctor has been in." He yawned.

"Okay, get some rest—you sound tired—and give Stacy our love."

I put the phone down and wiggled my striped-socked toes.

Twins! Wow! Where did they come from?

Chapter Five

CLOAK-AND-DAGGER &
A ROW OF SHOES

Lying in bed the next day, my thoughts were full of the twins and Doris.

The phone rang, and it was Stacy.

"Hi, love, how are you doing?"

"Okay," she mumbled quietly. "I feel terrible but I'll survive."

"What did the doctor say today?"

"I have to stay off work for the next month!" The disgust was obvious in her tone.

"I'm sorry. Will they give you the time off?"

"I've already talked to my boss. She's fine with it. But the problem is with Chris. The doctor doesn't want me to be alone, and he has to go on that important business trip to China the week after next. I also have a really important client coming to meet with me at the San-Bay Conference here. I'm going to have to find someone to come with me or the doctor says she won't let me go . . ."

Her voice trailed off. I knew the end of this conversation. She still found it hard to keep friends.

"Could you come down?" she finally said, meekly.

Sitting down hard on the sofa, I took a deep breath. It wasn't that I didn't want to take care of her. My heart was breaking, and I hated being so far away. It was just things never worked out well when we got together for any extended length of time, and I was hesitant to make our fragile relationship any more distant.

"I'm not sure I can, honey. There's a lot going on here at the library, and your dad needs me . . ." I never got any further. It was as if I'd sprung a bear trap.

"I'm sorry. I suppose I'm just not as important as the library!"

"No, darling, you know I didn't mean it like that. It's just I have work, and you know I hate to fly."

"Hate to fly" was an understatement. I was petrified, always had been. In fact, my parents had once taken our family to Disneyland when I was a child. I had screamed so hard all the way there that my dad had rented a car to drive us back. At that time, we lived in the Midwest, and it was a standing joke between my brother and sister about the time we went to Disneyland and spent most of the vacation driving home. In fact, my dad had just laughed about it with me the last time he and Mom had called me on his weekly call from Florida, where they now lived. They had moved there a few years ago and already had a more active social life than we did.

"Surely they would understand at work," Stacy

said in her whiny, six-year-old voice. "And I'm sure Dad could take care of himself for a week or so, couldn't he? And you love to drive. You could be here in just a few days. Mom . . . I really need you."

There it was, the "guilty pull" that came with the umbilical cord. I sighed deeply and found myself saying, "Let me get myself together here and see what I can do."

When Martin came home that evening, he found me on the sofa starting on my second glass of wine.

"Hard day?" he asked with a smirk.

I filled him in on the news.

"Are you going to go down?"

"I don't know. I've just been sitting here hoping that this would all blow over in a week or so."

"Or it could escalate into a hurricane. Want me to go down?"

I huffed at him. "What would you do with a pregnant woman? You upset her when she's not pregnant."

"Good point." He helped himself to a cup of coffee. "What about work?"

"I'm owed about a month's vacation, and this is usually a quiet time of the year for us. I'll talk to Karen tomorrow."

"So, you would drive down then?"

"All the way," I said sarcastically.

"You probably should give yourself four or five

days to get down there. Then you would only have to drive a couple of hundred miles a day."

"There's still a few days for the weather to change, then," I said optimistically.

"It's Stacy, remember. When she has an idea, she's like a dog with a bone. It's going to escalate. I would start packing your rescue remedy and tranquilizers now."

When I talked to Karen the next day, she was extremely sympathetic and said they could manage without me for a couple of weeks if they needed to. It was around lunchtime that I found myself down on my knees staring at Doris's shoes again, except this time they had bred—now there were three other pairs lined up next to them. Looking up, there, indeed, was Doris. Beside her, standing to attention, was Ethel, as happy as ever and still dressed as an alien as far as I could tell, plus Annie and Flora.

"We need to meet and talk urgently. This is important."

When wasn't it important with Doris?

"Okay," I agreed, not even trying to make an excuse this time. "My lunch break is in about an hour. Why don't I meet you over at the Crab?"

Doris nodded and then she and her posse were gone.

When I arrived an hour later, I looked around the restaurant. The theme of the Crabapple Diner, understandably, was apples. There were apple menus, apple tablecloths, apple motifs on the water glasses, and every kind of apple-tree-picking picture you could imagine, all ripe and choking the walls. The owner also did a play on the word "apple" on the menu, with creations like the "Apple-y-Dapple-y Pancakes" and the "Happily Apple-y Daily Special."

I didn't need to look around long to find the group. Lavinia and Lottie had joined them, and they had all managed, somehow, to squeeze themselves into the back booth. Doris sat looking like a tube of toothpaste just waiting for someone to remove her cap so she could spray the walls.

Gladys, the Crab's oldest waitress, was behind the counter. She was a permanent fixture there. Rumor had it she'd started working at the Crab as a young thing from college. Let's just say Lincoln must have been president about then. She walked over and greeted me.

"Happily apple-y day," she muttered without the faintest hint of sincerity. Then, shoving her pencil behind her ear, she stuffed her notepad into her bra and handed me a menu. "They've been squashed into that booth like a tin of sardines, waiting for you," she sniffed. "To be honest, I'm recommending salads all around, or we're gonna need a can opener to get you all back out!"

I followed her to the booth, and before I could find a chair, Annie jumped up, pushed me into the hulking mass, and squeezed herself in next to me.

"Wouldn't we all be more comfortable at a larger table?"

Doris scowled at me. "And be overheard by every flapping ear that just happens to be passing by? No! This is the best booth. It's close to the kitchen, and all that cooking clatter will drown out our conversation."

Why did she always make it sound as if she was about to divulge state secrets? Succumbing to my squished fate, I jumped in. I wanted to get this over with as quickly as possible.

"What can I do to help you all?"

Doris bowed her head and beckoned us all in closer. This was not easy, as I was having trouble breathing, and I wasn't sure which arms or legs were mine anymore. But we all obediently bowed our heads and drew closer toward her.

Waitress Gladys appeared at the table.

"Don't mind me," she grunted. "I can wait till you've all finished praying. By the looks of the meatloaf today, praying might not be such a bad idea!"

Lottie raised a brow. "I've prayed for it many a day," she murmured under her breath.

Doris yanked open a menu, glossing over Gladys's praying comment, saying, "I think we're ready to order."

Gladys pulled out a pencil and her curled-up notepad. She looked us over, sniffed, and then grunted. "Well?" She was just too old and tired to care about anything more amicable. "Just to let you know, the salad is looking real good today," she said, winking at me.

"I would like a patty melt," said Doris, ignoring her, "with french fries and an iced tea."

"Me too," said Ethel.

"What a surprise," muttered Gladys.

"Lottie and I already ate," said Lavinia, "but I'm sure we would both love an iced tea too."

Lottie agreed. Gladys wrote it down as Annie ordered a chicken salad sandwich, and Flora ordered a green salad.

"What about you?" she asked, pointing her pencil in my direction without looking up.

"A cup of your tomato soup and half a turkey sandwich."

Gladys trundled off to put in our order, and Doris resumed her conversation in a hushed tone.

"Let me get straight to the point," she said, bowing her head close to us all again. "We have our rejection group to save, and I have invited Janet here because she has offered to help us in any way she can."

I suddenly felt unusually warm.

Ruby arrived at the table, windswept and breathless. She was adorned in a full tie-dyed kaftan with huge pink and orange splotches that was cinched at her waist with a faux-alligator belt. Her hair was scooped up high into a beehive knot, a silk green-and-pink scarf woven through it creatively. From her ears dangled long, feathery pink flamingos that matched her shell-pink nail varnish and lipstick, and around her neck, an oversized silver peace symbol hung to her navel.

"Sorry I'm late," she said, grabbing a chair and joining the end of the booth. "Big rush on scarf and glove patterns today. Cold weather's coming in." She looked around the table. "Is your momma coming?"

"Momma is resting," said Doris.

"Recovering from the Island Lurgy," stated Lottie.

"Ohhh," said the rest of us, nodding in unison, acknowledging the Southlea Bay nickname for the flu that was sweeping through the island faster than a California wildfire.

As Gladys approached the table with our drinks, she stopped dead in her tracks when she saw Ruby and didn't hide the fact that she was checking her out with disgust. "Will *you* be requiring anything?" she asked with obvious annoyance at the growing table. "Like maybe a mirror or something," she added sarcastically.

Ruby ignored her comment. "Water is all I need. Oh, unless the chef has those little nut cutlets and the beansprout salad on the menu."

"I'll check. I'm not sure if we're catering to the hippies today."

Gladys left.

Doris whispered, "This is the plan."

Gladys shuffled back with Ruby's water, and Doris slammed her hand down on the table with an exaggerated, "Shhh."

Gladys didn't skip a beat. She glared at Doris. "If you and Sundance"—she gestured at Ethel with her pencil—"and the rest of the Hole in the Wall Gang are planning on robbing the place, I should let you know it's been a slow morning. There's only about sixty-seven dollars in the till." She sucked in her cheeks and hitched up her nylons with her free hand. "Plus, I get off in twenty minutes. If you could wait to rob the place till after that, it's more of an even fight with Geraldine. She's younger and enjoys the drama."

Doris, unruffled, ignored her comment and sipped her iced tea. "Could I get some extra sugar? I like my tea a little on the sweet side."

Gladys sniffed, pulled some sugar packets out of her well-worn apron pocket, and dropped them in the center of the table. "Your wish is my command, your ladyship!" Then, without so much as a backward glance, she shuffled off again, mumbling to herself.

Doris beckoned us back in closer once again. "We all know how much anguish this most unfortunate incident has caused our little group."

"I haven't slept for days," said Lottie.

"Me neither," said Annie over the clack of her knitting needles.

"Exactly," said Doris. "It's like all these years we've been bonded in our failure, and now that's all in jeopardy!"

She talked about success as if it had kidnapped her firstborn child.

"I have a plan. We're going to launch an attack."

"Right on!" rallied Ruby, pumping an arm into the air.

An attack? On a publisher? What was she going to ask me to do? Drive the getaway car?

Doris paused as Gladys came back and topped off our water glasses, saying to Ruby, "No rabbit food today. Jim's cooking, and he's strictly a red-meat-and-potatoes guy. Shaping peanuts to look like little pork chops just isn't part of his skill set."

Then Ruby nodded, as Gladys scuffled away again.

Doris moved. "I've been calling them ever since I got the letter, and no one ever seems to answer the phone, so this is what we're going to do. We're going down to see that Shrew and Gavy person, and we are going to demand that he give me back *Love in the Forest* and that he writes us a nice, gilded rejection letter instead."

"And an apology," added Lottie. "You know, for liking it in the first place!"

Everyone nodded her own approval.

"This time we need to act fast." Doris seemed encouraged with determination. "Writing them a letter and waiting for their response is just not going to cut it. You all remember how long those can take to come back. Remember letter one hundred and thirty-three?"

Everybody, except me, nodded in remembrance.

"Letter one hundred and thirty-three?" I asked, tentatively taking a sip of my water.

"Eighteen months!" said Lavinia with disgust.

"Eighteen months after we sent in the manuscript before they finally replied!" added Doris. "No, we are going to hit this head-on." She dropped an octave, as if she were about to share a deep dark secret. "I have been researching all about them on the World Wide Web."

All the ladies looked impressed.

In between the food starting to arrive, Annie asked a question. "What if they refuse to give us a letter?"

"Then," said Doris, with a flourish of grandeur, "we will go to plan B!"

"Plan B?" I asked in a tight voice, not really wanting to know what that was.

Doris sucked on a piece of ice from her tea. "Ruby has agreed to chain herself to one of their toilets. It would be like the Occupy Movement. Except this will be handy in case she needs to 'go.' So, Ruby is on Occupy the Toilet Movement, no pun intended," she said seriously, "and Ethel will be there as my right-hand woman."

Flora fluttered her white lashes nervously as she delicately sipped her water through a thin straw and spoke for the first time. "What about me? How can I help?"

"I thought that would be obvious," snapped Doris. "You're the youngest in our group. If we need some womanly wiles to seduce this Gaveston fella, that will be your job. You'll bring him around to our way of thinking by the oldest trick in the book."

From Flora's expression, she hadn't the foggiest idea what Doris was referring to.

Doris became irritated. "You know, the femme fatale. A low-cut blouse and some sass."

I thought Flora was going to pass out on the spot. The blood visibly drained from her face, and she started to cough uncontrollably.

"What I need from you all now is commitment and solidarity."

Ruby put her fist in the air again, like a salute, and they all followed. Doris's was the only fist still in the air when Gladys arrived back with the last of our order. As she placed down Doris's food in front of her, she quipped dryly, "Can I get you some greasepaint to go with that patty melt, Rocky?"

"Just some ketchup," replied Doris curtly.

I must admit this had all been immensely entertaining, but it was time for me to gracefully step off this carousel ride and go back to the real world. I was actually grateful for my daughter's emergency. It was about to come in really handy.

As soon as Gladys left the table, I started on my exit speech. "I don't think there's really much I can do to help your group," I said, winding up gently.

"Nonsense," Doris replied through a mouthful of patty melt. "You're a book person. You're an insider, and you know the trade. We're going to need you to help us strategize."

"I would really love to help you—honestly, I would—but unfortunately I have to drive down to San Francisco next week to help my daughter. She's having some complications with her pregnancy, and she needs me there while her husband's away. So I'll have to bow out of this little adventure. I wish I could be there to help the cause. I really do," I lied, adding my most contrite expression.

Doris looked at me, and her eyes narrowed. I was getting used to her facial expressions. This meant she was thinking.

"Did you say San Francisco?" she asked intently.

"Yes," I said as I scraped at the bottom of my soup bowl. Something about the turn of this conversation was starting to make me feel uncomfortable.

"When did you plan on coming back?"

"Oh, about a week or so later, I'm not really sure yet . . ."

"Perfect," said Doris, getting excited. "You'll

be glad to know there *is* something you can do." She paused, taking a long sip of her iced tea, then added, "You can take us with you!"

Her words appeared to jumble as they entered my brain. I could have sworn she had just said, "You can take us with you."

Doris was exuberant: "You can drive us all down to San Francisco, where this publishing person has his main office. We can meet with him while you take care of your daughter and maybe catch some sights, and then we can all drive back together. It's a perfect plan." She slapped her hand down on the table abruptly, bouncing condiments, unable to control her excitement.

This was about the point I stopped listening. I stopped listening because I could hear a strange woman's voice in my head screaming. Was it mine?

As she outlined the rest of her plan to the others, I pulled myself together and tried to back-pedal as fast as I could, only it appeared someone had stolen my bike chain.

"I can't think how to . . . make . . . it . . . work . . ." was all I managed to squeeze out as my voice dried up and trailed off.

I was completely flummoxed.

"We'll make it work," said Doris with renewed confidence. "I can help with the driving, and we'll all chip in for gas. It's perfect because I don't like to fly. In fact, I haven't flown on an airplane since the seventies, ever since they started making their seats smaller to save money."

Making their seats smaller? Here was a woman in denial. I didn't want to mention that I didn't think the seats were getting any smaller.

"So. That's all settled," said Doris. "Annie, can you get someone to take care of your dogs? Annie boards dogs," added Doris, stating the obvious.

"Trevor can do it," Annie said decidedly. Even her needles seemed to be clicking together with excitement. As she talked through her plans, they moved faster and faster. "He likes to get himself in front of my propane heater whenever he can. I'll freeze him some TV dinners. There's nothing more attractive to an old bachelor than a warm house, a satellite dish, and homemade pot roast."

Still glued to my seat and listening to that crazy woman who kept on screaming in my head, I tried to think of anything else I could do to get out of this. I drew a blank.

Doris was in full flow. "Flora, can you get some time off from Stems?"

"I think so," said Flora as she picked at her salad. "I get vacation days with my hours, but I never, ever get to take them. I have nowhere to go. Mrs. Bickerstaff will be more than happy to see me take a vacation."

"Good," said Doris. "So we're all set then. Let's get together soon to make our final plans."

Walking back to the library, I was in shock. Oliver Hardy's voice had replaced the screaming woman in my head. He kept saying, "That's another fine mess you've got yourself into," over and over again.

At the end of the day, I trudged to my car, thoroughly miserable. As I pulled into our driveway, Martin was out on the lawn. He seemed happier than a pig in muck.

"Hey there, library lady! What do you think?"

I eyed his creation like a plate of yesterday's leftovers. I was too miserable to get excited over a monstrous cratelike thing with chicken wire across the front.

"What is it?" I asked glumly.

"Isn't that obvious? It's the raccoon trap I've been building."

I snapped and kicked at the corner of it with my foot.

"I hate raccoons! It's just another thing on this island taking over my life," I ranted over my shoulder, making a beeline for the house and bursting into tears.

He found me about two minutes later, the bath water running as I sat on the top of the toilet clutching a bottle of my favorite bubble bath.

"Are you okay? This isn't about the raccoons, is it?"

Twenty-plus years had obviously taught him a thing or two.

"I'm going on a five-day road trip with a bunch of crazy people."

He stared at me, a bemused look on his face. "What?"

"I'm going to California with Doris's rejection group."

His face registered that he was no closer to understanding. "Why don't I make you a cup of tea and you can tell me all about it?"

After my bath, we sat side by side on the sofa, and I recalled the day's conversation with Doris and her group.

"You sure do manage to get yourself into some interesting situations," he said. "My life with you has been many things, but never boring. Remember the time you took in our neighbor's five dogs when they went on vacation, when I was away working for Lockheed in Santa Barbara?"

"They all looked so sweet over the garden fence, and I thought they would be company for me," I said defensively.

"As I recall, you ended up sleeping on the bedroom floor and chasing the 'hounds from hell' as you described them off the furniture for two weeks. When I arrived back, you looked as if you had just been through World War III, and so did the garden."

"How can I forget—oh, what am I going to do?" I whined.

He wanted to fix the problem. "You can tell her no!"

"That's impossible!" I snapped back. "It's like dealing with a Rottweiler. Once she's got ahold of your throat, she won't let go until you're dead."

"Well, then, it looks like you're going to San Francisco with the Rottweiler and her pack," he said through a suppressed grin. "In some ways, I'm glad you'll have some company on the road. Besides, it might be fun, all you girls together. You did say when we moved here how you were looking forward to making friends and being part of the community."

"But that was back when I was envisioning *Steel Magnolias*. You know"—I tried my best version of a Southern accent—"here's some pie, honey, and you are just the perfect person to sew a panel with us at our quilting bee. It hasn't been quite like that, has it?"

"I know you haven't met anyone you feel close to yet here, not like you did in California, so . . ." His eyes blazed with mischievous excitement. "Maybe a rejected girls' club is a perfect fit for you. You could band together with all the other losers who can't find friends."

I punched him playfully on the arm.

He pulled me in closer, saying, "Maybe you need to give these girls a chance. Who knows? They might grow on you."

I envisioned the "girls" my husband was referring to: Doris the Rottweiler, Ethel dressed as an alien, the bejangled hippie chained to some corporate toilet, and the shrinking violet dressed as a classic femme fatale. Picturing them like that actually made me laugh.

"It's only a few days," he reminded me.

Chapter Six

FAIRY BELLS &
HOT-PINK JOGGING PANTS

The next day at work I heard a *psssssst* sound coming from the car maintenance section. Curiosity got the better of me as I followed it. Suddenly, the book *How to Service Your Carburetor* started to wiggle and was then replaced with Doris's face. She was staring out from the other side of the bookcase, framed between a book about changing brake shoes and how to select your next SUV.

"I just wanted to let you know we're all on track for Operation Shrewy Guy. That's the code name, so no one knows what we are talking about," she informed me in hushed tones.

"Okay," I said in my regular voice.

"Shhh! You never know who's listening. With a small town like this, you only have to sneeze on First Street, and someone will rush over with a tissue from Third! I just wanted to find out what time we'll all be setting off. We should meet at my house. That way we can take on all the supplies!"

"Supplies?"

She removed the SUV book to make some more room. "I've left Ethel over at the house, cooking up a storm! I'll freeze lots of good food in little plastic containers. That way, we'll have plenty of food for our expedition."

She made it sound as if we were going on safari. I stopped myself just in time from saying, "I'll bring the tranquilizer gun."

"I was planning on leaving early so we could get off the island and through Seattle before rush hour. So how does six a.m. suit you?"

"Six a.m.!" she spat out with disgust. "I'm not a toddler! How about we meet at my house at nine a.m.? That's much more civilized."

"Okay," I mumbled genially. It was beginning to be acutely apparent that I was not in charge of any part of this trip.

"Remember"—she leaned into the book space for emphasis—"keep this all to yourself. I have to go. I'd better get back before Ethel overcooks the hog's trotters for the road, or they'll be tough as old shoe leather!"

With those parting words, she shoved the books back into place, then disappeared as fast as she'd appeared. Hog's trotters! What had I gotten myself into? My heart sank as I stood there for a moment, staring at a book cover titled *The A to Z of Changing Oil*. It had a photo of a man holding a small metal can.

I told my husband all about my concerns after dinner that night. He raised his eyebrows.

"You've been telling me how you want to lose a few pounds. I can't think of a better time than when someone is serving hog's trotters for dinner."

"It's not funny," I said, following him outside to the garden as he picked up some tools to work on the raccoon trap. "That kind of food is going to stink my whole car up, not to mention all the room it will take up in the trunk!"

He leaned back, put his hand in his pocket, and pulled out two small silver bells. I was momentarily distracted.

"Are you hoping to earn an angel her wings?" I asked, unable to keep from teasing him.

He looked confused as he sat back on his heels with the two little silver bells pressed between his thumb and forefinger.

"What?"

"The bells, getting an early jump on Christmas? Or is this a special decoration just for the raccoons?"

"No, this is so that I'll know when the trap is sprung."

I wished I'd never asked, because then he went into lengthy technical instructions about how the raccoons would set off the bells once they were inside. He then took me on a tour of the trap. Crouching down, I peered inside. It looked like a four-star hotel for rodents, including a hefty box piled with straw, a bowl of dog food, and water.

"Not bad. All it's missing is room service. Ah, now I understand what the bells are for."

"You'll be glad of this trap when you get your trash can back," he said defensively. "You wait and see."

The next week or so was a whirlwind of activity, punctuated by lots of covert conversations at the library with Doris through different sections of the bookshelves.

She hadn't mentioned the local person or the story in her manuscript again, but I couldn't help wondering about it. Instead, we had important discussions consisting of such topics as: What clothes did those folks down there in California wear? What was the best sunscreen to stop her burning to a crisp? And would she need to buy some jogging pants? Jogging pants! The woman could barely get herself up the library steps without breathing heavily. But apparently, she'd heard somewhere that everybody jogged in California, so she didn't want to look out of place. She added, as she informed me of this nugget, that she believed she had less chance of being mugged if she blended in with the rest of the natives. I didn't want to say anything, but I couldn't think of anything odder than seeing Doris's frame squeezed into some jogging pants, and I pitied the mugger that would attempt to take her on. However, even though I tried to convince her otherwise, she said she would take a hot-pink pair "just in case. They might come in handy."

The day before we left, she popped her head through the shelf on handicrafts to inform me that Ruby was down with the Island Lurgy, and Annie was taking her place.

"It's so unfortunate. We really needed our radical player," she added, shaking her head. "But Ethel has already offered to step in at the last minute and be chained to the toilet instead."

I nodded, hoping no one was listening to this very odd conversation.

It was extremely early morning the day of the road trip when I heard Martin rustling around in the bedroom.

I opened one eye and looked at the clock. It read 2:30 a.m.

"Are you okay?" I croaked. "What are you doing?"

"I'm looking for the emergency flashlight," he whispered back. "You'd think we'd keep it in an easy place, you know, so we could find it before we burnt to death in our beds."

"It's in my sock drawer," I yawned.

"What do you need it for? And why are you whispering?" Sitting up, I watched him amble over to my drawer and start rifling through it.

"I just heard the bells tripped on the trap.

Finally, we're getting somewhere," he announced triumphantly.

"Are you sure it isn't just the wind?" I said, putting on my slippers and pulling my robe from the bedroom chair. I must admit I was more than a little curious to see the critter that had been holding my trash can for ransom.

"There's only one way to find out." He smirked, finding the flashlight, clicking it on and off, and striding down the stairs. I shuffled after him, putting on my robe. I hovered over him as he pulled on his boots and coat.

Just then, I clearly heard the distinct sound of bells tinkling across the wind.

"Oh," I cooed. "It sounds like Santa's here."

As he opened the back door, the biting cold Northwest November morning cut me to the core. Cinching my robe tighter, I followed him into the garden. He stalked up to the cage like a big-game hunter, and I crept behind him.

As we got closer, I could see there was actually something inside. It was moving around and sniffing at the food bowl. Martin shone his flashlight into the trap, and my first thought was how small this raccoon seemed, but as my eyes adjusted, I realized it didn't seem like a raccoon at all. It looked much more like . . .

"A cat!" My husband finished my thought out loud, the disappointment in his voice unmistakable.

"It's the Joneses'." I shivered.

They were our neighbors down the street. The poor thing looked petrified, frozen in the light. I was sure it was more than happy to have found a nice bowl of food in the middle of the night, but performing on Broadway had not been a part of its plan.

Martin groaned and opened the cage door. "Come on," he said gruffly. "Come on out of there."

But the poor thing just sat rooted to the spot, frozen with fear. I yawned again and plodded back up the yard toward the house. "You could always leave it in there. I've heard that raccoons are extremely partial to cat."

Hurrying back upstairs, I climbed back into the warm sheets. Martin joined me presently, snoring again as soon as his head hit the pillow. But I just lay there, staring up at the ceiling, a million things going through my mind.

When I finally did get to sleep, I had a nightmare. I was dressed in a safari outfit and was stalking prey with an enormous rifle in my backyard. A fairy flew by and thanked me for her wings. It was then that I realized in my dream that the raccoon trap must have been sprung, so I crept up to it ever so slowly. I could hear something chomping away inside the cage. I carefully came around, and as I aimed my shotgun at the prey, about to fire, it turned its head and looked at me.

It was Doris. She was down on all fours in a pink pair of spandex jogging pants, feeding on a bowl of hog's trotters. Then, as she waved at me, the bells on the cage started ringing louder and louder. I woke up with a start, and I realized the ringing was my phone.

Running down the stairs, I picked it up. It was Stacy.

"So you *are* there," she said, disgruntled.

"I had a bad night," I responded defensively.

How could this one person rattle me just by saying four words? I looked at the clock. It was 7:30 a.m.

"Aren't you starting out today?" Stacy asked, clearly irritated by the pause.

"Yes, in about an hour. Is everything okay?"

Boy, was that the wrong question.

She went into a thirty-minute rant about how frustrated she was to have to rest all the time, how her job wasn't being managed effectively while she was gone, and how Chris didn't understand how hard it was to be pregnant, especially as she was either peeing or throwing up all the time. She started to cry with frustration and in between snivels told me she would call me back later.

My head began to whirl. I felt like crawling into the raccoon trap with the Joneses' cat, and you wouldn't be able to get me out either. This was not going to be an easy visit.

I finished packing the car and came back in for

one last check. As I looked around at my cozy little cottage, my heart sank like a stone. I was going to miss it. Deep down in my boots, I was a homebody, and it wasn't easy to tear myself away. The shabby-chic interior with its cool blue-and-white-painted furniture just made my heart happy.

As I passed the raccoon trap, I glanced in. The Joneses' cat was still there, curled up in a ball, sleeping.

Driving toward Doris's, I started to feel upbeat as I reveled in the changing season. The late fall sun was dazzling, and along the roadsides, the leaves blanketed the ground like multicolored quilts. My sentimental mood disappeared like Scotch mist as soon as I pulled into her driveway.

I felt as if I'd joined the circus. It was chaotic. I made my way inside, going past heaped piles lining the hallway. Doris was marching around with a clipboard, barking out orders as Ethel ran around doing her bidding. Wading in, I made my way into the living room.

Flora was slung across the sofa like a bag of laundry, wearing layer upon layer of clothes, which included a hat, gloves, and a scarf. Scattered around her feet on the floor was an odd assortment of carpet and string bags. Clasped in her rice-paper hand was a weatherworn satchel and a copy of *Wuthering Heights*. She looked like she'd run away from home. She also looked unconscious.

Sitting on the sofa next to her was Annie. Compared to Flora, she looked positively radiant. She was wearing a pink poodle-knit sweater and brown rayon pants, and her short, gray hair was sporting a new, tight permanent. Her sparkly pink knitting needles clicked away rhythmically as she sat glued to the early news on the TV.

"Good morning." I nodded at Annie. Flora didn't even move. She was lying remarkably still, with her eyes firmly closed. "Is Flora okay?"

Annie chuckled to herself as she knitted.

"She's fine. We had a good old-fashioned girls' sleepover last night. We ate dinner, drank my homemade cherry brandy, and played cards till late. These young folk just aren't made of the same stuff we are."

I tried to imagine a sleepover at Doris's. The poor girl was probably stuffed full of cholesterol, with alcohol poisoning from potent homemade brandy. I was hoping that brandy and cards weren't going to be the trend.

The front door opened, and Lavinia's singsong greeting rang down the hallway. "Knock, knock, it's only us." The twins arrived in the living room looking like a breath of spring air and smelling like it too.

"It's a new scent I had flown here from Paris," said Lavinia, outstretching her wrist toward us.

"Lovely," Annie reflected.

"Lottie hates it, so I wear enough for both of us."

Lottie screwed up her nose. "It's just too musky for me. I prefer something more flowery."

Doris appeared in the living room with her clipboard.

Lottie straightened. "Here we are, reporting as ordered for Momma duty."

"Great." Doris tore off a sheet and handed it to Lottie with a bag of pills. "Here's a list of Momma's meds and when she needs to take them. Make sure she takes the blue ones in the morning and the red ones at night. The blue ones wake her up and the red ones help her sleep, and don't get them in reverse, otherwise you've got yourself a whole bunch of trouble."

"I like the sound of those blue ones," mused Lavinia. "I might have to try a couple of those myself."

As if on cue, Gracie floated into the room, wearing a pink nightgown, blue mud boots, and a red turban. Around her neck dangled a sparkly pink feather boa.

"Well, don't you look lovely," cooed Lavinia, taking Gracie by the hand and twirling her around in a circle.

"I'm going to a party," announced Gracie with a twinkle in her eye.

Doris sighed. "Momma, I told you to get dressed. Lavinia and Lottie are here to take you to their house, remember? You're staying there for a few days while I'm away."

"I am dressed," pointed out Gracie defensively. "Can't you see I'm wearing my party outfit?"

Doris was obviously agitated, but before she could comment, Lavinia took Gracie by the hand. "Come on. Let's see if we can find the rest of your party clothes, shall we? I don't think I've seen all of your wardrobe."

The two of them went off down the hallway toward Gracie's bedroom, Gracie gliding along on her toes.

Lottie then took Doris's arm. "Now, I don't want you to worry a jot. We have it all in hand. Your momma is going to be fine with us."

Doris nodded her thanks, then scanned her clipboard again.

"Okay, where was I?" Doris went on. "Oh yes. Flora, Annie, you two ladies are next. We need all your things out in the yard, ready to load into the car."

There was a sudden flutter of movement in Flora's ruffles, and she came to life. The two of them jumped to attention and started hustling. They'd obviously been part of one of Doris's military campaigns before. They seemed to know the drill.

I followed everyone outside. It looked as if we were about to have a rummage sale. The back of my ten-year-old forest-green Suburban was already open, and Ethel, beet-red, was pushing bags into every corner of it. The assembled troops lined up and stood to attention as if there was going to be an inspection at any minute.

Taking in the whole picture, I closed my eyes for a second. I had had such a different vision in my head of what this would be like. It seemed silly now thinking about it and bearing in mind the company I was traveling with, but I'd always had this kind of idyllic 1950s vision of going on a road trip. I had conjured up images of good-looking middle-aged women in lipstick and headscarves laughing and joking along an open highway. A bit like *Thelma & Louise*, without the attempted rape, killing, and suicide leap. However, the notion of the suicide leap seemed almost appealing now.

I opened my eyes. Doris and her clipboard were in front of me.

"Did you bring toilet paper?" she inquired in an extremely serious tone.

"Toilet paper?"

"Yes, toilet paper." She checked off other items on the list on her clipboard.

"Why would I need that?"

She looked up at me as if I'd lost my mind.

"I never travel without my own roll!" she said in a tone that made me sound like she thought I was a caveman. "You need it for the woods and those little box toilets along the road. I would never put myself in a position of getting caught short without my own paper."

"No, I haven't got any. I never travel with it normally," I said, a little bewildered.

She gave me one of those looks as if she were trying to work out if I were joking or just an idiot and then shook her head.

"Never mind. I'm on it." She yelled at the top of her lungs, "Ethel! We'll need an extra roll of toilet paper from the bathroom cupboard. Mrs. Johnson forgot hers."

Ethel marched into the house, emerged with a roll of toilet paper, and thrust it unceremoniously at me.

I got in the car to wait, sitting with "my roll" balanced on my knee. Presently, Flora and Annie joined me, each armed with their own rolls too. I guessed I wasn't the only unenlightened one.

Lavinia opened the door and poked in her head. "I just wanted to say good-bye to you and good luck." Seeing us all sitting there clutching our "rolls" she stopped in her tracks. "Let me guess," she said, touching a pink, manicured nail to her lips. "Plan C is to TP the publishers?"

"Don't ask," I replied as Flora and Annie's expressions echoed the same sentiment.

Gracie stuck her head in the window. She was now suitably dressed in a powder-blue lounge suit and her white wispy-wool hair had been combed into captivity, but she was still sporting her pink, sparkly boa.

"Guess what? I'm going for a sleepover at

Lavinia's. Won't that be fun?" Her eyes danced wildly with the excitement of it all.

Doris squashed herself into the passenger side of the car, saying, "Looks as if we're ready to roll. I have the maps and directions, so I'll ride shotgun."

"Oh, goody," I said under my breath.

Ethel got in the back as Lottie appeared at the other passenger window.

Doris issued last-minute instructions. "Now, don't forget Trevor has the dogs at Annie's place, so they should be fine there. I'll try and call to check in on them and Momma. I don't own a cell phone—they fry your brain—so if you need to get a hold of me, Annie has her iPad. You could e-mail us, or Janet has her cell phone. Could you write down the number for them?" She looked over in my direction.

I did as I was told, handing Lavinia a hastily written note.

I could hear Gracie's singsong voice in the wind as we drove away. "Good-bye, everybody. Come and visit me again soon!"

The clock on the dashboard informed me it was already 11:30. We might just make the noon ferry off the island if I put my foot down.

"First things first," said Doris as I pulled the car onto the road. "Let's stop at the Crab for some lunch."

"But don't you want to get on the road?" I asked, mystified.

"Without lunch? Why, I would barely have the energy to turn the map pages."

I tried to find a compromise.

"What if we get going and find a restaurant on the mainland? At least we'll be on the road."

She screwed up her eyes and peered at me, then snapped, "I know what I'm getting at the Crab. I don't trust a mainland patty melt the same way."

"They add hormones!" declared Ethel, wrinkling up her nose.

Doris nodded in agreement. "Exactly. I have enough of those myself. I definitely don't want any more hormones!"

What could I say to that?

Gladys watched us, bemused from behind the till, as we all burst out of the car, an act that I'm sure resembled a ripened boil about to pop. We all trudged in. She pulled out a bunch of menus, sniffed, and eyed Doris mischievously. "Will you and your renegades be wanting your usual war bunker?"

The joke was wasted on Doris.

"The back booth," she demanded.

As I passed one of the tables, I spotted my husband, who was just finishing off what looked suspiciously like a cheeseburger and fries. He looked a little sheepish. He knew my views on cholesterol-laden foods, especially for lunch.

"Hi, honey. I didn't expect to see you so soon."

"Obviously," I smirked, reaching down to his plate and stealing one of his leftover french fries.

"My thinking was I would have a large lunch, to save me from cooking later."

"Hmmm," I murmured. I had a pretty good idea the Crab would be seeing a lot of my husband over the next few weeks.

He quickly changed the subject. "How come you're still here?"

"Oh, our fearless leader couldn't face the world on an off-island patty melt!"

"Sounds as if it's going to be a long journey."

"Yes. And one that hasn't even started yet!"

We finally made it out of the Crab at around 12:45 p.m. and headed out of town. I wasn't even a mile out of the village when Annie leaned forward and whispered, "Are you stopping at the gas station at the end of town?"

"I wasn't planning to. I got gas last night."

"I just need to . . . go. That iced tea went straight through me!"

"No problem," I said through clenched teeth.

I had left home four hours before, and we had barely made it to the end of town. It was worse than a kindergarten field trip.

"We don't have time," boomed Doris. "We're scheduled to get the one o'clock boat. You'll just have to hold it until we get on the ferry!"

So much for lipstick and headscarves. We were

just pawns in Doris's outlandish plan. We missed the one o'clock ferry and boarded the one thirty. As soon as we parked, Annie made a dash out of the car and ran upstairs to the bathroom. Doris followed, muttering something about getting herself an iced tea, and Flora and Ethel tagged along.

I decided to stay in the car. Alone with my own thoughts, I drew in a deep breath. I'd always loved traveling, which I'd found challenging over the years with my fear of flying. But there was nothing to compare with the experience of meeting new people and seeing new landscapes. Now, with the craziness of the planning of this trip behind me, I looked out at the waves of the Puget Sound as they broke at the foot of the ferry. As I absorbed their hypnotic rolling, I felt myself starting to relax, unwind, and actually feel excited. I marveled as a seagull hovered on the wind then dove down into the water and retrieved a fish. I ruminated on the fact that there was nothing more refreshing than experiencing life fully in the moment. An open road was good for clearing the mind, with nothing to distract you, nothing to pull you from the one goal of getting from here to there.

I had mixed feelings about how the visit would go. I was looking forward to seeing Stacy, even though the last time we had been to stay was still a painful memory. While she had been at work,

Martin and I had decided to surprise her by filling her garden with beautiful pink, yellow, and purple spring plants to soften all the depressive straight lines of her yard. On returning home, she had shrieked, dropped her shopping, and burst into tears. Apparently without realizing it, we had "unfenged her shui." We had apologized, digging up the offensive tulips and daffodils and giving them to one of her grateful neighbors, but it had made the rest of our visit very frosty indeed. I sighed knowingly; having children would change her, that was for sure. There was no time for monitoring complex chi patterns when a toddler is tearing through your yard covered in toilet paper and ketchup. The realization hit me once again: my little girl was about to become a mommy, and I was going to be a grandmother.

I found myself in a thoughtful and forgiving mood when they all arrived back at the car twenty minutes later. As they got in, I wondered if we would bond on this trip. Who knew? Maybe in ten years' time we'd all be laughing and talking about how much we'd enjoyed our first road trip.

My foolish illusions were quickly shattered.

"What's wrong with you?" asked Doris suspiciously. "Why are you smiling in the mirror like a Cheshire cat?"

"Oh, nothing," I said wistfully. "I was just thinking."

"You keep grinning at yourself like that, and

someone is going to come along and haul you away to the funny farm."

I sighed deeply, put the car into drive, and left the ferry to join the traffic on the freeway. Doris scrutinized her maps and looked at her watch, Flora listened to her iPod and looked out the window, Annie quietly read a woman's magazine, and Ethel peered forward, stone-faced.

It was slow going on the road, and I hoped we weren't going to hit traffic downtown. But my fear was realized when, thirty minutes later, we were bumper-to-bumper with the downtown traffic, crawling along slower than a herd of snails moving through molasses.

The women amused themselves. Annie knitted and read and punched Flora on the arm, yelling, "Slug bug" every time we passed a Volkswagen Bcetle. Flora did her best to ignore her as soft tones of classical music floated from her iPod. She wrote poetry in a small leather-bound book, staring endlessly out the window with a pencil poised at her lips. Then suddenly, as if one of the passing trucks gave her the answer to life, she would start to scribble away. Ethel, who'd fallen asleep, snored softly, her head thrown back and her mouth open. Doris felt the need to feed us after only twenty minutes from the numerous plastic containers she ordered us to pass around as we went along.

It was 4:30 p.m. before we saw the back of

Seattle, and I breathed a sigh of relief as we left the city behind us. We pulled off to get coffee, and on returning to the car, Doris slammed her map book closed and looked hard at me.

"Okay, I think I'll take this leg of the journey," she said in her demanding manner and threw her bulk behind the wheel. "Ethel, you ride shotgun and help me with the map reading. Janet, you take the backseat." I must admit I was tired from driving through traffic and was happy to give up the wheel, though I was also a little nervous.

"Have you driven an SUV before?" I inquired as I climbed in beside Flora and Annie.

"Of course," she said, not sounding terribly confident.

"Because they can be tricky things if you—"

She shut me down. "I've been driving for forty years. I'm sure I can figure it out." With that, she threw it into reverse.

We lurched to a stop, she put it in drive, and tested the gas pedal fishtailing all the way across the parking lot. Dear God, it was going to be a long journey with her at the wheel. She finally managed to get the hang of it and screeched off down the road.

Once we were on the freeway, Doris punched the buttons of the radio until she found a country music channel. Tapping the steering wheel and singing out of tune at the top of her voice, she settled into her groove as the car nipped along at a clip. I looked around the car as we traveled. Having not traveled in the backseat much, I had a different perspective sitting there. I noted the gray fabric interior was starting to look worn and scuffed, and the carpets muddied from island living could do with a cleaning. Also, there was the little hole in the backseat upholstery that Martin had punctured when carrying tools in my car once. As Doris drove, my eye was drawn to the little angel good-luck charm that hung from my mirror. It glinted as it swung back and forth in the light.

It was a beautiful evening, crisp and cold but clear, and my spirits started to soar. We'd been traveling for about an hour when Annie put down her knitting needles and pulled out her iPad.

"Time for my soap," she said, her eyes twinkling.

I had to admit I'd never been into TV soap operas. I didn't know what all the fuss was about, and Flora didn't look that impressed either. After about five minutes, I was totally hooked.

There was this doctor, and his secretary was pregnant with his baby. She wasn't telling him, but she felt there was something wrong with it. The doctor's wife was a witch, and the secretary was also dating a guy who had just come back from the war and was having flashbacks . . . I got so engrossed in the show that I didn't see that the traffic had started to congest.

Then I felt a sharp pull and heard the screeching of the brakes as they strained to stop. A minibus loomed large and ominously in front of us. I felt Doris hit the brakes again harder as I held my breath and closed my eyes. Flora screamed beside me as Doris spun the car off onto the hard shoulder with a crunch of gears and the smell of burned rubber. We had missed the back of the minibus by a hair's breadth.

As Doris started moving again, it was obvious something was not right with the car. It was making a strange grinding noise and felt sluggish. Just outside Portland, it was definitely limping along.

"I think we need to get the car checked out," I said nervously from the backseat.

Reluctantly, Doris pulled off the freeway to look for a garage.

Chapter Seven

A KNIGHT UNDER A WHITE CAR

After about a half a mile, we came upon Jim's Automotive. Annie disappeared to find a bathroom, and the rest of us entered the garage. A radio was playing softly, and someone was singing along. A large heater radiated warmth, and the rich, earthy aroma of black coffee mixed with engine oil filled the air. There were a couple of cars in various states of repair, a red Honda up on a ramp, and a white Alfa Romeo on the ground. Tools were strewn around haphazardly. Under the Alfa Romeo, someone with long legs wearing blue work overalls tapped and hummed along with the music.

"Excuse me, young man," Doris said as she knocked on the hood of the car.

The humming stopped. The mechanic stood up to greet us; he was tall, well over six feet, with thick black hair and striking emerald-green eyes. His overall sleeves were rolled up, and from his elbows to the tips of his fingers he was covered in grease. His name was Dan, according to the label on his breast pocket.

"Oh hello," he said. "What can I do for you today?"

He addressed us all, but his eyes found Flora's and held them. We all noticed it, especially Flora, who blushed and lowered her own.

"There seems to be a problem with my car," I said, cutting through the extended "Moment in Time" pause.

"Well, you've come to the right place."

He listened intently as Doris explained the symptoms but looked directly at Flora, saying, "Let's get you back on the road. Can you give me about an hour to look at it?"

I looked at my watch. It was nearly six o'clock. "I think we should try and find a hotel and check in for the night. Are there any nearby?"

"Actually, my parents own a lovely B&B just up the road. It's very quiet at this time of the year, so I'm sure they'll have rooms. And I may have some sway to get you a reduced rate," he added with a coy smile.

"That sounds perfect." I was relieved.

"Okay. Let me clean a little of this grease off. I'll call my parents. Then I can walk you down to their house."

With a final glance at Flora, he walked off toward the bathroom, and she let out a breath beside me. I was pretty sure she'd been holding it since we'd arrived.

Ten minutes later, Dan was back, washed and

wearing jeans, a denim-blue shirt, and a black leather jacket. He closed up the garage, and we followed him up the road, carrying our overnight cases.

"So, where are you coming from?" He directed his question at Flora.

She just blushed and looked at her feet.

Annie answered him. "We're from a little town called Southlea Bay. You've probably never heard of it."

"On the contrary, my aunt lives there. Do you know Karen Shore at all?"

"I do," I answered in surprise. "She works with me at the Southlea Bay library. It's a small world, isn't it?" I mused.

"She loves it there, and I don't blame her. I love to read too," he added. "She always says no one could be unhappy while they're surrounded by books."

"I know what she means," answered Flora in a small, tight voice. "I feel the safest surrounded by my books. They're like my friends." She bit her lip nervously, as if worried perhaps she'd revealed too much to him. But he murmured agreement as she added, "Friends that are always there for you . . ." Her voice trailed off as we arrived in front of a little swinging sign that read "Primrose Hill Bed and Breakfast," and Dan unlatched a white picket gate.

The house was an impressive Queen Anne–style

Victorian, complete with a turret, gables, and gingerbread detailing. Its clapboard walls were painted a soft blush pink and its gables a creamy white. A stunning lattice arbor lush with crimson foliage invited us onto the scrubbed white deck adorned with overflowing planters and a couple of well-worn rocking chairs.

"How lovely," said Annie, clapping her hands as Dan trotted up the steps and rang the bell.

Dan's mother greeted us at the door as if we were long-lost family, and Dan offered to carry our overnight bags up to our rooms.

"How gallant," remarked Annie once he was out of earshot. "Just like he fell right out of a romance novel." She bumped Flora with her elbow.

Flora blushed to her toes, burying her face deeper into her long paisley scarf.

"I don't trust him," snapped Ethel, who'd insisted on clutching her bag. "Him being a man and all!"

Dan left to return to the garage. His mother commented, "You ladies look half-frozen to death. I'll go and get dinner started right away."

Beckoned in by the heat emanating from a magnificent white marble Corinthian-style fire-place, we made our way into her sitting room. The room was impeccable, elegantly decorated with sumptuous fabrics and tasteful antiques. A highly polished mahogany coffee table centered the room, surrounded by overstuffed armchairs and plump footstools. From the ceiling, tiered crystal chandeliers reflected sparkling white light into every corner of the room. Annie planted herself in front of the TV and turned on the evening news as Doris opened her map book and made notes. Ethel seated herself at a high, glossy card table and began to work on a half-finished jigsaw of marine life as Flora wandered thoughtfully about the house.

We polished off a fabulous home-cooked meal of chicken pie, mashed potatoes, and vegetables before Dan arrived back. He joined us in the dining room just as his mother appeared with a decadently layered chocolate cream pie, and his father served us coffee.

Dan poured himself a cup and sat down next to Flora, who colored for the umpteenth time that evening.

"Well," he said, taking a sip, "I have good news, and I have bad news. Which do you want first?"

Doris and I spoke at the same time.

"The bad," she said.

"The good," I said.

Amused, he looked at us both. "Which one?"

"The good," said Flora, daring to look at him for a moment.

His gaze lingered again.

"The good news is the problem you came in with was your tracking. When you swerved hard on the freeway, you must have knocked it out of alignment. That was very simple, and I've already put it right."

"Wonderful!" said Annie, clapping her hands together.

"Not so fast," said Doris, ever cautious. "What's the bad news?"

"It's going to cost us five thousand dollars!" spluttered Ethel. Then she squinted her eyes at Dan as if she were about to bite him.

"No!" he said and sounded shocked at the thought. "That was a quick job. I wasn't even going to charge you for it. The thing is you have a much bigger problem with your engine. I checked all your systems while I had your car up, and your ECM is damaged."

"ECM?" asked Doris, puzzled.

"It's our Engine Control Module," said Flora. "It controls all the workings of the engine . . ." Then she blushed beet red. We all looked at her, utterly surprised. Dan looked impressed.

"Exactly," said Dan as we all continued to stare in wonderment at Flora.

Self-conscious of our gaze, she responded in a whisper, "My father used to restore cars." Then she returned all her focus to her teacup.

Forcing his gaze from her, Dan went on, "To be honest with you, the engine could go at any minute. It's amazing you got this far without a problem."

"Are you sure?" I asked, puzzled. "It's been running okay."

"Did you notice any warning lights on your dashboard?"

Now I could feel my own cheeks starting to color. "Well, yes. But my husband said we probably just had a loose connection or something . . ." my voice trailed off pathetically.

"To be fair, he would probably be right half of the time, but unfortunately this time there actually is a problem."

"Can you fix it?" asked Annie over a mouthful of chocolate cream pie.

"Technically, yes." He took another sip of his coffee. "But unfortunately I don't have the right parts. I phoned around, and the quickest I could get them out here would be two days."

"Two days!" we all echoed.

"But I need to be in San Francisco. My daughter needs my help." I couldn't help sounding petulant.

He was instantly reassuring. "I do have a solution, but it's a little bit extreme, so you may want to think about it before you decide."

"What is it?" said Doris. "We really need to get back on the road."

He made circles in the sugar bowl with a spoon. "Tomorrow, I have to go down to southern Oregon to pick up a car from a friend's garage. I called and asked, and he happens to have the

part you need. I was going to take the train . . ."
Then sounding more self-conscious, he said,
"But if you wouldn't be too uncomfortable"—he
afforded himself a quick sideways glance at
Flora—"I could travel down in your car with
you tomorrow. That way, if you have any
problems I could patch it up as we go."

Doris responded immediately. "That's very
kind of you, young man. Are you sure we won't
be inconveniencing you in any way?"

"The way I see it"—he finished the dregs of his
coffee—"is that we would all be helping each
other out." His voice petered off as his eyes met
Flora's once more.

It was like watching two sixteen-year-olds.

"I think that sounds great," said Doris.

After dinner, we insisted on helping clear away
the dinner dishes. Dan and Flora lingered at the
sink as they slowly dried the plates. I joined
everyone else in the sitting room and settled to
read a magazine.

Flora arrived back in the main room wearing
her coat and hat.

"Dan and I were thinking of going to see a
movie . . ." Her voice trailed off.

For a split second, there was complete silence in
the room as the reality of what she was saying
sank in. Flora was going on a date, the first of her
life, for sure. I smiled to myself.

After they left, Dan's parents joined us in the

sitting room and chatted comfortably about running their B&B. They spoke fondly about raising their family, especially Dan. They told us in hushed tones that he'd suffered a serious breakup the year before and they were thrilled to see him taking an interest in Flora.

"She seems very sweet," said his dad. "Have you known her long?"

"I've known Flora her whole life, and her parents before they died. She's a lovely girl," said Annie. "As far as I know, this is the first time I've seen her show interest in anyone."

"How sad that her parents passed away," sighed his mom. "She seems so young to have lost them."

"Don't you worry about Flora," reassured Doris, tapping Dan's mother's hand and knocking back a glass of cherry brandy in one gulp. "She has us."

Doris set up a card table in the dining room, and the group started a lively game of poker. I excused myself and returned to the sitting room with a book.

Later, I was in the kitchen fetching myself a glass of water when I heard the gate open in the front garden.

Glancing out the window, I noticed Jack Frost had woven his magic spell. All about the garden, the bright porch light reflected crystalized flowers and sculptures of frozen blades of grass. Through the icy pane, I saw that Flora and Dan were back and outside under the arbor. They seemed oblivious to the arctic temperatures.

She had her upturned face to him, and her eyes were alive and sparkling. She appeared to be listening intently to every word he was saying. Just then, he must have said something witty because she burst out into a delicate ripple of laughter. It took me by surprise, as I realized it was the first time I could honestly say I had seen her really look joyful, let alone laugh.

They fell in the front door ten minutes later, giggling. There was undoubtedly the presence of young love in the air. It permeated the house like the fragrance of wild roses, bringing an added sweetness to the evening. Flora was glowing; I couldn't believe it was the same girl who had left the island with us that morning. They joined us in the sitting room, talking excitedly about their night, finishing each other's sentences as they recalled the terrible movie they'd just seen.

I listened for a while then excused myself to make my way to bed. As I wandered up the stairs, I glanced back one more time. The lovebirds were quietly talking and laughing together as they toyed with the jigsaw puzzle Ethel had abandoned.

I sat on my bed and dialed Stacy. Chris answered and said she was doing much better but was exhausted and had gone to bed early and then reassured me, telling me not to worry as he was taking care of her. I told him to give her my love before I hung up and dialed home. As I waited for the call to connect, I thought about how much I liked Chris. He met Stacy at UCLA while he was getting his computer science degree and Stacy had been studying business. He was quiet and thoughtful and made a good match for Stacy's volatile nature. They hit it off from the beginning. After graduating, it was only a matter of time before they moved back to his home in San Francisco. Stacy started a job she loved in advertising, and Chris had found a fantastic job working for a major computer technology company. He traveled a lot for work and sometimes was even able to take Stacy with him.

After a couple of rings, Martin picked up, and I filled him in on the events of the afternoon. He seemed taken aback by the fact that the red check engine light, which had been illuminated for the past month, had, in fact, actually meant we were supposed to check the engine.

"Really?" he said, not meaning to be comical. "That's the last thing I would have thought of doing. It seems to flick on and off like a Christmas tree light. I was sure it was just a loose connection."

He paused for a moment. He was probably standing like a statue in our hallway, thinking, staring at his shoes. In the silence, I heard the distinct sound of a cat meowing.

"What was that?" I asked, already suspecting the answer.

"What was what?"

"It sounded like a cat."

There was a hesitant pause.

"Do you remember how the Joneses' cat got into the raccoon trap?"

"Yeeess."

"The thing wouldn't come out all day, and I finally managed to coax it out with a piece of cooked salmon. I took it over to their house earlier this evening. But, as it turns out, it's not their cat after all. Theirs is a boy, and this is a girl! So, I thought it was cruel just to turn it out when it was so cold . . ."

"Don't tell me," I said, finishing this story. "It's moved in!"

"Just until I can find its owner. I've been asking around." He was trying to earn some extra points. "I also called the animal shelter, but they're full right now. She's on their waiting list."

Here it comes, I thought, I could feel it in my bones . . .

"She's such a sweet little thing, really, lovely and good company. I was worried that the raccoons would eat her for breakfast."

My husband's love of cats was obvious in his concerned tone.

"So, let me get this straight. You were supposed to be getting rid of one wild animal and instead you've taken in another one!"

"Yes," he answered sheepishly.

"I just might have something to say about that."

"I thought you might." Then he added quickly, "But, unfortunately, I have to go. I think I hear Dwayne at the door. Love you. Bye." He hung up. He was being playful, and it made me laugh. It was well after ten, and I was sure there was no one at our door.

Under that "I've got it all together" exterior, my husband had always been a big teddy bear. I was pretty sure that the cat had come home to stay.

I fell into bed exhausted, but at about three o'clock, I woke up again. I often had trouble sleeping the first night away from home. I was also worried about Stacy. I put on my robe and slippers and went to get myself a glass of warm milk.

When I arrived downstairs, I was surprised to find that Doris was also awake. She stood in pink curlers, staring absently out the kitchen window.

"Doris, are you okay?"

I seemed to bring her back from a faraway place.

"Oh, Janet, I couldn't sleep. I have a lot on my mind."

"Anything I can help with?"

"I don't know," she said. "It's all . . . too awful."

There was a deep sadness in her eyes. This was a very different Doris than the one she presented to the world. She seemed utterly forlorn and lost. It was quite disconcerting.

I tried to buoy her spirits as I prepared my drink. "Why don't you tell me about it?"

She looked at me intently, as if once again she were trying to figure out if she could trust me or not, then, appearing to make up her mind, she sighed deeply.

"Do you remember when I told you there was another important reason that I needed to get back the manuscript from the publishers?"

I nodded and sat down at the table. Doris joined me.

"I did some more investigating, because I just couldn't believe this scandalous story could be true. This evening I made a phone call to a person that could help me confirm some of the facts, and they told me something that has made me believe more than ever that the story must be true."

"We'll just have to make sure we get that manuscript back from the publishers," I said optimistically as I took a sip of my milk.

I had to admit I had been hoping she'd divulge the story to me. I plucked up the courage to ask her a question I'd been wondering about ever since she'd confided in me.

"How did you find this story?"

Doris narrowed her eyes again as if she were trying to figure out how much she wanted to share.

"I was given it. The person who wrote this particular piece has passed away and often wrote many fictional short stories. I just assumed it was fiction just like all the others."

"How did you find out it wasn't?" I took another sip of my milk.

"By accident." She wrung her hands slowly. "There was some information in the story that was mentioned to me in passing the other day. And so that's why I decided to do some more checking."

"And where is the original story now?" I asked, finishing my drink.

"It's totally safe. As soon as I suspected any-thing, I hid it in a very safe place. I didn't want it to be found while we were away. The story is about . . . someone very dear to me and . . ." She paused then, obviously trying to collect herself.

I took the opportunity to reach out and take her hand. "It's one of your rejected ladies, isn't it?"

Doris's expression confirmed my suspicions, and ever so slowly, she nodded her head.

"The person who wrote this story lived in our village for a spell and, yes, it's about one of my ladies."

"Don't worry, Doris. We'll be in San Francisco in two days and you'll get it back and this will all go away."

She nodded. That thought seemed to cheer her a little, but I could tell there was still something behind her hesitant smile. I sensed there was a lot more to this story by the way it was affecting her, something much deeper.

Chapter Eight

THE LITTLE RED WAGON THAT COULD

The next morning I lay half-awake, roused by the intoxicating smell of coffee mingled with waffles. I pondered the conversation Doris and I had shared in the middle of the night. The fact it was about one of the rejected ladies now had me wondering. Jumping into the shower, my mind was alive, trying to figure out which one it involved.

Lavinia? There wasn't much she hadn't done that could be devastating to her life or that we didn't already know about. Or Ruby for that matter. She would be proud of her own scandal. Could it be Lottie? She had a very spotless reputation. If there had been something in her past, it would be devastating for her. What if Ruby wrote horror because she really killed people as a hobby? Or maybe Ethel was really just quiet because she had a secret illegitimate child she kept in a closet at home.

I grinned to myself as I rinsed off. My husband was always remarking about my wild imagination. Maybe I should start writing books too, and if I joined the Rejection Club, they wouldn't even need to be good.

I dressed and made my way downstairs.

Dan's mother was busy in the kitchen. She wore a flowery apron and her hair pulled up in a chignon. Doris was by her side, helping. She nodded at me but didn't acknowledge the conversation from the night before as she poured waffle batter into the iron.

Dan and Flora were already seated at the table in the dining room. Flora looked like a different person. Her pale, long hair was smooth and flowing about her shoulders instead of in the usual tight braid, and rather than a hat and layers, she was wearing a cream chiffon dress, pretty earrings, and a light perfume. Flora turned to me, excited as I entered. "Can you believe it?" she enthused. "Dan adores sea turtles and Italian opera, just like me."

"And Flora loves saffron rice," added Dan, equally in awe of his new muse.

"Ummm," I said, trying to keep the cynical tone out of my voice.

Oh, to be young and falling in love. I wanted to tell them turtles and rice were all well and good, but if Dan wanted to build a raccoon trap in their garden in twenty years' time, don't let him because they would probably end up with a cat.

After breakfast, we said our good-byes to Dan's parents, and Dan brought the car from the garage. We were a jovial party as we got into the car that morning, and even Doris, who had been thoughtful over breakfast, had cheered.

Even though it was large, I knew it would still be a squeeze in my ten-year-old Chevy Suburban. As my front car door greeted me with its usual grinding creak, I got behind the wheel, and Ethel squashed in, petulantly, beside me on the front bench seat. Doris squeezed in next to her and started scrutinizing her maps. In the back, Annie got in one side and the lovebirds got in the other. As we settled, Annie put on her soap. I drove along, listening to the story as it drifted from the backseat of the car.

The doctor character had found out his secretary was having his baby and was putting pressure on her to give it up for adoption. The other guy she was also dating was now having delusions and believed he was still undercover during the war. In the meantime, the wife of the doctor had suspected her husband's affair after stealing the secretary's medical chart from his office and had decided she was going to put a hit on him.

I was totally engrossed. So were Dan and Flora behind me, as Ethel periodically huffed her disapproval.

Once it had finished, Annie was about to turn off her iPad when a little bell went off. She looked at it mysteriously. It was obvious she had no idea what it meant. She waved it in front of Dan, who responded matter-of-factly, "Someone is FaceTiming you."

Annie blinked and shrugged. Chuckling, he took

it from her and pressed a button. All at once, the car was filled with the voices of Lottie, Lavinia, and Gracie.

"Surprise!" they shrieked as their faces appeared on the screen.

"Oh!" squealed Annie. "It's the girls."

"It is!" said Lavinia.

"Look how tech savvy we've become since you left. It took us a while to figure it out, but here we are, larger-than-life and beaming to you all the way from Southlea Bay."

"How y'all doing?" asked Lavinia. "Whizz me around the car so I can see how you're all holding up."

Annie obliged. I waved at them as Annie flashed it in front of me.

"Wait, hold everything!" Lavinia shrieked. "Go back! Is that a man you have in the car?"

"Yes, it's Dan," giggled Annie.

"Ethel," said Lavinia in a mock disapproving way, "you didn't sneak a man under that duvet I saw you stuffing into the trunk, now, did you?"

Ethel's eyes became as large as saucers. It was obvious how she felt about that comment.

Annie filled them in on how we'd ended up with Dan and about the rest of our adventures so far.

"My, you girls are having so much fun. I wish I could have come along," sighed Gracie.

"Next time, Momma, when you're not recovering from the Lurgy," Doris shouted from the front.

They caught us up with all the village gossip. Ruby was feeling much better, and the rest of the rejection group was planning a mini group meeting while we were on the road.

"Just for fun," added Lavinia. "But we gotta go. Gracie and I are planning an old-fashioned tea dance, and we have a lot to do. Bye."

We all shouted our good-byes, and Annie hung up.

Having Dan in the car certainly changed the dynamics of our group. He was fun and playful, and all of our interactions seemed easier and more comfortable as we settled into our second day. It was confirmed to me when Doris leaned across and gently tapped me on the hand, saying, "Let's pull over and get some lunch, shall we, dear?"

Dear? Her whole face lit up, and I realized it was the first time I'd seen her cheerful since the day of the rejection meeting. It made me realize how serious this was for her.

Seeing a sign for a little mom-and-pop-style café, I pulled into the parking lot. A dainty silver bell tinkled as we opened the door. Cheery red-and-white-checked tablecloths dressed the dozen or so tables. Behind the counter, a middle-aged woman wearing an apron of the same red-and-white check was putting delicious-looking pies into a glass display case. We practically tiptoed across the polished oak floor, which creaked as we made our way into the center of the room.

Smiling sweetly, our server came over to greet us.

"Welcome to the Little Red Wagon. I'm Betty," said our host in a soft, singsong way. "Are you here to eat?"

I wanted to say, "No, actually I'm here to stay for the rest of my life," but found myself nodding instead. She led us to a large table in the back, close to the fireplace. Behind it, a quaint picture window framed a peekaboo view of a bubbling brook that ran behind the café. It was delightful.

"It's warm and cozy over here," she sang, placing menus on the table in front of us. "Now what can I get for you all?"

"I would like a patty melt," said Doris decisively.

"You're in for a treat," enthused Betty. "That's our chef's specialty."

Doris looked pleased, and the rest of us ordered. Betty went off to get our food.

Dan turned to the group. "So, tell me more about what you'll be doing in California."

Doris straightened up. "We're on our way to save our rejection group."

"Yes, Flora told me about that," said Dan, and his eyes flashed in her direction. "Tell me, how did your group get started?"

Doris launched into her story with gusto. "Three years ago, Lottie, Lavinia, Momma, and I decided to start a group to support each other as we wrote together. So I wrote *Love in the Forest*. It's sort of a mix of Jane Austen and Stephen King, if you know what I mean."

I didn't know about Dan, but I certainly had no idea what she meant. I couldn't connect those two authors together in my brain no matter how I tried. But Dan just nodded and appeared to be intensely interested.

"For over a year, we laughed and cried together reading excerpts of our books, and it was like a little party every month. We were actually genuinely sad when the day came for us to send our books off to the publishers because we were going to miss our little group. So, we decided to get together once we heard back."

Betty came back with our drinks, and Doris's enthusiasm was so infectious that even our server seemed to be drawn in.

"I actually received my first letter about a month later and was so excited because it would mean another party for us. We had such a fabulous evening reminiscing about our year and were having such a good time that we almost forgot to open the letter. But just before the girls left, Lottie reminded us. We gathered around the fireplace to open the envelope."

I noticed Betty was hanging around topping off waters that appeared to be already full. She then started to wipe off the already clean table adjoining ours, fully engrossed. As I sipped my water, I could tell Doris had told this story many times before.

"Inside, I found a thick, creamy-white piece of paper. You know, the sort you get at those fancy stationery stores, with the embossing on it?"

Doris closed her eyes and recited it, word for word:

"Dear Mrs. Newberry,
Thank you for sending us your manuscript, *Love in the Forest*. Unfortunately, we feel there would not be enough interest in a book where aliens abduct Elizabeth Bennett and she time travels, only to go back with a dishwasher. If you would like your manuscript returned, please send us the postage, and we will be happy to send it back to you."

"How sad," sighed Betty as she served our food.

I looked around the table; Dan was listening to every word as he started eating his hamburger.

Doris carried on. "We all sat there for a while. We let the news sink in. Then Lavinia broke the silence. She said, 'It's a real shame the way this turned out, because it was a lovely party. At least we'll be able to spend some time together again if we get another rejection letter.'

"And that's when it hit me. Finishing our books had left a void in our lives, as we no longer had a reason to be together. And that was when the Rejection Club was born.

"We made a pact that every time a rejection letter came in we would have a party and see them as a blessing because it would mean we would still have a reason to get together, even though it was to share in our failure. Before long, we heard of other writers who were getting rejection letters and wanted to join our group. Now there are many of us."

"That is such a beautiful story," said Betty, blowing her nose on a napkin.

"Anyway, from then on we've kept all of our letters."

"And believe me, we had some doozies," added Annie with a chuckle.

A man from the other side of the restaurant held up an empty coffee cup. "Can I get some more coffee, Betty?"

"In a minute, Joe," she responded, a little irritated, filling up our water glasses again. "Are you still meeting?" asked Betty, eagerly.

Doris's eyes dropped to her hands folded on the table in front of her, and her voice softened. "We were. Then, just recently, tragedy struck."

"What!" Betty slammed down her water jug in alarm. She pulled up a chair close to our table.

Doris opened her purse, pulled out the now-crumpled acceptance letter, and placed it firmly down in front of her.

"Some publisher wants to publish my book. So, that's why we're going to San Francisco. We're going to face this publishing guy and ask him to give us a rejection letter instead."

"Have you tried calling them?" inquired Dan.

"Oh yes," said Doris indignantly, "but they never get back to me. I'm not taking the chance of anything going wrong. I want to talk to them in person," said Doris. Then she began sucking on the ice from her water.

Joe shouted once again. "Hey, Betty, a man could die of thirst over here."

"I'm coming, I'm coming!" she called back reluctantly. Then she leaned forward, pulled a Little Red Wagon business card out of her pocket, and gave it to Doris, taking her by the hand. "You are a really brave person. You have been a true inspiration to me. That was a wonderful story, and I hope you get that letter for your group. Anything you need, I want you to call me. Anything! You understand?"

Doris was visibly touched by the gesture and nodded her head, putting the card away.

Betty left the table, adding with all the excitement of a child who'd just learned to spell her first word, "If you want, you can tweet me. I'm on Twitter too!"

As we made our way out into the parking lot, Dan asked if he could drive.

"Sure," I said gratefully, handing him the keys and slipping into the backseat.

"I can map-read for you," offered Doris, all sweetness and light. "I prefer the old-fashioned way. I don't believe in those electronic GSPs or ESPs or whatever they're called."

Dan raised his eyebrows playfully. "Do you mean a GPS?"

"I guess so. I could never trust some electronic woman, with her voice all dripping in honey, telling me which exit to get off."

Dan laughed. "Sounds good. I'm happy to have you with all your words dripping in honey instead."

"Saucy," responded Doris with a laugh, and I do believe I saw her blush. She, like all of us, appeared to have a little crush on our new companion.

I looked over at Flora, who was beaming and watching Dan fondly. Oh, young love. I remembered it. Wouldn't want to go back though. It was like holding someone's brand-new baby. You knew you loved the sounds and that baby smell and the way it felt in your arms as it made sweet baby noises. But it was always nice to give them back, knowing that you wouldn't swap all the sweetness of a newborn for a good night's sleep for anything.

Once Dan was behind the wheel, it was as if we were at a party. He sang old fifties songs and made us join in. We played I Spy and all manner of car games. Out the window, we watched the roving landscape change from the misty evergreens of Washington State to the rolling hills and vineyards of the Oregon Umpqua Valley. We ate a lovely lunch in the beautiful historical town of Roseburg and even took a quick detour to covered bridges in Grants Pass that Dan insisted we saw. We were like a group of excited schoolchildren on our way to camp. Even the car seemed to be behaving well.

Before long, we were in Medford. Somehow, in all the frivolity, I'd forgotten that this would be where we'd say good-bye to Dan. I thought everybody must have been feeling it as we stepped out of the car in silence; only Dan seemed chipper as he shook hands and greeted his friend at the garage. Flora looked totally forlorn. Dan finished chatting and came over to us.

"Ian is having a slow day, so they offered to help me replace the engine part for you. I'll drop you first at your accommodation for the night. There's a hotel nearby, but Ian's parents are out of town right now, and they have a beautiful lake house just about a mile away. He's offered it to you to stay in if you'd like."

Everybody perked up, except Flora.

"That would be great," I finally said in response.

"There's only one condition," Dan added. "Unfortunately, I would have to stay there too. There's lots of room, but I have to warn you, I do snore."

He looked at Flora, who lit up like a Christmas tree. The idea of having Dan with us for the evening had brought her to life.

"That's a splendid idea. I could make us dinner, and then I can set up one of my poker and brandy nights," responded Doris.

I felt myself gulping hard before I could catch myself.

"And then maybe we could all play charades," added Annie.

"That absolutely won't be possible," said Dan, in mock seriousness. "I have a surprise for you. I've just been talking to Ian about it. If you're game, I would love you all to be ready to go out about seven o'clock."

"Sounds great," I said, quicker than I intended.

Doris screwed up her face. "A surprise?"

"I think you'll like it, but my lips are sealed," he smirked.

Doris's eyes narrowed. "Could you at least give us an idea of what to pull out of our suitcases? I mean, do we need to dress up as if we're going out to a fancy restaurant or to stalk elk?"

Dan started to laugh.

"Though I feel that an elk wouldn't stand a chance against you, Doris, the former is more appropriate, and that's all you're getting out of me."

I heard Annie giggle behind me; the group was becoming younger by the minute.

"I'll take you over to the lake house to get settled in then bring the car back so we can get started."

When we arrived at the lake, I stepped out of the car, inhaling deeply the crisp, clear scent of nature. The lake was a heart-shaped, glimmering body of water with gentle waves rippling leisurely onto the shore. The trees reflected a rich patchwork of autumnal flourish as they drifted toward their seasonal finale. Somewhere nearby, loons called, and in the hazy distance, ducks babbled their own greetings to one another.

The lake house was a delightful old building, possessing the charm of an era gone by. Its timeworn, shingled roof hung low and heavy over large picture windows and aged, brown walls. In front, a quaint English garden was a riot of color. Behind it, a wooden dock stretched out into the water. Bobbing merrily alongside it, a quirky little rowboat was named in red swirling letters: *The Ladybug*.

I followed the group around the back to a rosy, covered porch, brightened with white wicker furniture and a porch swing.

As he hunted for a key under a hand-painted flowerpot, Dan explained that Ian's family had owned it for over fifty years. They used it mostly in the summer when extended family visited from back East.

Ian had apparently offered it to him when he knew he would be coming down to pick up the car.

"But," he said with a chuckle, "he hadn't expected me to turn up with five women."

He located the key and unlocked the back door.

As we entered the house, its brightness and warmth were a cheery welcome. A rich, honey-toned wood floor, warmed by the late afternoon sun, stretched into every room. In the main room, a lovely white-bricked fireplace was set for a fire and a line of antique wooden ducks greeted us from the mantle. A gilded mirror above reflected the afternoon sunlight that bounced off the lake, forming little silver ridges of light that danced playfully around the room. A sturdy pine coffee table heaped with colorful periodicals and nature books stood in front of a vast, well-stocked bookshelf. I drooled; I would definitely be hitting that before I went to bed to see if any of my favorite classics were hiding on the shelves.

A charming blue-and-white kitchen opened out from the main room. Ornately carved cupboards displayed dainty blue-and-white English china and more little ducks that peeked out curiously from every corner.

Dan offered to show us our rooms. He led us

down a narrow corridor, where spotlights punctuated dazzling white light, reflecting a warm glow from the buttery-colored floor. The paneled walls were crammed with family photos taken around the lake: people in boats holding up fish, jumping off the dock, or seated around a fire pit at the bottom of the garden. We each took a room, Flora the last.

I peeked in to take a look. It was smaller than the rest of ours, but extremely pretty, decorated in white wicker with a large patchwork quilt folded at the foot of the bed. It had a little door that led out onto the covered porch overlooking the lake. She blushed as she looked at Dan, and in a quiet voice said, "This is perfect."

Dan beamed down at her, saying in a soft tone, "You can sit right out here in the morning and write your poetry. The morning wildlife will be a great inspiration for you."

Her face upturned to his. "Where are you going to sleep?" she inquired gently.

"There's a little converted boathouse close to the water. I'll be more than comfortable out there. I could join you in the morning for coffee out on your little porch here if you like."

Flora sounded enchanted. "I would love that."

Oh, was that girl in trouble.

I joined Doris in the kitchen. "I'm getting a head start on dinner," she stated, pulling out a bag of carrots and a vegetable knife.

"Do you need any help?" I asked.

Ethel scowled at me.

"No, I have Ethel. We know each other's kitchen rhythm. We should be fine."

"Okay," I said, yawning. The new blast of fresh air had worn me out. "I think I'm going to take a nap before dinner."

"We're eating at six o'clock sharp," shouted Doris after me as I moved toward my bedroom.

I was in a deep sleep when my cell phone rang. Thinking it might be Stacy, I forced myself awake and snatched up my phone.

"Sorry to bother you, Janet, I can't get Doris on Annie's facey thingy. I just needed to ask her something." It was Lottie.

"Right," I said trying to rouse myself back to the land of the living. "Hold on. I'll go and get her."

Starting to climb out of bed, I heard Gracie's sweet voice in the background, raised in excitement. "Found it!"

"Oh, never mind! Sorry to have bothered you. Gracie and Lavinia have been up in the attic searching for some old gramophone for about thirty minutes. But it looks like they just found it. No need to bother Doris. Sorry, Janet." I heard Lavinia's voice shout down to her sister. "That's that sorted. Now all we need to do is find ourselves some handsome single men."

I guessed Lottie covered the receiver with her hand, because as I lay back down and closed my eyes, I heard a muffled version of, "Lavinia!" right before she hung up.

I yawned and turned over to finish my nap.

I woke up feeling much perkier and in plenty of time to eat dinner, after which there was a mass exodus for various bedrooms and bath-rooms as we tried to pull together an outfit from our overstuffed suitcases of creased clothes. Excitement crackled in the air. Annie put on some jazz music in the living room, and we moved about the house getting ready to the soft lilting sounds of Ella Fitzgerald reminding us, "It was just one of those things."

Passing Doris's bedroom, I noticed her sorting through bracelets and earrings. Ethel was helping her get on her "sling-backs," as she called them.

Managing to find a little black dress that I'd packed just in case crumpled up in the corner of my suitcase, I hung it in the bathroom, and thankfully most of the creases fell out as I showered. I added black stockings to my outfit and the heart locket my husband had given me on our twentieth wedding anniversary. Holding it in my hand for a second, I felt a connection to my family.

Inside, it had one of those silly pictures of our family that you allow a photographer to take to get all the nerves out at the beginning of an official photo sitting. We'd been trying to get a photo taken for our Christmas card. Stacy was about twelve, and we had all turned up in our Christmas sweaters for the session. We had been giggling about the fact that Martin had arrived for the sitting wearing a very humorous hat that lit up and said, "Ho, ho, ho" whenever he moved. We'd eventually gotten just the right photo for our card, but I'd always loved this natural one of us all being silly and laughing hysterically.

Thirty minutes later, all of us were a pretty package, decidedly different from the bedraggled bunch we'd been earlier.

Flora sat wringing a little lace hankie as we sat in nervous silence. It was as if we were *all* waiting for our first date.

Chapter Nine

AN OLD FLAME &
A BROOM SALESMAN

Dan arrived just after seven, looking dapper in a black suit and tie. We all jumped up in unison, as if we were on the same line-dancing team. He stopped dead in the center of the room and let out a long, low whistle.

"Wow, you all look so lovely. I'm not sure I'm going to be able to trust myself tonight."

We laughed and that broke the awkwardness in the air.

Flora beamed. She looked charming in a calf-length lace dress, white with little pink rosebuds running through it, and cream pumps. She'd managed to get her long hair into a chignon that suited her heart-shaped face. I also noted she'd been experimenting with makeup, just a little, just enough to define her gentle features. She looked like a very elegant china doll, and even though her outfit would have been more appropriate for an afternoon tea party, she still looked lovely.

"Are you ready to tell us where we're going?" inquired Doris. "My mind has gone from crab fishing to bingo."

"We could go and play bingo on my friend's

crabbing boat if you want, but I think you'll like this a lot more. Also, I think I'd like to keep the surprise just a little bit longer. By the way, I have another one waiting for you all outside."

We all bustled out the door, grabbing hats and coats as we exited, intrigued to discover our latest surprise.

It didn't take long to figure out what it was. Instead of my Suburban on the driveway, there was a sleek, black limousine. I heard Annie whoop with joy behind me.

"I'm afraid," said Dan in mock sadness, "your car was still being worked on, so, as Ian's family also owns a limousine company, we had to settle for this old thing to go out in tonight."

He opened the passenger door and produced a chauffeur's hat that he then placed on his head.

"I have more bad news. I was the only chauffeur we could find at this short notice."

He smiled broadly and held out his hand to help us into the car.

Doris was the first in; she was wearing a long, flowery dress. The pattern was a little garish, but she still looked quite elegant in her hose and slingbacks. Her hair was coiffed neatly, and for the first time I'd ever seen, she was also wearing makeup, which, apart from rather brassy red lipstick, actually suited her.

The rest of us playfully rushed to be next in line for the door, enjoying our own version of a middle-aged prom night, everyone scrambling and giggling, except Ethel, who watched disapprovingly as we became this frothing mass of teenage energy.

Inside the limo, a polished walnut interior set off the smoked-glass windows and sumptuous black leather seats. In the center, the minibar came complete with a bottle of champagne chilling in a silver ice bucket.

We oohed and aahed as we took it all in. Then, as if we were a bunch of five-year-olds on their first field trip, we couldn't resist the urge to press every button and open all the windows.

"Help yourselves to a beverage," said Dan in a very official-sounding tone as he climbed into the driver's seat.

Doris popped the champagne cork and started pouring it into the crystal glasses arranged on a silver tray. It gushed up and frothed out as Annie and Flora giggled uncontrollably. Once the glasses were filled, Annie raised hers, saying, "To our wonderful chauffeur. This has to be the best way to travel to bingo ever."

We all laughed and clinked our glasses together.

Twenty minutes later, Dan pulled smoothly into a parking lot next to a large redbrick building. Excited groups of people milled about, decked out in their evening finery.

Dan opened our door, and then in his deepest chauffeur voice, he announced, "I would be honored if you all would accompany me to the hottest event of the season here in Medford."

Linking arms with Doris and Annie, he then led us up broad stone steps and through stately mahogany doors.

"Good evening, Ernie," said Dan to one of two sixtyish men seated in front of a cash box. "How are you this evening?"

The larger man jumped to his feet. "Well, if it isn't little Danny Cohen. How good to see you."

The other man blinked twice. "Danny Cohen?" he asked in expectation. "Bob Cohen's boy?"

A light bulb came on behind the blank shutters, and he also jumped to his feet.

"Little Danny Cohen!" he exclaimed. "You sure grew up fast. What the devil are you doing in Medford? I thought your mom and dad had moved north to open up a bed and breakfast?"

"You thought right. I happen to be down here on a mission of mercy, saving damsels in distress."

"Enough of that," said Doris, nudging him in the ribs. "You're all full of hot air."

Ernie was drawn in immediately. "What do we have here?" he asked, eyeing Doris with a glint in his eye. "Seems you've got yourself a feisty one here, young Dan."

"Too feisty for the likes of you," she joked back.

"I wouldn't be so sure about that," he responded, showing a row of pearly white teeth and a couple of gold caps. "I, myself, like a little chili sauce on my steak."

"Oh, get away with you," quipped Doris.

But I swear I saw her blush as she said it.

"How much do we owe you?" asked Dan.

"I think you can have your tickets on the house," said Ernie, not taking his eyes from Doris. "But you'd better take your group, including this jalapeno, inside before she starts a fire out here in the foyer."

We laughed and thanked them, and Dan led us into the main ballroom.

The room was vast, illuminated by dozens of sparkling white twinkle lights that dangled from the ceiling, casting a lively glow onto a highly polished dance floor. Arranged about the room were clusters of round tables elegantly draped with white satin ribbons and adorned with flowers. An enormous stage dominated the far end of the room, where a roving spotlight spun spirals of brilliant white light in hypnotic circles around couples dancing on the dance floor.

On the stage, dressed in white shirts and black tuxedos, was an impressive-sounding thirty-piece jazz orchestra. Each performer was fully engaged, brass instruments glinting and glimmering as they stood tapping and swaying in the sparkling lights. The music was so incredible, its magical sight and sound brought tears to my eyes.

A pretty, young woman approached to inform

us she would help us find a table. But then her eyes widened.

"Danny? Danny Cohen!" she squealed. "Is that you?" She threw her arms around his neck, demonstratively hugging and kissing him on the cheek.

Dan's face registered shock, then surprise.

"Wow, is that you, Marcy? Little Marcy Campbell?"

"Not so little anymore," she gushed, bobbing her hair with one hand and thrusting out her voluminous chest. "How lovely to see you. I'd heard you'd moved up north to be by your parents."

The rest of us seemed to vanish as Marcy seemed to dominate the whole room. I looked over to Flora, who'd turned into her old, shrinking violet self. She stared at her shoes.

"Yes. Yes I did," said Dan, apparently aware of how uncomfortable it had become, and he appeared to want to stop the conversation there.

Doris blurted out, "Hello, I'm Doris Newberry. I'm a friend of Dan's. In fact, we all came with him this evening."

Marcy took a step back. She was having one of those "youthful" moments, where younger people only see anyone their own generation. Anyone over the age of forty was just window dressing, like old curtains.

"I'm sorry." She was obviously annoyed by the interruption.

But Dan tactfully disentangled himself and began to introduce us one by one. She was polite, but there was a little more ice in her tone.

"Oh," she said as he finished, the disappointment obvious in her voice. "Let me see if I can find you all a table, then."

She wove us through and across the dance floor, where we took our lives in our hands.

She did find us a really nice table with a great view of the band and then excused herself with a long, lingering glance back at Dan that none of us missed.

The music that filled the room was a welcome relief from the need to converse. Flora had shrunk, looking awkward in her own skin.

Annie leaned forward and spoke to Dan. "So, you used to live here? Have you been to this event before?"

Dan went on to explain about the annual jazz dance in Medford and how he and his parents had attended it. He recalled the year when he'd been fifteen and had spent the evening sampling his parents' punch only to be sick all the way home. We all laughed, except Flora, who looked miserable.

An announcer informed us that the next dance would be "ask a new partner." As the spotlight roved and the drums rolled, people got up from all over the room and walked to different tables, asking people to dance. It was fun to watch shy young men approaching girls they may have had their eyes on all night.

A tiny man in an oversized suit shuffled up to our table. He had wisps of peach fuzz on the top of his head and circular glasses that emphasized his round face. He seemed incredibly bashful and hopped from foot to foot as he worked up his courage. Looking directly at Ethel's feet, he stuttered out, "My name is Osborne. Would you do me the honor of dancing with me?"

Ethel was horrified and looked about the table for our support. Even though the woman spoke fewer words than a starling, the pleading in her eyes was obvious as she pierced Doris with her gaze.

Doris opened her mouth to speak, and Ethel seemed relieved, thinking her friend would save her. That notion, however, was short-lived when Doris said instead, "Nice to meet you, Osborne. This is Ethel. She's a little shy but would love to dance with you."

Doris then rocked Ethel's chair back onto its back legs, causing Ethel to jump up to save herself.

Osborne, now believing he was accepted, wasn't slow. He took a firm hold of Ethel's arm and started to lead her to the dance floor.

She looked back at us pathetically, like a horse sensing it was about to be shot. I watched her as she disappeared. She was wearing a white frilly blouse, smart black pants, and sensible shoes. And as if she had had an afterthought, there was a little diamanté hair slide in her hair. It actually made her look quite sweet.

We were so engrossed in watching Ethel being led away to her execution that we didn't see who was approaching the table from behind us.

"On your feet, chili pepper," someone barked from behind Doris.

It was Ernie, the gentleman from the door. Doris didn't miss a beat. She swiveled herself around and barked right back at him indignantly, "I don't know how to dance!"

But before she could object any further, he'd grabbed her by the arm and had her on her feet. "There's never been a better time to learn than right now," he said.

"Well, I never!" sputtered Doris. And that's when it dawned on me. Doris Newberry had just met her match.

His eyes twinkled as he beamed a white-and-gold grin in her direction, adding, "See! You don't scare me. I can be just as feisty as you." And before she could say another word, he was leading, half-dragging her onto the dance floor.

Obviously stirred into courage by the moment, Dan was on his feet.

"Flora," he said in a very official tone, "would you do me the honor of being my partner?"

Flora looked as if she were going to crumble and disappear under the table.

"Oh, I don't think so," she said hesitantly. "You see, I don't dance or anything. I would look silly and be awkward out there with all those *real* dancers."

She said it as if he were asking her to compete on *Dancing with the Stars*.

"Those real dancers you're talking about are people like you." He cast his eye over the crowd and then lifted a finger to point out an awkward-looking man who appeared as if he'd been vacuumed-packed into an extremely snug-fitting suit. "People like Mr. Jefferies over there. He runs the local hardware shop."

Then he nodded his head in a different direction, toward a rather heavyset woman who was moving in a decidedly odd fashion, as if one leg couldn't quite keep up with the other. "And there's Mrs. Hendrix. She runs the cat sanctuary and is always complaining about her clicky hips."

As if on cue, Mrs. Hendrix's partner swung her around in a circle, and she threw back her head and laughed heartily.

Dan looked down at Flora tenderly. "These are just local people having some old-fashioned fun."

He gently took her hand in his and gracefully, she was up and under his spell. Before she knew what had hit her, she was on the dance floor, twirling in circles.

Sighing gently, I thought of Martin. He would have loved this big band sound. I could almost

166

hear him tapping his feet and humming along beside me; Glenn Miller was one of his favorites. He had been an eager, though not very accomplished, trombone player in our middle school jazz band. I could still remember him performing, years before we'd even dated. His usual boyish cowlick slicked back and his reddened cheeks working hard to keep up performing his favorite version of "Chattanooga Choo Choo."

As the music picked up its pace, we watched all the couples moving around the dance floor, seeming to be having a genuinely good time, everyone except Ethel, who still looked mortified. Doris was enjoying herself so much that she stayed up for the next dance. So did Flora and Dan as the music moved into a boogie-woogie rhythm.

Ethel, however, bolted from the dance floor like a whippet the minute the band played the last note of the song. She passed our table at a trot, muttering something about the restroom as she went. No doubt she was off to strip down and wash to get rid of the man cooties.

I felt sorry for Osborne, who looked forlorn, a Prince Charming dumped on the dance floor by his Cinderella. Annie called out and invited him to have a drink with us. I reassured him that his date was just extremely shy and not to take any offense at her fleeing the scene. He sat and seemed relieved at that knowledge, though he watched the door that Ethel had bolted through like a spaniel awaiting his master's return.

Flora and Dan appeared back at the table, laughing, and her cheeks were flushed. She took a swig of her drink, trying to get her breath back. But just as she was about to sit, the band started up again with another boogie-woogie, and Dan had her back on her feet.

"Come on," he said imploringly. "I'm just getting the hang of this one."

"Dan, I can't. I'm exhausted."

"Pleeease," he pleaded.

After the second boogie-woogie, both couples came back to the table, flushed and breathless.

Ethel arrived back from the bathroom too. She looked horrified to see Osborne was now sitting with us, looking like a hopeful puppy. She sat as far away from him as possible and glared at him across the table.

I distracted him, asking him about his job. He told me how he'd been a broom salesman for many years, until the company had gone out of business because of all those "infomercials," he said with obvious bitterness. He went on to explain how he now worked at a chain home improvement store.

The announcer from the stage cut across our conversation.

"Okay, ladies! Now it's your turn to be brave. The next one will be the Ladies Excuse Me dance.

Time to ask the man of your dreams to dance, but remember, at any time another lady can come and ask him too, stealing your partner away from you."

There was a general sound of merriment all around us as people plotted whom they were going to ask and whom they were going to steal.

Doris was first on her feet. "Come on, Ernie," she said decisively. "You can dance with me, and with any luck, someone will come and take you right off my hands."

Ernie chuckled and was up on his feet too. "That I don't doubt, me being as good-looking and such a catch as I am. You may just be sad to let me go!"

Osborne looked hopefully at Ethel, who had her arms firmly folded and her eyes boring a hole into her water glass. I was just about to ask Osborne to dance when Annie beat me to it. "Osborne, would you care to join me? I would be really honored if you would dance with me."

As they left, I overheard Annie whisper to him, "Let's see if we can make her a little jealous, shall we?"

He beamed, taking Annie tightly by the arm as she threw back her head in an exaggerated laugh as they headed toward the dance floor.

Ethel watched and appeared to fume.

Flora had just stood up when Marcy suddenly appeared. "Danny!" she said, full of sparkles and light. "Would you do me the honor of dancing with me? It's been a long time."

Dan gulped back his drink. He appeared to be playing for time.

Flora slumped down next to me. I wasn't sure how this was going to play out, but it wasn't going to be pretty.

"Oh, I'm not sure," said Dan. "I just got off the dance floor. I'm pretty tired."

Marcy threw back her head and screeched with laughter.

"Danny Cohen, tired? If you were planning to get rid of me, you'd never do it with that line. You can outlast all of us. I could tell you some stories about Danny, especially back when he was dating my sister. We all had a little crush on him back then. Remember, Danny? Now, Danny, are you going to dance with an old friend or not?"

Dan reluctantly rose to his feet.

Flora looked as if she might cry at any moment. She picked up her water glass, and her hand was shaking so hard she spilled it straight down her dress. "Dammit!" she berated herself and burst into tears. She ran from the table in the direction of the bathroom.

I followed her to the powder room. She was sitting in front of the vanity, dabbing at her eyes with a hankie.

"It's a stupid dress anyway. I mean, everyone is here in evening wear, and this is the only thing

I have that's even a little appropriate. I look ridiculous!"

"No, you don't." I took her hand as I would my own daughter. "You look beautiful."

"But all these girls here looked sophisticated and elegant."

I suppressed a grin because even though the girls here all seemed to look nice, they were far from my idea of sophisticated.

"It's not what you wear," I reminded her gently. Then, edging toward the real issue, "Dan seems to like what you're wearing. He hasn't taken his eyes off you all evening."

"I don't know why," she said quietly. "There are so many pretty girls here, and it sounds like he's very popular with them here in Medford. I can't compete with that."

"Who said anything about competing? As far as I can see, if his actions are anything to go by, his heart is already won."

Flora allowed herself a bashful smile. "Do you think he really likes me?"

I was back in middle school.

"If he doesn't, he's a masterful actor. Everything I'm seeing in his eyes and his actions is saying so."

"I just feel so plain and silly. I never really had a relationship before, and I can't think what he sees in me when there are all these confident, attractive women that have been in his life!"

"Listen to me, Flora. You are kind, gentle, genuine, and lovely. And I can't think of qualities that are more attractive in a human being. Dan sees all of those amazing things about you and likes them too. Don't let self-doubt rob you of at least seeing where this relationship could go. If he had wanted the likes of Marcy, he would still be living here, wouldn't he?"

Flora cheered a little and blew her nose.

"Come on. Dan went to a lot of trouble to give us all a wonderful evening. Let's not let Marcy spoil it for you."

"You're right."

She blew her nose again, then was suddenly on her feet and out the door. She strode back into the ballroom, a new confidence in her step. As we started toward the table, it was as if she suddenly headed for the dance floor instead.

I watched her walk up to Dan and Marcy and say in a clear, strong voice, "I believe this is a Ladies Excuse Me, and I would like to dance with your partner."

Dan's face lit up.

Marcy reluctantly let Dan go, and Dan took Flora's hand. They danced off into the crowd, leaving a very disgruntled-looking Marcy.

I was walking back to the table when I caught sight of a red-faced Ethel watching Osborne and Annie like a hawk. I couldn't resist giving Osborne an extra boost.

I tapped Annie on the shoulder, saying, "I'd like to steal your partner from you, if you don't mind." I gestured with my head to our table and the beady-eyed Ethel.

Annie understood instantly. "I'm not sure," she said in a rather loud voice so Ethel could hear us. "He's a marvelous dancer," she gushed.

Ethel huffed and folded her arms harder across her chest.

But Annie played along. "I suppose I have to, as this is the Ladies Excuse Me."

Osborne seemed ecstatic to be fought over and eagerly escorted me around the dance floor. When we returned to the table, all seemed right with the world. Osborne was walking with his head a little higher, Doris and Ernie were convulsing in laughter, and Flora and Dan floated back to the table, all love and light. Flora looked different somehow, as if that one heroic act of confronting Marcy had opened up the door to a new strength in her.

At the end of the night, Doris and Ernie exchanged phone numbers, and Osborne informed us it had been the happiest night of his life. He gave a sideways glance at Ethel and said, "I would love to see you all again sometime."

Annie gave him her home phone number, adding, "Give us a call sometime. We would all love to see you in Southlea Bay if you're ever in the area."

Back at the house, I put on the kettle in the kitchen. Walking past one of the large picture windows overlooking the lake, I stopped to admire the full moon shimmering over the water.

Gentle voices floated in from the porch. It was Dan and Flora. I couldn't hear what they were saying, but I peeked out and saw him slowly cup her face with his hands and kiss her gently on the lips. Smiling, I crept away.

I saw Doris as she made her way into the kitchen and Ethel followed.

"I think we should have more dancing in Southlea Bay," said Annie, as she and I walked down the hall together.

"That's what Lavinia and Gracie are doing," I said. "They called and told me they were up in Doris's attic today getting the gramophone player, I think for their tea dance."

Suddenly, there was a crash. We both jumped. Dan and Flora hurried in from outside. In the kitchen, we found Doris, pale and sitting in a chair. Ethel was fanning her with a dishtowel, and on the floor was a smashed mug of hot chocolate.

"Doris, are you okay?" I was really concerned.

She was sweating, breathing heavily, and couldn't seem to talk.

"What is it?" implored Flora. "What's wrong?"

Doris finally spoke. "Did I hear you say Momma was up in the attic?" she asked desperately.

"Well, yes, Lavinia said they were looking for a gramophone player."

Doris loosened the collar buttons on her dress, and Annie got her a drink of water.

She looked right at me. "That's where they are."

I knew instantly what she meant. The stories. She'd hidden the stories in the attic.

"What?" asked Flora.

"They shouldn't be up in the attic. I have valuable things up there. I need to call them."

"Call who, Doris?" inquired Annie as she also got a cold cloth to put on Doris's forehead.

"The twins. I have to call them and see what they did up there."

Everyone looked utterly confused.

"They're probably asleep," I said. "It's after twelve."

Doris was adamant, and as she took my cell phone, I felt guilty for not telling her earlier about their call.

She punched in the number. It rang a few times; then we all heard Lavinia's sassy voice on the answering machine.

Doris hung up, despondent.

I tapped her hand. "There's nothing you can do tonight. We can call first thing in the morning."

Doris reluctantly nodded, and we all went to bed.

Chapter Ten

CINNAMON ROLLS & COIN TRICKS

The next morning I woke up early. I had hardly slept a wink.

Doris was sitting in the kitchen, looking between my cell phone on the table and the clock on the wall.

"It's going to be okay," I assured her.

She nodded, but I could see she didn't seem convinced.

"I've been calling since five. No answer."

As the clock struck six, she called again, and this time we both heard the phone pick up and then Lottie's soft Southern drawl. "My," she said once she realized it was us, "you girls are up early. I like to be up early too so I can spend a little time with God before Lavinia gets up and all hell breaks loose, but this morning you seem to be up even before him."

Doris came straight to the point.

"What did you take out of the attic yesterday?"

"Pardon?"

"The attic, what did you take out of the attic?"

"Oh, the gramophone, of course. We're having our own little tea dance and—"

"Anything else?" snapped Doris.

"Why, no, I don't think so," said Lottie, sounding as if she were trying to think. "Wait. Gracie also bought down some records, I believe. Why? Doris, dear, are you hiding your crown jewels up there?"

"No," responded Doris, a little too quickly for it to sound truthful. "I just . . . don't want anyone up there. It's dangerous. Someone could get hurt."

"Okay, honey, we won't go up there again if you don't want us to. We don't want you to worry while you're away."

"Good. Now, will you promise me?" The relief was now evident in her voice.

"Of course," said Lottie, her tone indicating she was a little put out that her integrity was in question. "Is that all you wanted?"

"Yes." Then she added, as if it were an afterthought, "How's Momma doing?"

"She's having a marvelous time. I think she thinks she's at summer camp."

"Good," said Doris, going back to her usual brusque self. "I'll call again later."

"Okay, bye-bye then." Lottie's stilted tone implied that she was obviously a little confused by the early morning interrogation.

The relief was plain on Doris's face.

"I told you it was going to be fine," I said, yawning. "Now, I'm going back to bed to try and get some sleep. I suggest you do the same."

Doris shook her head. "Ethel and I have

cinnamon rolls to raise," she said, and the declaration of that fact seemed to bring her back to life. I noticed the color had also returned to her cheeks.

Back in bed, I passed out, finally finding sleep after such a restless night.

When I woke, my face felt the chill of the first unmistakable fingers of frost while my body felt cozy and warm under the down comforter. All I wanted to do was turn over, pull the covers over my head, and go back to sleep. However, as I lay there contemplating that very thought, the unmistakable smell of cinnamon wafted under my doorway. I pushed my feet into my slippers, pulled on my fleecy robe, and headed for the bathroom.

The rest of the house was a hive of activity already. Annie was planted firmly in front of a roaring fire, knitting and watching the morning's news. "Morning, sleepyhead," she said playfully, then added in a quieter tone, "What was all that about last night?"

"Doris was worried about her momma being up in the attic," I lied.

Shuffling toward the fire, I inhaled the scent of the fresh-brewed coffee. Ethel was setting the table with a charming tablecloth patterned with blue delphiniums and placemats to match. In the kitchen, Dan was wearing an apron, and Flora was seated up on a counter, smiling at him. He had a spoon to her lips, offering her a taste of something.

Doris was at the stove, pulling a fresh batch of cinnamon rolls out of the oven. My "trying to keep it healthy" self was beaten into submission by the ten-year-old in me. I was salivating.

"Look who's up. No point asking you if you got back off to sleep okay," chuckled Doris.

"Why?" I inquired, yawning. "What time is it?"

"Nine thirty," shouted Annie from her perch on the sofa.

"We were just going to come in to resuscitate you."

"Nine thirty!" I repeated with surprise.

There was a hard rap on the front door.

"That will be Ernie," piped up Doris with the kind of excitement reserved for Christmas Day visitors.

"I'll get it," called Dan, wiping his hands on his apron and heading for the front door.

I raced back to my room to get decent. I was back out, washed, and dressed in record time.

Ernie was holding court in the kitchen, telling jokes to Flora and Dan. As I came in, he'd obviously just delivered his punch line, as all three of them roared with laughter. They were extremely boisterous and obviously overwhelming our cook.

Doris raised a wooden spoon. "Now, all you kitchen do-gooders aren't worth anything at all just hanging around visiting. Get out so the real workers can finish preparing the food. I can barely hear myself think, never mind turn in a full circle with you all cluttering up the place."

Ernie raised his eyebrows and let out a low whistle. "Yes, sir," he said as if answering a superior in the army and made his way out into the living room, saying over his shoulder, "I wouldn't want to get in the way of anyone who intended to feed me."

I quickly poured myself a coffee and then joined the rest of the group, who'd settled themselves around the fireplace. Ernie had started doing coin tricks to keep everyone amused.

"It's in your right hand," shouted Dan, guessing the latest place Ernie was hiding his nickel. "I already know this trick. You showed it to me when I was a kid."

"Keep it quiet, young'un," said Ernie with mock hostility. "I am trying to fool a whole new audience here."

"It's in your right hand," repeated Flora, joking along.

"Well, I know you know that now," scoffed Ernie. "Your boyfriend already told you."

I saw Flora and Dan exchange glances and smile knowingly at each other. It was the first time anyone had referred to them as a couple.

Doris yelled from the kitchen as she removed her apron, "Get it while it's hot!"

We gathered around the table like a happy family. It was chock-full with bacon, sausage, eggs, and toast, not to mention hot, steaming cinnamon rolls. Doris heaped delicious hot food onto our plates and placed a basket of warm bread rolls in the center. I inhaled the delightful aroma and realized I was ravenous.

Dan lifted up his glass of orange juice to us in a toast.

"To all the wonderful ladies of the Rejected Writers' Book Club for being brave and determined. May all your letters be rejections and all your manuscripts be duds."

We all laughed, and Doris echoed, "Hear, hear."

As he polished off his second helping of bacon and toast, Ernie commented, "I don't think I've seen a spread like this since last Thanksgiving. I sure hope you're planning on staying around awhile!"

"Actually, we're on our way today," said Doris, tapping Ernie's hand as he tried to reach for his third cinnamon roll. "You've had enough of those, mister!" she added sternly.

Ernie was jovial. "Oh, you don't miss a trick," he quipped back. "I like a woman who's not only on her toes, but is also on mine."

He brushed her leg under the table playfully. Doris was obviously taken aback but recovered quickly. "And don't think you'll be getting around me playing footsie like that. I'm not sixteen anymore."

"You might not be in your teens," he poked back

at her, "but everyone knows the sweetest peaches take longer to mature."

I was amazed they were flirting. Something about this area had brought Cupid out in force, with a stack of arrows to boot.

We washed the dishes all together, like the Waltons. "Here's a spoon, Jim-Bob. Thanks, John-Boy. Into the drawer, Mary Ellen."

Soon after, Ian walked in.

"Your car is all ready to roll and . . ." Then he stopped in midsentence as his nose caught up with him. "Wow," he said, sniffing the air. "Looks like I missed a good brunch, by the smell of it."

"There's one last cinnamon roll I managed to wrestle away from Ernie," shouted Doris from the kitchen, "and the coffee is still hot!"

"So, you're the young man who fixed their car, are you?" Ernie said. "Could I pay you to unfix it? I can't bear to see the back of the chili pepper and her beans. That is the best dang brunch I've had in a long while."

Ian beamed and swallowed a mouthful of cinnamon roll, saying, "It'll cost you. But you're on if this cinnamon roll's anything to go on."

I stepped out for one last look at the lake before we left. It was magical. The frost was still heavy on the ground and glistening on the grass like frosted diamonds through muted sunlight. A lazy fog was just starting to roll out across the water. It gave the loons an eerie sound as it muffled their cries.

As I walked back toward the house, I noticed Flora sitting on a bench, staring pensively at the water, no doubt thinking about her new relationship. If I were a painter, I would have wanted to capture that moment on canvas.

We were all a little somber as we assembled in the driveway, each one of us quiet with our own thoughts.

Ernie broke the silence by admiring the limousine. "Nice wheels."

"Thank you," said Ian. "That's our transportation back to the garage today."

Ernie's eyes twinkled as he asked, "Would you mind dropping me on the way? I would love to get under the skin of that old woman who lives across the road from me. 'The curtain twitcher,' I call her. She'll bite her hand off at the wrist just to find out why I'm coming home in a limousine on a Sunday morning."

"I would be delighted." Ian laughed. "I'll even wear my chauffeur's hat if you want!"

Ernie smacked his hand across his knee. "That's the spirit. That should keep her wringing herself in knots for weeks."

We got into the car. Everyone piled in except Dan and Flora, who were in each other's arms, saying their final good-byes. Eventually, climbing in, she sank into the corner of the backseat.

"It's been wonderful meeting you all," said Dan. "Maybe I'll see you on your way back through Medford."

Ian added, "You're all welcome to stay here again if you want."

We voiced our thanks and appreciation.

Then, suddenly, Ernie stuck his head in as well. "I can always do with a good feeding if ever you're passing this way again."

Doris thumped him playfully on the arm, saying, "You shouldn't need feeding again until we come back in a week! But you have my phone number in case you need to remember me."

"I'll remember you whenever I pass a cinnamon roll," he joked back.

Dan reached in and grabbed Flora's hand for the last time. She thrust a piece of paper into his, which I surmised was probably one of her poems, and we drove away.

I looked in the rearview mirror as we did; the men were all lined up on the driveway, smiling and waving to us, all except Dan, who looked crestfallen. As soon as we rounded the corner, Flora burst into tears.

We all tried to cheer her up, but everything seemed to fall flat. It was like having a lovesick teenager. When we stopped for a bathroom break two hours later, Flora inside, Doris pulled us into a huddle.

"You know that girl has never been in love

before. That's what the problem is. She's going to be hard work for a few days, no doubt."

When Flora came back, Ethel suddenly sneezed. "I don't feel so good," she said, blowing her nose on a coffee shop napkin.

"I hope you haven't got the Lurgy," said Doris unsympathetically.

"I have an aspirin," said Annie, fishing one out of her purse.

Ethel eyed it distrustfully before eventually giving in and taking it as she sneezed again.

Doris offered to drive, and as we started up again, I must admit I was relieved. I hated mountain driving, and I knew that would be the next leg of our journey.

We got underway again. Ethel sniffed and Flora sobbed. I personally couldn't think of anything better for a poet's work than a little pining. Doris tried to find a country music channel, which was almost impossible as we started to climb into the mountains. Next to me, Annie flipped on her soap. I didn't want to admit it, but secretly I couldn't wait to find out what would happen next.

The doctor's wife had arranged a secret meeting with the guy she'd hired to put the hit on her husband, who coincidently just happened to be the same guy back from the war, who now believed he was an assassin. He, the assassin, was unaware that his girlfriend, the secretary, was having an affair with the doctor he was being hired to kill. In the meantime, the doctor had mysteriously gone missing, and the big clincher to the episode was . . . that the baby the secretary was carrying may or may not be even human at all. Apparently, the secretary may have been impregnated during an alien abduction in which her memory had been wiped clean.

Annie and I watched intently as the envelope containing the test results of the baby was slowly opened. The camera closed in on her shocked face, and as she opened her mouth to speak . . .

A loud bell rang out. Both Annie and I screamed. It was the FaceTime alert.

Annie hit the "Accept" button, and the faces of the other ladies from the Rejection Club swam into view.

"Hi, y'all," said Lavinia. "Here we are again."

Ruby's face popped onto the screen. She still looked a little under the weather. She was wearing what appeared to be a white turban adorned with gold-sprayed fruit and looked like a red-nosed Christmas Carmen Miranda.

"Look, it's me, back in the land of the living."

We all shouted our hellos.

It was hard to hear very well, as the car was starting to climb, and the strain of the engine noise was drowning out all other sound. Ruby was waving at us, as were Lottie and Gracie, who was still wearing her pink sparkly boa. I made out that they were having an impromptu meeting of the

Rejection Club and were going to share some stories. The engine roared.

"What are they saying?" bellowed Doris from the front.

"They're having a Rejection Club meeting," I shouted back.

"How are the dogs?" she yelled. "Ask how they are."

All I could see were moving heads on the creen, but I couldn't hear a thing over the engine.

Annie laughed at something Lottie had said, then shouted back, "Okay, have fun!"

The picture went dark.

"Darn, lost the signal," said Annie. "That was fun, wasn't it," she said, putting her iPad away in her bag.

We kept on climbing. As I looked out the window, the scenery around me was beginning to change significantly, as well as the temperature. Doris shouted back to us, "We should be getting to the top soon, and then we'll hit three thousand feet."

We journeyed on for another twenty minutes. All we had to listen to was the high-pitched strain of the engine as it climbed higher and higher.

As I looked out on the view, I was overwhelmed by the sheer majesty of it all. Thick forests of emerald-green trees reached skyward from snow-laden peaks. In between, forging their way through jagged gray granite, craggy brooks and waterfalls frothed and spluttered down the mountainsides.

"Isn't it pretty!" said Annie.

I nodded. It truly was an awe-inspiring sight, nature at its finest, unspoiled and raw, without any footprints of civilization for miles around, and that made me just a little nervous. My ears started to pop as we adjusted to the altitude. The car clock read 3:30 p.m. It would soon be getting dark.

As we started to crest the top, a battered sign marked the entrance to a desolate rest stop. Doris pulled in.

"Oh, good. Potty break!" said Annie, putting down her knitting and grabbing her roll of toilet paper. Flora had used most of hers up sobbing quietly in her corner.

I stepped out and took a deep, slow breath of the frigid air. It was silent and isolated, as if we were the only people left on the planet.

"It's cold enough to snow, don't you think?" noted Annie, joining me as I stood looking out at the incredible view.

Doris brought out some sandwiches she'd made that morning, and Ethel sat blowing her nose as she fed a group of chipmunks right under the "Do Not Feed the Wild Animals" sign.

"How long till we hit a town?" I asked Doris. The anxiety was obvious in my tone.

Doris fetched her map and took the opportunity to spread it out on the picnic bench.

"As far as I can see, we have about another twenty miles of mountain driving, and we should make it into northern California before six o'clock. There are lots of nice hotels there, and we should easily be in San Francisco by tomorrow afternoon."

I took another deep breath. Just thinking about a large city made me feel as if we were close to safety.

"Right," said Doris decisively. "If we want to get over this pass before dark, we should get moving again."

Back in the car, Annie remarked absently, "It sounds like the stories Lavinia found will be an interesting read."

I went ice-cold.

"What did you say?" I asked, shouting over the whine of the engine.

Annie raised her voice. "Lavinia found some stories that she's going to read to the group and said they're pretty raunchy."

"What!" Doris and I shrieked in unison.

Doris slammed on the brakes. Behind us, drivers skidded to emergency stops and honked their displeasure as they pulled around us.

Doris was bearing down on Annie, who was looking from one of us to the other in bewilderment.

Doris found her voice. "What did you say?"

"That Lavinia said she'd found some raunchy

stories that she was going to share with the group."

"What kind of stories?" demanded Doris.

"I don't know," said Annie weakly. "It was hard to hear."

"Where did she find them?"

"I don't know."

"Get them back on!"

"I can't. We don't have a signal."

"Try, dammit!" bellowed Doris.

"Don't shout at me!" screamed back Annie. "I haven't done anything wrong."

Doris matched Annie's pitch. "You should have told me about the stories. Why didn't you tell me straightaway?"

"Why?" yelled back Annie. "What's the big deal about some racy stories of Lavinia's?"

Annie's voice was starting to crack as Doris delivered the final blow. "Because they could be about my momma, that's why!"

The car became deadly quiet as the reality of what Doris had just said sank in. Annie burst into tears, and she and Flora started to sob in unity; then, right on cue, Ethel sprayed the car with an immense sneeze, causing Doris to swear and smack the steering wheel.

"Why don't we all just calm down?" I said, trying to be the voice of reason.

Doris swung open her door and jumped out of the car.

I got out to talk to her. "Doris, I know this is hard, but you don't know what stories Lavinia is talking about. For all we know, they could be from one of her romance magazines."

"But if they're from that terrible journal I hid in the attic, then they're about Momma. Horrible lies about her. I just don't know what she'll do if she hears them."

"Look, there's nothing we can do here. Once we get to the other side of the pass, we'll get a signal again. It's still early. We can ring the twins and warn them not to read them."

Doris nodded. Her face reflected all the fear and worry she felt.

She was in no condition to drive, so I climbed into the driver's seat. I started the car and, gripping the steering wheel, desperately tried to focus on the road ahead.

The one thing I hated above traveling through the mountains was actually driving the passes. I looked at the group in my rearview mirror. We were a mess. Annie and Flora sobbed; Ethel, red-eyed, sniffed; and beside me, Doris seethed. So much for the fifties fantasy, because compared to this road trip, *Thelma & Louise* was starting to look like a soppy love story.

Chapter Eleven

A ROCKSLIDE & A HAUNTED HOUSE

We drove for another twenty nail-biting minutes, and the silence in the car was eerie, only punctuated from time to time with a sob or a sniff. Out of nowhere, we suddenly hit traffic. As we started to inch along, I noticed cars and trucks appeared to be turning back toward us.

"Looks like trouble," said Ethel as she blew her nose again.

This new turn of events seemed to break the deadlock in the car.

Doris turned to Annie, squeezed her hand, and apologized.

"What do you mean about your momma?" croaked Annie, her voice hoarse from crying.

"I can't talk about it right now. It's just too hard."

Flora nodded, took Doris's hand, and squeezed it too.

After a one-hour crawl, we hadn't even gone ten miles. As we crept forward, we could see a state trooper ahead waving a flashlight and turning drivers back. By the time we inched to the front of the line, it was almost 5:30 p.m., way past dusk, and a damp, heavy fog was starting to swirl ominously around the car.

Rolling down my window, I asked, "What's going on, officer?"

"Landslide. We have heavy equipment down there right now moving it as best we can, but it was a doozy. There's no way we're going to be able to secure the road tonight. Your best bet is to make it back to Ashland or Medford for the evening."

"Medford," I repeated, a note of hysteria creeping into my tone.

"Sorry. There's no way I can let you through here this evening. It's just not safe."

Before I could say anything else, he was waving us on with his light and walking toward an RV behind us.

Wheeling the car around, I started to double back. I looked at the gas gauge. We were nearly on empty. I'd meant to remind Doris to fill up when we'd left the coffee shop, but with the upset with Flora and Ethel being sick, I had quite forgotten. It would be touch and go whether we would make it back anywhere close to civilization. We would be coasting on fumes before we hit the bottom of the mountains.

"What's it going to be, then?" asked Annie, as if we were making a decision about dessert.

"The first thing we need to do is find a gas station."

Trucks along the route had pulled over onto the hard shoulder, settling down for the night.

"You know, there was a little convenience store about five miles back," mentioned Annie optimistically.

"Yes, they may know where we could get gas." I recalled the place; my spirits lifted.

"And maybe they have a phone I can use too," Doris added.

We drove back and pulled over. The store appeared to be closed, so Doris and I peered in a window and saw a hodgepodge of camping and fishing paraphernalia. Way in the back, there was a light shining from what seemed to be a back office. The faint strains of a TV floated from it. I rapped on the door. Nothing. I rapped again harder. The TV turned off.

A dark head poked out from the back office door, and a man shuffled toward us. He was older, with a leathery, weathered face and heavy wrinkles that seemed to roll over each other. He was wearing an oversized woolen sweater and khaki pants. On his feet were well-worn hiking boots. As he looked up at us, I thought I caught a wry twinkle in his gray eyes, as he gently unlocked the door.

"Did you want some bait or something? Because officially we close at five o'clock."

"We don't need anything except some help."

He nodded as if he'd known that all along and that digging people out of trouble on the mountainside was his real life vocation.

"I need to use a phone," demanded Doris urgently. "We don't have a signal up here."

"Then I suppose you'd better come in."

He pointed to a payphone just inside the door. Putting on lights as he went, he eventually positioned himself behind his counter, which was stocked with a dusty display of fishhooks, chocolate mints, and Beanie Babies.

"My name is Joe. Welcome to the Fish and Cut Bait Store. How can I help you?"

"There's been a landslide about five miles from here on the way over the pass."

"Yes, I know," he said nodding nonchalantly. "Happened about two hours ago. It happens a lot this time of year. It won't be cleared tonight. Your best bet is to make your way back to Medford till the morning."

"That's just the problem. I'm going to need gas to get back there. Do you know if there's a gas station nearby?"

Joe rocked back on his heels and let out a low, long whistle and shook his head slowly, as if he were thinking.

Just then, a younger version of the man in front of me came through the same office door. In his hand, he had a blackened pan that contained what looked as if in a former life used to be baked beans.

"This is my son, Tom," said Joe. Then with a hint of impishness, he added, "As you can see, he's our cook around here." He turned to Tom. "They're looking for a gas station."

Tom also let out a low whistle. "Did you tell them we're all diesel up here?"

"No, I was just about to. Nearest gas station is on the other side of that rockslide."

They both stared at the floor and started shaking their heads in unison. I would have laughed if I hadn't felt so desperate.

Doris arrived by my side, shaking her head and whispering, "I've called both numbers. No reply."

"Let's hope for the best, Doris."

She sighed deeply, nodding, and then knitted her brow as she caught a glimpse of the pan in Tom's hand. "Is that what you gentlemen call dinner?" she asked, eyeing the pan with disgust.

"Yes, ma'am," responded Joe. "We're just two old bachelors living up here. Nothing to work with except a microwave and one gas ring."

"That's no way to eat!" she sniffed. "You're doing a manly job; you should be eating a decent meal."

They both smirked, appearing to appreciate her forthrightness, but neither of them commented. They were men of few words. It must be quiet living in the back of beyond with no one to talk to but trees and fish, I thought.

I tried again. "Is there anywhere nearby that we could stay for the night?"

"Not up here," said Joe, shaking his head again,

"unless you've brought your tent. There's an old lodge close by for skiing in the season, but that place isn't open till after Thanksgiving. It doesn't make sense to open it till we have some snow."

"Do you think the owners would be willing to let us stay so we could get a decent night's sleep?" I asked desperately. "We could be on our way early in the morning as soon as the pass clears."

"I don't know about that," said Joe. "It hasn't actually been aired out or anything yet. The last party was up there last April."

"And there will be nothing to eat there except a bunch of canned vegetables," added Tom.

"Is there a reasonable kitchen?" inquired Doris.

"Oh, yes, ma'am, it's very equipped. It even has two sinks," added Tom in a tone that hinted that he thought even one sink was an indulgence.

"Perfect," said Doris. "I have all my own food supplies with me."

I noticed she'd started to cheer up. Cooking always seemed to do that for her.

"How do we get a hold of the owner?" I was starting to see a glimmer of hope.

"It's just owned by a father and son," Joe said with a hint of a grin. "I think we could get a hold of them this evening."

"We're very clean and willing to pay for the accommodation. And I'll cook a meal they won't forget in a hurry," added Doris.

"You've got yourselves a deal. I'll go and fetch

the keys. It's been a long time since we've had a meal we'll never forget."

As I followed Joe and Tom, my headlights illuminated a pile of tools under a scruffy brown tarp in the back of their immense white pickup truck.

After about half a mile, they turned off the highway, and we started to climb. My engine labored again as we headed up a goat trail of a road. It was now pitch-dark, and we inched along the steep path that had thick brush on one side and a sheer drop on the other. I tried to concentrate on the taillights in front of me. The road suddenly flattened out, and an old log cabin came into view. Joe and Tom stopped, and we pulled up and parked beside them. I exhaled and released the steering wheel I'd been gripping for dear life.

Tom got out of his truck and walked over to us. "Why don't you all stay in there awhile so we can get a fire started and the lights on?"

Thanking him, we watched the building gradually fill with the flicker of candlelight. Eventually a slow circle of gray smoke curled out of the chimney silhouetted against the dark sky.

All at once, there was a rustle in the bushes to the right of us, just a few feet from the car, as if something large were scrambling to hide. We all looked in the direction of the disturbance, but it was too dark to make anything out. The bushes rustled again, and it sounded as if whatever it was had lunged away to hide in thicker brush.

"What was that?" asked Flora in a whisper.

"Oh, probably just a possum or a raccoon," I answered, not even convinced of that myself but not wanting to take my imaginings any further.

"Too big for a possum," said Doris as we heard small branches snapping underfoot.

"Sasquatch!" growled Ethel with a conviction that implied she'd met him personally.

Tom came trundling out. He explained there was still a bit of work to do before the season began, but it would keep us warm and dry for the night.

"A bit of work" was an understatement. As we entered, I felt a strong camaraderie with Snow White when she'd first entered the dwarves' cottage. Though from what I could see, that chick had it easy. This place was a cauldron of gloomy walls, hanging cobwebs, sticks of ugly furniture, and threadbare carpets. As we stepped inside the front door, Flora froze and anchored herself to the spot ahead of me as if she planned to put down roots right there. I nudged her gently in the back to keep her moving. We shuffled in together in a huddle, none of us wanting to leave the safety of the pack or, in fact, touch anything.

The men were working on the fire in the main room. Dominating the one main wall was a monstrous, heavily carved fireplace that was just missing a country squire and a couple of dogs flanking it. Above the mantel, a somber picture of a hunting scene was complete with mutilated animals, and on top of the ramshackle mantel sat an old brass candelabrum with nubs of gnarly candles they'd lit.

We shuffled our way in as if we were joined at the hip and gravitated toward the fire, the only warmth in the room. In front of it sagged a humungous sofa that sported ugly, wood-carved gargoyle armrests and a dirty brown ticking. It was the least inviting thing I'd ever seen. Speechless, we sat down on it all together, like five nuts in a sack. The sofa screamed out, and we jumped back to our feet.

Tom turned around, saying matter-of-factly, "Oh, that old sofa's springs are on the way out. Don't worry about it. It only bites people on Sundays."

Doris opened her mouth to say something but nothing came out. I think we were all thinking the same thing. We'd traded a beautiful lakeside home for the Hammer House of Horror.

Tom put wood onto the fire, and Joe offered to show us around the "old place."

"It belonged to my grandfather," he explained with pride. Raising the candelabrum above his head, he led us toward a long, dingy passageway.

"Is there no electricity?" I asked, hoping for the best.

"Oh, yes, we have electricity up here now," he

said with assurance. "But a fuse must have blown. We'll take a look at it."

We followed him down the gloomy hallway, where every few feet of wall space was punctuated with the head of some poor animal. We couldn't help being wide-eyed and terrified. I noted that Ethel had disappeared somewhere beneath Doris's coat, and Flora seemed to be wrapped around me like a scarf. For five women, we were so interlaced that we took up the space of just one.

"My grandfather really used it for hunting. In fact, he shot most of what you see on these walls."

Joe opened up one of the corridor's paneled doors, and it creaked desperately.

We all peered inside as if we were expecting a ghost to jump out. But actually the room looked quite comfortable and clean. Joe walked in and drew the dark, heavy curtains.

"I have a woman come out and clean up before the season starts. She was here yesterday and has already made headway on the bedrooms. But she won't be back till next week to finish off the rest of the house."

The woman needed a medal as far as I was concerned. It was still gaudy and dark, but it had a breath of spring life about it. A large four-poster oak bed dominated the room, with crisp white sheets. A cozy handmade patchwork quilt was folded at the foot.

"Ethel and I can take this room," said Doris,

marking her territory by throwing her huge flowery purse onto the bed. "We don't mind sleeping together."

Ethel scuffled in and perched on the edge of the bed like a little bird.

"Okay," said Joe. "Let me show the rest of you the other rooms."

Our optimism was short-lived as Joe opened the next bedroom door. The room was freshly cleaned and possessed a simple charm, but it lost all of its appeal once we looked up at the wall over the bed. Hanging from it, bearing down on us, was an enormous moose head. It fixed us with its glassy stare, as if it were telling us that it had no intention of letting anyone sleep. I heard Flora catch her breath beside me as Annie tightened her grip on my arm. Why was I suddenly the strong one?

Joe walked into the room and adjusted a mat, oblivious to our discomfort.

"This was my grandmother's room," he mused, fondly. "She loved it in here. I remember as a small child hearing her sing as she sat sewing or reading in that chair over there."

He pointed to a heavy, dark, carved chair with a tapestry seat that looked more like a throne.

"Yes, she loved it in here," he repeated, reminiscently. "In fact," he said with a sigh, "she died right here in the bed in the middle of the night. God bless her soul."

I heard Flora gasp. No doubt Grandma probably

died of shock as she'd turned over in the night and saw that moose head staring down at her.

Joe looked over at us expectantly. I looked at Annie and Flora. They both had their mouths wide open and were glued to either side of me, their eyes locked on the moose. Neither of them seemed to be breathing as far as I could tell.

"I'll take this one," I said in a tight voice.

I knew that Flora would have probably succumbed to Grandma's fate if we left her in here.

"Great," Joe said. Then he added, "That means you two other ladies will have to take the nursery."

Just the word "nursery" made them both visibly relax. It was hard to imagine children had actually been in this space, but the mention of it seemed to enable them to breathe again. I put down my overnight things on Grandma's bed and was eager to get out of the room to see the nursery.

Joe opened up the next paneled door, and it was utterly enchanting, totally out of place from the other rooms, created for children from an era gone by. Two charming little beds stood side by side. Surrounding the room on painted shelves were china dolls, wooden soldiers, and overstuffed teddy bears. In the corner of the room was an enormous white-and-pink dollhouse. In the center, a group of china dolls in Victorian whites was seated around a pretty miniature wicker table that was set for a tea party.

"I'm sorry there are only two single beds, and you two girls will have to share," added Joe. "I hope that's okay with you."

"It's perfect," squealed Flora.

All at once, the room burst into glorious electric light, and we heard Tom's voice shout from a distant room, "Got it!"

"Lovely," said Annie, picking up one of the dolls.

"Oh, yes," said Joe nostalgically. "My grandmother brought a lot of the toys from England when she came here as a little girl. Mrs. Jameson, the lady that cleans, loves this room. She takes all the doll clothes home, washes, and presses them before the beginning of the season. I think she looks after these toys better than she does herself."

As we made our way back out into the corridor, Doris was waiting there.

"I would like to see the kitchen."

"Of course," said Joe, blowing out the candles. "This way."

"Do you have any meat in this place at all?" asked Doris.

"There's some venison in the back freezer that's on a different circuit so it should still be okay. I'll go and check for you."

"Good," said Doris as she breezed past him toward the kitchen.

We all walked to the kitchen but stopped in

our tracks. It had obviously been designed with a fifties theme in mind, with a stunning monochrome floor and red-and-black wall tiles.

"Oh, good. It looks like Mrs. Jameson made it in here too!" said Joe as he dropped a lump of frozen meat on the counter.

As we all stood in awe of the room, Doris was practically salivating at my side.

"This is very different from the rest of the house," I finally said, trying to be tactful.

"Yes," sniffed Joe as Tom joined us in the kitchen. "My son, Tom, got himself married for a while back there. And *this* is the result."

Joe didn't seem too impressed.

Tom picked up the story. "My ex-bride decided this place needed some updating and started with the kitchen. She had planned to modernize the whole lodge."

"Turn it into some yuppie chateau," added Joe with obvious disdain. "It would have taken away all its character."

"Fortunately, the remodel was as short-lived as the marriage."

And then, as if on cue, they both looked at their feet.

Joe broke the silence. "It takes a certain kind of female to live up in these parts."

He said the word "female" as if he was sexing goats. I wanted to laugh, but instead I said, "I'm sorry to hear that, Tom."

"Oh no, I dodged a bullet, alright. Otherwise who knows what else she would have changed."

Looking around the gleaming kitchen, I tried to imagine how "terrible" that would have been. It wasn't my favorite style, but it was stunning, like something out of *Good Housekeeping* magazine. A shiny, state-of-the-art cast-iron range with double burners and two ovens stood against one wall. To its side, multiple slick, open stainless steel shelves housed every conceivable piece of kitchen equipment. A large square island topped with a thick slab of smooth black granite dominated the center of the room.

Under the window, which was cheerfully decorated with black-and-white polka-dot curtains, sat a shiny black-buttoned booth. Above it, an oversized neon-pink backlit wall clock. It depicted a cute, smiling fifties-era waitress wearing a short pink uniform and a pretty white apron. Skating on roller skates, she carried a tray of Coca-Cola as her long, pinlike legs hung low below the clock and swung back and forward as a pendulum.

"This will do nicely," said Doris with an approving sniff.

She washed her hands and started barking orders to us to retrieve certain boxes out of the car. Ethel got to work peeling potatoes.

It wasn't long before we were all gathered in the kitchen, ready to eat. We polished off the venison stew that Doris had created for us in record time. Then she produced a huge pan of moist, hot brownies.

"I just had to try out that fancy kitchen mixer," she drawled as she handed out plates of the warm, chewy dessert. "It had one of those baker hook attachments and everything." Only Doris seemed impressed.

Between them, Tom and Joe managed to polish off four bowls of stew and six brownies. But as soon as they were done, they stood up to go.

"Unfortunately, you don't have a phone up here, but we're only twenty minutes down the mountain if you need us," said Tom.

"There's only one road," joked Joe. "You can't miss it."

"We'll be gone in the morning," I assured them, confidently. "We'll stop in to say good-bye and pay you for the night."

"Oh no," said Tom, "the house isn't really set up yet. We wouldn't dream of taking a penny off you, especially after a dinner like that. However, we would be happy to take some of your leftovers, if you have some to spare."

"Of course," said Doris, a twinkle in her eye.

She had dishes wrapped for them in aluminum foil before they'd finished putting on their coats and boots. Eagerly they took their packages and made their way to the door. As we followed them outside, I noted there was a severe nip in the air.

Joe got in his truck, wound down the window,

and shouted out to us, "It's supposed to rain hard tonight, so take your time getting back down the mountain tomorrow. Oh, and the back door doesn't close properly, so make sure to set something heavy against it to stop any critters from wandering in during the night. You're in bear country now!"

That was all we needed to hear. Before their taillights had even disappeared, we were back inside with the front door firmly bolted behind us. We wandered into the peculiar living room, and Doris made us all hot cocoa. Sitting down on the lumpy furniture, we peered into the fire in silence.

Doris stood up slowly, her large stature illuminated by the glow from the fireplace.

"I guess I owe you all an explanation."

No one dared speak for a minute, though I think we all knew what she was referring to.

"You don't owe us anything," I eventually answered.

"Yes, I do. I need to talk to somebody, and where else would I be safer than here with . . . my friends?" She cleared her throat. "I did a very foolish thing, and Momma may end up paying for it."

Sighing heavily, she turned her back to us and stared absently at the hunting scene above the mantel as she began. "A couple of months ago, my mother's only living relative, her sister, Regina, died. They had a very tumultuous relationship.

Regina never married or had children and always appeared to be just a little jealous of her sister."

Doris let go of a long slow breath and sat down in one of the side chairs.

"Momma is more of an extrovert, and Regina preferred to retreat to the world of her books and her writing, eventually becoming a teacher in a private girls' school. When she died a few months ago, I inherited all of her things. I got rid of a lot but decided to keep all the volumes of her stories. They were crafted in beautiful books and so eloquently written. One day I was bored and wanted to spice up my manuscript—you know, change it up a bit. I was stuck about what to add when I remembered Regina's stories. I searched through her journals. Many of them were inappropriate, about goblins and fairies. But then I found this one about a young girl embarking on an illicit love affair during the Second World War. It was exactly what I was looking for, a love triangle with a British girl, her Scottish lover, and an American GI stationed in England during that time."

Doris sat back, her tone more relaxed now she'd decided to unburden herself.

"The story started with the young woman falling in love with this GI stationed in her hometown. They got engaged before he had to leave her to fight the war in Europe. While he was gone, she stole her best friend's Scottish boyfriend, whom she met when he'd rescued her from a pond where she'd fallen in, drunk and unable to swim. However, she spurned his love, and the young Scottish man died heartbroken and alone in a hospital. When the GI eventually came back from the war, she told him nothing of her affair and married him. I thought the story was an interesting addition, and I managed to work it into one of Jane Austen's time-travel adventures, and it fit nicely with the rest of the book. I then sent it off in this last manuscript."

Doris got up then and started to pace.

"Then, a few weeks ago, Momma and I decided to try out that new aquatic place that opened up on the island, as I know how much she loves to swim. On our way there, she just happened to mention that she didn't learn to swim till after she was married and that my father had taught her. She went on to tell me how she'd once nearly drowned in a pond in her village and a friend had saved her life. Her recollection was eerily similar to the story I'd just sent off to the publishers. So, I tentatively asked her a few more questions. She couldn't remember much else, but she did mention her best friend Mary's maiden name. After this conversation, I was really concerned. It bothered me. Surely the story I'd just read in Regina's journal couldn't be based in fact. Momma had never mentioned anything about a story like this. And you know we've heard so many of her stories set during the war. The thought just wouldn't go away, so I decided to do some checking to see if I could locate Mary."

Doris paused.

"Did you find her?" asked Annie, finishing her cocoa.

"Yes and no. The morning we left on this trip, I eventually tracked down a phone number for Mary's granddaughter. I tried to call her straight-away, but with the time difference in England, it wasn't easy. Then the other night when you'd all gone to bed, I asked Dan's parents to let me use their phone and managed to talk to her. Her name was Sarah. She informed me her grandmother had passed away quite some time ago, and unfortunately she didn't know an awful lot about Mary's childhood. However, she did remember Mary had spoken of a friend called Grace and that her grandmother had once been engaged to someone from the north. She didn't know the details of why they'd split up, just that Mary had gone on to marry her grandfather, whom she'd nursed during the war.

"It seems like the north could be Scotland, and now instead of putting my mind at rest, I'm now really worried, more than ever, that all this is a true story. I can't stop wondering, if so, how come Momma has never told me about it."

We sat quietly and listened to the fire as we finished our cocoa.

"It could still all be a story," said Flora gently. "A love triangle? It doesn't even sound like something Grace would do."

Doris nodded. "I know. I have thought of that too, but it's how the story ends that has me most concerned. At the end of the story, the girl decides to marry the GI even though she doesn't love him. She marries him for one reason only . . ." She paused then, before saying quietly, "She marries him because she was pregnant with the Scottish man's baby."

We all seemed to realize at once the implication of what she was saying, and heaviness descended on the room like a blanket.

Doris clarified it for us. "Which means if this story is about my mother, the man I knew all of my life may not have been my father."

I tried desperately to think of something reassuring to say.

"And where is the story now?" asked Flora in alarm.

"It was hidden in the attic. I wish I'd destroyed it before we left. But those books are the only things of my auntie's I have. I just didn't want to destroy them until I'd spoken to Mary's grand-daughter. I didn't want to overreact. I thought they would be perfectly safe while we were gone, as Momma never goes up in the attic, and she was going to be staying at the twins' house. Now, in my foolishness, I may have exposed my momma to something she has felt the need to keep hidden from me all these years."

Doris sighed deeply.

I tried to encourage her. "There are a lot of 'what ifs' here, Doris," I reminded her gently. "Regina could have just set her tale in the same village she grew up in, drawing on experiences from her childhood, and Lavinia might have been talking about completely different stories at the group. We'll have your manuscript back by tomorrow, the day after that at the latest. Then you can destroy both that and the journal when you get home, if you want, and no one will be any the wiser."

Doris nodded at that wisdom as she collected our cups and headed for the kitchen before adding, somberly, "Yes, it would all go away, except for knowing for sure that my father was really my father."

We sat quietly for a while, each with her own thoughts, before an antique clock on the mantel chimed ten o'clock. We decided to call it a night.

I patted Doris's hand as I left for my bedroom.

"Try not to worry about all this, Doris. There's nothing we can do tonight, and in the morning you can call Lavinia and get her to destroy the journal if it will make you feel better."

She nodded and seemed to cheer a little before making her way to her room.

We all said our good nights.

I opened my bedroom door and there it was . . . staring at me . . . Mr. Moose. I had momentarily forgotten about him with all that had happened, but now he was staring down at me as I shivered. Preparing for bed, I felt his two beady eyes following me all around the room, silently questioning: "Why did you do this to me? What did I ever do to you?"

I looked at him as I brushed my teeth while standing in the tiny gray-and-white-tiled bathroom. Something had to be done. The thing was humongous, too bulky for me to lift off the wall. I looked around the room. As I searched, I heard the gentle tinkle of a music box coming from the nursery and the unmistakable giggle of Annie. I was glad someone was having fun. Opening an enormous blanket chest at the foot of the bed, I found a clean white sheet. That would have to do. By standing on the throne, I managed to throw the sheet right over the moose's head and cover it perfectly. It looked better already. What I couldn't see wouldn't hurt me.

Getting into bed, I suddenly missed Martin and my own cozy bed at home. Checking my phone, I could see there was still no signal. At least by tomorrow we would be back in civilization. Battling with the stiff white sheets and the bedspread, I eventually managed to burrow myself inside.

Replaying the day's events as I lay there, I felt

deeply sad for Doris. This was hard. The only other thought that preoccupied my mind as I drifted off to sleep was . . . what if the secretary's baby was really an alien?

Chapter Twelve

RONALD TRAMP, THE GRIZZLY BEAR

In my dream, there was a girl floating about in a white wedding dress, holding a candle and calling my name. She reached toward me with an outstretched hand and shook me. It felt so real. Opening my eyes, I tried to focus through the darkness.

The girl in my dream appeared to be standing right next to my bed. Was it a ghost? Maybe this was Grandma coming back to punish me for covering up her moose head. As the girl moved closer, I realized it was only Flora in her nightgown.

"Are you okay?" My voice was dry and rasping.

She bent down and whispered to me, "There's something in the kitchen. I think it might be a bear!"

Annie arrived behind her, yawning as she put on her own robe.

"Someone needs to investigate," added Flora.

"It's probably just this old house settling." I yawned. I did not relish the thought of leaving my bed. "I don't think a bear would come all the way inside. Besides . . ."

I never finished my sentence because all of a

sudden there was a clear, dull thud in another part of the house. It sounded like a book or a log being dropped to the floor.

Suddenly, one thought rendered me fully awake: the back door. I couldn't remember if any of us had set anything heavy against it as Joe had advised us to do. Jumping up out of bed, I followed Flora out into the corridor. Switching on the lights, I looked down the hall toward the noise.

"Maybe Doris is up," I whispered to them both.

Doris's door suddenly opened.

"Up where?" inquired a curler-clad Doris.

We filled Doris in on the situation. She nodded and then went back into her room for a second, arriving back in the hallway with a pile of her pots and pans.

"What are we going to do with these, cook it an omelet?" I asked, bewildered.

"If you see a bear," hissed Doris as she started to tiptoe down the hall, "you're supposed to make yourself very large and make a lot of noise."

Ethel's head popped out of her bedroom door and made us all jump. Doris gave a pan and lid to Ethel, who didn't seem the least bit fazed by being handed kitchen equipment in the middle of the night and then being asked to join the end of the Scooby-Doo line that we were forming.

"So here's the plan," hissed Doris. "We'll walk up the hallway, slowly. When we reach the kitchen, we'll run in and bang our pots together as hard as we can."

We started to creep behind Doris. I looked back at our old lady battle line and didn't hold out much hope for Ethel. The bear would probably see her as a delightful little snack.

As we tiptoed into the main room, I couldn't help myself.

"Doris, why do you have your pans in the bedroom?"

She stopped and looked back at me as if I were an idiot. "They're my best ones!" she said indignantly. "I don't want anyone stealing them."

"Who are you talking about? We're not exactly at the end of the world, but we can see it from here!"

Doris looked back at me again as if the thought had never actually occurred to her. She appeared to be about to answer me when we heard another noise from the kitchen, and it sounded as if something were exhaling. We were all frozen to the spot for a second, and then Doris raised her pot above her head, holding her pan lid up in the other hand as if she were about to crash an enormous pair of cymbals. She gestured for us all to do the same. As we lifted our arms, Flora's lid slipped from her hand and clattered to the ground. Doris rolled her eyes as Flora hastily picked it up and mouthed her apologies. Signaling us to follow, Doris charged toward the kitchen, banging her lid on her pot and screaming at the top of her lungs.

"Aaaaaaaaaarh!"

We all followed behind, banging and yelling at the top of our voices too.

"Aaaaaaaaaaaarh!"

We saw a flash of movement and a jumbled mass of matted fur running for its life toward the back kitchen door, screeching. Somehow, it managed to miss the doorway and run smack into the kitchen wall instead. Ricocheting off it, it hit the floor hard, and then it just lay there. The impact of the crash shook the walls and knocked down the "floozy clock," as Doris had nicknamed it. The Coca-Cola girl lay on the floor, smiling up at us, her legs still rocking back and forth.

We all looked down at the mass of fur with concern. Whatever it was, we had just killed it. Scared it to death, no doubt. It lay on the black-and-white-tiled floor, fearfully still. We put down our pans, and Doris turned on the light.

"What is it?" asked Annie.

"It's an extremely odd shape for a bear," added Flora.

"That's because it's Big Foot," snapped Ethel.

We all walked slowly toward the animal lying on the floor. As we got closer, I noticed it didn't have paws, but fingers. Oh no, this ragbag of jumble definitely wasn't a bear.

"It's a man!" said Flora, moving closer.

We gathered around and looked closer. He was wearing what looked like flour sacks pulled together as a sort of cape and tatty pants being held together with a piece of string. He had long, matted, sandy-colored hair and a ragged beard. The newest, cleanest thing on him seemed to be his boots.

"Should we try and wake him?" asked Flora, leaning even closer to his face.

Suddenly, a sticklike hand shot out of the cape and grabbed Flora's arm. We all screamed, except Flora. She seemed to be frozen in shock. He opened his eyes and screamed too.

Flora was incredible. She came to life, put her other hand on his shoulder, and reassured him. "Don't be scared," she said soothingly. "It's okay. We're not going to hurt you."

He stopped screaming, his wild brown eyes flicking fearfully from one of us to the other, like a caged animal in terror. He seemed to be summing up the situation extremely quickly and deciding if we could be trusted.

"Can you sit up?" asked Doris, starting to take command.

He just stared at her.

"Ethel, get him a glass of water."

Flora gently patted his shoulder; I reached down and took him by the arm.

He slowly started to sit up. It was like lifting

a tiny bird. He was really bundled up, but I was guessing he was just a pile of skin and bones.

Ethel came back with water and handed it to him. His grimy, shaking hand stretched out and took the glass. He took a couple of gulps, then opened his mouth and said, "What y'all doin' here in my house?"

"Sorry?" said Doris.

"My house," he said, sounding braver. "Why y'all here?"

We all looked at him in bewilderment.

"We're guests of Tom and Joe at the Fish and Cut Bait Store," I said.

"Who?" he said, screwing up his eyes.

"Down the mountain," I added, weakly.

"Never heard of 'em! This is my cabin. I've been using it for years."

The man was obviously a little deranged, so I decided to play along. "Oh. We thought you wouldn't mind us staying one night. We ran out of gas on the road, and it was very cold to sleep in the car."

He eyed me cautiously over his glass of water, then said, "S'pose that'd be okay. But you can't go around yelling and hollering like that. You darn near gave me a heart attack."

"Oh no, that's because we thought you were a bear."

"A bear!" he screeched, incredulously. "How could you think I looked anything like a bear?"

He sniffed then, as if he believed we were all obviously a little stupid.

Doris picked up the kettle. "Would you like a cup of coffee or something?"

His eyes narrowed. "As long as you don't poison it or anything," he snapped gruffly.

Doris held her tongue, but the disapproval was obvious on her face.

With Flora's help, he climbed to his feet. He folded his arms and huffed, then sat himself firmly down on the edge of the booth and started picking at his teeth. He looked ridiculous sitting there, a bundle of rags and matted hair on the shiny, buttoned buffet seat.

We all congregated around the stove to talk as Doris made coffee.

"What should we do?" asked Annie, concerned.

"What can we do? We're all stuck up here in the middle of the night with no phone," I answered.

"He could be an axe murderer," sneered Ethel with a look as if she were half-hoping that was exactly what he was.

I looked back at him as he now picked at his nails. "I don't think he's dangerous. Besides, he's as light as a feather. Ethel could take him down."

She looked up at me, then back at the man. She wrinkled her nose and sniffed.

"There's nothing we can do now. It's four in the morning," I said, glancing at the floozy clock that was still rocking her way around the kitchen floor.

"We may as well wait until it gets light. Then we can go down the mountain and get Joe or Tom."

"What are ya birds whispering about?" shouted our scruffy guest from the booth. "I don't like all that whispering. Makes me nervous. Makes me think you're plotting to kill me and throw my tired old bones in the creek."

"Oh, we would never do anything like that," said Flora, walking over and sitting opposite him. "Do we look like the murdering type to you?"

He looked straight at Flora, narrowed his eyes, and said with conviction, "Yes. You look exactly like the murdering type. Using all your feminine wiles to get on my good side and then you'd be killing me stone dead." He emphasized his words as he spoke. "Yes, siree," he said. "You are exactly the murdering type."

Flora just sat, blinking, with her mouth open.

Doris brought over his coffee and slammed it down in front of him. I could tell she was not putting up with any of his nonsense. "Would you like some sugar for your poison?" she asked sarcastically.

He just sniffed and begrudgingly took a sip.

I approached him and sat next to him.

"My name is Janet." I held out my hand. "What's yours?"

He looked at me like a lame dog that had just been beaten and was not sure whether to trust this hand of a stranger or not. Then his eyes twinkled, and he screwed up his nose, thrusting a darkened, scraggy, half-mittened hand into mine saying, "Ronald Tramp. You may know my brother. Pleased to meet ya."

Then, as if this were the funniest thing anyone had ever said, he rocked back, slapping his leg and laughing hysterically, baring all four of his blackened teeth in the process. His breath left something to be desired.

I placed my hand strategically across my nose. "Do you come from around here?"

He looked at me as if he'd never made small talk in his life, then, scratching at something in his hair, he said, "Do I come from around here? Course I come from around here! It's not like I got a Lamborghini parked out front, you know, so I can shoot off to Vegas on a whim. I live as far as these two walkers will take me. Normally up into town and back."

Fed up with listening to me beating about the bush, Doris went straight for the jugular. "What are you really doing here?"

"I told you, this is my house. I live here once or twice a year when the season changes and the snow comes, to shelter from it for a couple of days. There are usually a couple of cans knocking around in the cupboard to keep me entertained." He picked at his teeth again. "I leave the place as clean as a whistle when I go. It's kind of a game with me. I think of myself as the cat burglar of

Siskiyou Pass. 'Cept I don't steal anything, save a couple of old cans or so. I just like to live it up for a couple of days and let my bones catch up and then be on my way."

He narrowed his eyes then as if we were the intruders.

"Usually we don't see city folk up here till a couple of days after the snow comes. Then they all come up here in their fancy German cars with their little white snow suits and pink booties, cars all full of kids and skiing gear." He tutted heavily, like skiing was way up there with washing.

"We got trapped behind a rockslide," said Flora, smiling at him as she sat next to him on the bench.

Doris still wasn't having any of it. "I don't care who you are and where you came from. You need to leave once you finish your drink."

Ronald looked thunderstruck. "What! You would throw an old bag of bones like me out into the snow just like that?"

"Snow! What snow?!"

He looked at Doris as if she were stupid. "The snow. It's snowing outside! That's what snow."

"It isn't snowing outside," said Doris, gruffly. "It's raining."

Ronald rocked back in his seat and laughed again. "I'm a lot of things, but I am not stupid, and unless that is the fattest, fluffiest rain I have ever seen—and I wouldn't put it past my old eyes to trick me, but my bones will tell me every single time—it's been snowing out there for hours!"

Flora went to the hallway and pulled the door open. Doris and I joined her. Sure enough, it was bucketing down outside. There had to be at least a foot already, and it appeared to show no sign of stopping in the near future.

"No!" I exclaimed, suddenly feeling claustrophobic. This wasn't good. This wasn't good at all.

"We'll never get out today," groaned Flora, reading my thoughts.

"Never is about right," said Doris. "And what are we going to do about that piece of work in the kitchen?"

"We can't turn him out into this snow," said Flora. "He came in here to get away from it."

"We should keep our eyes on him," said Doris suspiciously. "One of us should watch him at all times."

Ronald joined us, standing in the hallway. We smelled him before we saw him.

"I hope none of you ladies are wanted by the law and need to make a fast getaway or anything," he said, looking up at the sky as he linked his arm in Annie's and mine. He gave us all a broad, gummy smile before adding, " 'Cause we could be trapped up here together for weeks!"

Ethel looked as if she were going to pass out on the spot as Doris muttered, "Nonsense," under her breath and moved away from the door. Then over her shoulder, she shouted back, "We have places to go, and as soon as it stops, we'll be out of here and on our way."

She sounded severe, but not certain.

"In the meantime"—she marched toward the bedroom—"I am going back to bed till it's a decent time to get up!" Then, as an afterthought, she looked at Ronald and added, "I'm locking my bedroom door, just in case you were wondering."

She disappeared down the corridor, Ethel following as they slammed the bedroom door shut.

Ronald didn't skip a beat. He shouted after her, "No need to get your panties in a bunch, there, Frosty the Snow Queen. You're not exactly my type."

"I'm going back to bed," I yawned, starting to feel tired again.

"I'm happy to stay out here and keep Ronald company," said Annie cheerfully. "Would you like some stew, Ronald?"

"I thought you'd never ask," he said with a twinkle in his eye.

Lying in bed, I alternated between looking at the sheeted moose head and out the bedroom window, where fluffy cotton snow fell silently. What was I doing here in the back of beyond when I should be at home with my husband? I looked down at my phone again. Still no signal. I was now well and truly homesick, and my fear about not being in touch with Stacy was escalating.

The next morning, there was a soft rap on my door. It was Flora.

"Am I disturbing you?" she inquired.

"No," I said, lifting myself up onto one arm and patting the edge of the bed, inviting her in. She perched like a wayward sparrow.

"I'm just a little blue," she said after a long pause.

"You're missing Dan," I responded with a knowing smile.

"We've only known each other for a couple of days, but . . ." She appeared to be searching for the right words. "But now I feel lost without him."

"Like the other half of you is missing," I filled in the blanks.

"Yes."

"Don't worry; that's normal."

"Can I share something?" she asked gently. "I'm entertaining the thought of moving off the island."

"Maybe to Portland?"

She nodded.

"I'm not making any major decisions yet, but for the first time in my life, I want something more than what the island can offer me. What do you think?" she asked, like a little girl.

"I think it's a little bit early to be thinking too seriously. But if in five or six months' time, things have progressed and you and Dan are getting further along in the relationship, I wouldn't think anything will be able to keep you on the island."

I slid to the end of the bed. "Let's get a cup of tea." I patted her hand. She nodded.

We made our way to the kitchen, passing Annie and Ronald, who were sitting at the small table in the front room. We were just in time to see Ronald slam down a playing card, then jump to his feet excitedly, shouting, "Snap again!" He threw back his head and laughed a hearty belly laugh, as if it were the funniest thing in the world.

I put the kettle on, and Flora climbed up onto one of the little black stools at the island just as Doris came in to make herself a drink.

"I saw Ronald Tramp is still here," she said as she stomped around the kitchen. "I suppose I'll be expected to feed him too." She sniffed hard. "I only hope we aren't here till spring. I only have enough food for a week or so. And he looks like the hungry type."

Chapter Thirteen

A GHOST THAT EATS PIE

We moped around the next day, drinking tea and playing endless games of cards. As the afternoon wore on, Flora shared her favorite poems with me.

"I love to write them," she informed me quietly as she opened the smooth leather cover of her journal, and handed it to me. "They help me say the things that are in my heart that I'm scared to say."

Annie passed around photos of her dogs. All fifty of them.

"They are all adorable," I admitted as I looked at their eager faces, shiny brown-button eyes, and lolloping tongues.

"And so much fun." Annie beamed, her face alive. "That's why I have to write about them; their little funny ways bring me so much joy each day."

We also ate Doris's creations. Cooking kept her busy, and that, in the process, also seemed to stop her worrying about her momma. Then at around four o'clock, without any warning, the lights went out and the fridge shuddered to a stop.

"Oh great," snapped Doris. "As if things couldn't get any worse, now the power's out!"

We lit all the candles we could find and placed them around. As the evening drew in, we gravitated like moths to the fireside.

I was standing in the kitchen when Flora came back in. She'd been walking in the snow. Her cheeks were reddened from the cold. "It's stopped snowing. I think we can leave tomorrow," she announced.

Doris balked. "I doubt it. Good thing I managed to cook an apple pie earlier today, but as I haven't learned how to cook over a candle yet, there's only bread and a bunch of cold cuts for our dinner."

Flora tried to rally us. "Let's eat around the fire," she suggested excitedly, like a child wanting to play a game. She ran to get a large woolen blanket from her room, laid it on the carpet, and then clustered candles together on the side tables.

"It's just like a little winter picnic," remarked Annie with delight as she settled down on the floor close to the fire to work on her latest project, a pair of thick woolen socks for Ronald.

His Highness at that particular moment was splayed out across the ugly gargoyle sofa, snoring loudly. Doris and Ethel brought in the supper and, as if on cue, like an old dog, Ronald stirred. "Is that food I smell?"

Doris placed meat, cheese, bread, and the apple pie on the table and fixed him with an icy stare. "Yes. Less than I thought, as I'm feeding more people."

Ronald yawned. "I sense the ice maiden is unhappy with me. How 'bout I pay you for my supper?"

"Pay me," Doris scoffed. "What a good idea."

"That would be fine," he said, scratching at something in his layers, then thrusting his hands into his pant pockets and pulling them inside out. "Unfortunately, I didn't bring any copper with me. But I could entertain ya if ya like."

"Oh, dear God. Tell me you're not going to sing," retorted Doris, horrified, as she handed out napkins. She made sure to give double the amount to Ronald, who just looked at them in bewilderment, then shrugged and stuffed them into his empty pockets.

"No," he said indignantly. "I sing as bad as a pig in a noose. But I do tell a mean ghost story."

"Oh, good!" said Annie, clapping her hands together. "I love ghost stories."

"Do we have to?" implored Flora. "I would rather play cards."

"Cards?" snapped Ronald, with disgust. "This 'ere story could save ya life, and you wanna play cards?" Then he added in an eerie voice, "You, my girl, would be the first to go . . . when he comes."

Flora's eyes widened. "What do you mean, *he* comes?"

"You'd 'ave to hear the story to know, won't ya?" said Ronald, reverting to his normal voice

232

and playfully popping a piece of cheese into his mouth.

"Come on," I encouraged. "It's going to be a long night as it is. We may as well enjoy a good yarn."

Doris huffed again as she handed out the pie and sat down to listen. Ronald leaned forward to take a slice, and Doris slapped his hand. "Story first, pie after. If I think it's worth anything," she said sternly, her lips set in a tight line.

Ronald screwed up his nose and snatched up a candle from the table. Then, ceremoniously, in true storytelling fashion, he took his place in front of the odious fireplace, in which Annie had managed to coax a roaring fire into life. Throwing back his potato-sack cape and pushing away matted dreadlocks from his grimy face, he stood still, and his voice became quiet and intentional as he began.

"This terrible tale I'm gonna tell y'all were told to me by me granddaddy, his granddaddy, and his granddaddy before him. It's told to every young'un along this side of the creek to warn 'em, so it never, ever happens again."

Nervously, he started to pace back and forth, and his voice dropped to barely above a whisper.

"This house you are sitting in is part of this very story. If these walls 'ere could speak, they'd say . . ." He paused, stopped pacing, and darted his eyes about the room, then he raised his arms and splayed out his sticklike fingers, his voice building to fever pitch as he said, "Travelers beware! Beware! Beware!"

He paused for effect. All that could be heard was the quiet scraping of forks on plates. We were riveted.

As the fire danced and crackled behind him, he resembled an odd woodland sprite, his silhouette casting a mischievous shadow across the walls as he stood there. He took a deep breath and began.

"It happened all the way back in 1845, during the gold rush. It were a mighty crazy time back then, and the mountains out here were full t' the brim with heaps of gold. So people came from all over, in droves like flies to shh—poop. They came to pan. One family that came up 'ere . . . were the Grants."

Ronald stopped, and his wild eyes danced around us as if he were hoping that name would mean something to us. As no one responded, he tutted, and continued.

"Well, Thaddeus Grant built wheels for carriages, and he had'ta leave his home in Kansas because there were no water there, nothing, zip. It t'all gone and dried up."

"I remember reading about that in school," mused Annie, taking a mouthful of pie.

Ronald picked up his story. "If there be no farmers, then there be no wagons for 'im to fix. So one day, he just made up his mind, he did. He decided to follow 'em. Thaddeus packed up everything he owned and took his wife, Beth, and their two biddy children, Theo and Ruth, on that terrible, long journey to Oregon. He had to watch ov'r his shoulder for Indians as he went."

Ronald started to pantomime a man packing and riding in a wagon, flashing his eyes from side to side as if he were keeping a look out. Flora clapped her hands together, obviously enchanted by the fun of it. Ethel just blew her nose, and Doris shook her head.

He brushed back a stray dreadlock. "He had planned to set up shop in Medford, but he never got there."

Ronald stopped to take a deep breath for effect; then he pulled the candle close to his face so it illuminated his dirty, ragged, sandy-colored beard. His tone became measured.

"Oh, if only he'd kept going." He looked across the room, above our heads, lost in that thought, and then ever so slowly he nodded his head.

This was quite a performance.

He snapped back into storytelling mode. "On his journey to Medford, Thaddeus was making his way over the top of the pass. It was an awful stormy night, and he and his family were badly in need of warming their bones in front of a roaring fire. Anyhow, as he rounded the mountain, suddenly outta nowhere a mudslide were upon 'em. His family were all a-yelling and a-hollering somethin' awful as the wagon was battered and buffeted by all the mud and rocks, like."

Ronald fought to control his imaginary horse as he continued.

"He rode the horse hard, pulling his carriage this way and more, 'n' once he nearly wenna fell clear off of the side of the mountain."

Ronald acted out pulling the horses hard left and then hard right before finally bringing them to an imaginary stop.

I let go of a breath. Ethel was perched on the edge of her seat like a squirrel about to pounce for nuts. Flora had pulled her blanket tightly around her shoulders, and she gripped a pillow to her chest. Even Doris seemed to be listening.

Ronald started again. "But Thaddeus were a-best of-a carriage drivers, and he saved all their lives. The only thing were-a broke was 'is wheel. They made camp for the night. In the morning, he set about fixing it. As he were-a working, another wagon came over the pass, struck a boulder, and cracked a wheel just like he had-a done. The driver was mighty happy to see a man that could fix 'em right up, right there on the pass, and Thaddeus saw it as a sign."

Ronald became animated again and started to pace.

"He made up his-a mind that he was a-gonna work right here on the mountain. He set up 'is shop just a ways down here, and he did alright.

There was plenty-a work for him, with folks hobbling up over the pass every five minutes. So much work, he had a pot of money, enough money, to build his wife a nice cabin up here on the ledge to raise their two young'uns in.

"Then it happened. November 1848, the night of the season's first snow . . ." Suddenly, he leapt toward us, clapped his hands, and shook his bony fingers at us, shouting, *"Just like tonight!"*

We all jumped.

"Less of the dramatics," warned Doris. "Or there will be no more pie!"

"Calm down there, starchy breeches. A story gotta have a little flare, ain't it?"

He wrinkled up his nose and treated us all to another gummy grin. "Anyhow, that-a night, a family had been struggling on the last leg of their journey. They were good folks named Barnes—Thomas; his wife, Sophie; their young'uns."

Ronald started to ride another imaginary horse. "The Barneses were just a-comin' over the mountain, which was slick with ice, when their horse, it a-lost its footing and reared up, and the carriage cracked an axle. Thaddeus was in his shop and heard all the commotion, surprised anyone was fool enough to come over the pass that late in the season. Fortunately, as Thomas thought t' hisself at the time, Thaddeus were there to help. It were mightily cold that day, so they moved Sophie and her young'uns up to this house with Beth and her children. Thaddeus looked at the wheel, but he got 'imself a-worrying 'coz he were running low on repair supplies. He hadn'a expected folks this late in the season. Thomas begged him to help, so Thaddeus did the best he could with what he had and patched it right up. But this is when this tale takes a darker turn."

Ronald stopped, slowly taking a long drink of milk. All that could be heard was the crackle of the fire and the clicking of Annie's knitting needles. I was flooded with feelings of nostalgia. There was something magical about a storyteller, even this ragged, foul-smelling one. It took me straight back to my childhood and a thousand fireside stories on the shores of Lake Tahoe, where my family spent every summer as I grew up.

"The repair had'da taken a couple of days, and a hard snowstorm blew in from a-nowhere as the Barneses started on'er their way. The snow fell deep around 'em, and the wind lashed at their-a carriage."

Ronald started to pantomime shivering on a carriage ride.

"Suddenly, as the blizzard went an' blinded him, that-a old wheel went and gave out again. That patch just wasn't a-strong enough to hold up under that awful mean weather. The horses, they started a-panicking and a-running a-this way and a-that a-way. Thomas tried his hardest, but he couldn't keep the thing together. The carriage broke loose of the horses and crashed onto its side, then ran right off'er the cliff. It rolled over and over all the way a-down that mountainside."

Ronald threw himself to the floor and rolled himself over and over across the floor toward us, before stopping dead in front of the side table. When he reached it, he helped himself to a piece of ham on the plate Doris had laid out before jumping back to his feet and continuing.

"Thomas was a-flung from the carriage and were a-knocked out, like. When he came to 'is senses, he rushed to the bottom of the creek, but all of his family was dead. He climbed the mountain and hobbled back to Thaddeus's house. Half-crazed with shock and grief, he banged upon the door, shouting that Thaddeus was gonna pay for the death of his family by the death of *his* own. Breaking down the door, he attacked Thaddeus with a spade. The men wrestled. Thaddeus managed to push Thomas back outside, and they fought like crazy men."

Ronald wrestled back and forth with an imaginary opponent. Then he stopped to take a breath.

"Beth was a-awful frightened and raced to hide herself and the children in the barn. The men fought hard, but Thaddeus, bein' a strong man, overpowered the likes of Thomas. But it were a-mighty dark by then, and neither of them saw a-how close to the edge they were a-fighting.

With a last mean blow, Thaddeus struck Thomas, knocking him backward hard, and he tripped over a boulder behind him. Before either man could do a thing about it, Thomas went straight over a-that cliff, falling right down to the creek at the bottom. It was just too dark to go down that night, so the next day Thaddeus went down to look for Thomas's body, but it was nowhere to be seen. He searched and searched, but no trace of that man were-a ever found. Well, Thaddeus found Thomas's carriage and buried Sophie and her young'uns in a small church cemetery about five miles from here. And life went on, for Thaddeus's family, as best it could. That is, until the following winter."

Ronald took a deep breath and looked carefully at each one of us.

"It was the beginning of November and snow came mighty early that year, not unlike this-a year. It 'er came down thick and heavy that first day. Thaddeus was awful sad remembering the year before and that poor family that had perished. After that terrible night, he-a always kept a bunch of extra parts through the winter; he never wanted that awful thing happening t' him again. Anyhow, Thaddeus had been out in the barn when the snow came, and no one knows for sure what the truth is, but this is the story that has been told.

"That first night of the snow, Beth was a-cooking

supper in the kitchen when there were a-knock at the door. She had'a her hands full, so she asked her son, who was ten years olds, t' open it. After he didn't come back to tell her who it was, she went and saw the front door was a-wide open, and her boy was nowhere to be seen. But here is the oddest thing about this whole tale."

Ronald pulled the candle close to his face again as he whispered, "Beth looked a-down at the ground but there weren't-a no footprints in the snow leading to or away from that house. Well, Beth was a-frantic, so she holler'd to her husband, and they hunted for their son all that day and many a-days after that. But young Theo was never seen again. They were a-both heartbroken and pined awful for him, but nothing could'a be done. It was the mystery of it all that kept them up nights. Who had taken him? And without no footprints? Slowly they started to recover as best they could. That is, until the following winter and the first snowfall.

"Beth was a-carrying their third child, and the snow, it a-started to fall early in the afternoon. Completely worned out, she told her daughter, who was now twelve years old, that she was going to lie down. She reminded her not to answer the front door for no one. Her daughter agreed and stayed in by the fire to play with her dolls. When Beth woke about an hour later, the first thing she felt, even before her eyes opened, was the bone-chilling cold. She jumped outta that-a bed, racing through the house like a crazed woman. When she got to the hallway, the front door was a-wide open. In there, her daughter's dolls were on the floor, but Ruth were a-gone.

"Once again there were no tracks to or from the house. They searched late into the night. But they never saw little Ruth again."

Ronald paused. I heard a sob slip from Flora, who now appeared to be chewing on a tissue, and Annie had stopped knitting and had both her hands to her chest. Ethel seemed to be holding her breath, and Doris's eyebrows were knitted in thought.

Ronald shook his head sadly, and his dirty, matted hair brushed roughly against his sack cape.

"Beth, she was a-heartbroken, and Thaddeus, he a-wanted to leave the mountain right away. But Beth wanted t' stay in case one of the children found their way back. She wanted to be there for 'em.

"The following winter, Beth had her hands full with a new baby. Then that first snow came again. This time Thaddeus was ready. He told Beth they would stay together no matter what, and guard that-a new baby of theirs. That first night they huddled together in front of this fire, neither of them sleeping a lick, Thaddeus with his pistol loaded by his side. They made it through that-a night and through-a the next day. They started to think that maybe the dreadful curse had been lifted, and Thomas's ghost had found its vengeance. The following night, they were feeling better, and Beth wanted to sleep in her own bed. Thaddeus went out back to get some firewood to keep 'em warm through the night, and he told Beth to stay in the bedroom. Beth nodded and lay back quietly. As Thaddeus left, three loud knocks came on the front door."

Ronald stopped to rap theatrically on the mantelpiece.

"Beth, she was a-mighty scared and a-pulled that-a baby's body close to her and closed her eyes. Then those knocks came again."

Ronald rapped again harder.

"Then suddenly she heard her son, Theo's, voice calling to her on the wind, then the voice of Ruth. Without thinking, with that baby in her-a arms, she leapt from the bed and ran to the front door. She could hear them. They had come home. She flung open that-a door, and the snow poured in.

"As Thaddeus left the barn, he also heard the voices of Theo and Ruth. Overjoyed, he dropped the wood and raced to the front of this-a house, but when he got-a there, there was no one. Desperate and with a mountain of fear, he raced into his bedroom, but his wife and baby were gone, and the only footprints leading into the house was-a 'is own. He dropped to his knees right-a 'ere in-a front of this fire, sobbing, realizing Thomas's ghost had taken all of his family. Then, half-wild with grief, he ran from this house and bolted into the snow and off into the night, calling for them.

"For years, he searched desperately for them all until, crazy and broken, one night during the first snow of one year, he couldn't a-take it no more so he threw himself off the mountain just outside here at the very same spot where Thomas Barnes had lost his life all those years ago."

Ronald's voice became a whisper again.

"It is said that the ghost of Thomas Barnes still roams these parts, looking for vengeance for his family. And that he still knocks at this very door on the night after the first snowfall."

Ronald blew out the candles for effect, and the room became darkened all around us. All we could see was his wild, fiery scarecrow silhouette, backlit by the fire.

Doris started to speak. "I have never heard so much nonsense in all of . . ."

But she never finished her sentence because suddenly, out of the blue, there came three loud knocks at the front door.

We all screamed.

Ronald lifted both his hands in the dark. "Don't open it!" he yelled. I could hear real fear in his voice. "As long as you don't open it, we'll be safe inside."

For a minute, I wondered if this was some sort of party trick and somehow he'd managed to make the door knock. But as I relit the candles, I could see the fear on his face too. We all froze to the spot. Someone knocked at the door again, now with more urgency.

"Someone had better open it," sniffed Doris, not quite as confident as she usually sounded. "We can't just all sit here like a bunch of scared camp kids."

"I warn you again!" pleaded Ronald, urgency in his tone. "It's Thomas's ghost. He'll take you away!"

Doris pulled herself out of her chair. "I would like to see him try. I am not exactly waiflike. It'll take more than a ghost to get *me* down that mountain."

She started to walk toward the door.

Flora jumped up. "We can't let her go alone," she implored. "It can't take all of us, can it? Let's all go."

We clustered together and slowly shuffled toward the door, Doris in front, a candle held high.

The person rapped once again, hard.

Ronald shouted after us. "I'll tell your story for years to come! The brave ladies from an island who brought pie."

Chapter Fourteen

HE'S COMING TO TAKE YOU AWAY . . .

As we crept slowly toward the front door, someone pounded again even harder. Doris reached
for the latch, then flung it open. There, wrapped
inside a hat, scarf, and winter coat, was Dan. As
we enveloped him with a group hug, more out of a
sense of relief, I believe, Flora spoke his name
with fondness.

"Dan."

He seemed bemused by us all as we huddled
around him on the doorstep with nothing but a
candle.

"Look at this greeting. I thought I was going to
freeze to death standing out here for ten minutes.
Then you treat me like your long-lost son."

"You *are* our long-lost son," said Annie, smiling
and pulling him inside. Following behind him
were Tom and Joe.

We all arrived back in the main room just in
time to see Ronald stuffing the rest of the apple
pie into his mouth, straight from the dish. He eyed
everyone curiously, saying in a muffled voice
as he sprayed crumbs all over the place, "Did
anyone disappear?"

"The only thing that seems to have disappeared

around here is that pie!" said Doris, planting her hands on her hips.

Tom noticed our guest.

"Hey there, Ronald, you're up here late in the year. I thought you were normally down in town by now."

"That snow caught me. Came in fast," mumbled Ronald as he swallowed down the rest of the pie in one gulp.

"I'd put the kettle on and make coffee," said Doris, "but there's no power."

Joe nodded. "That's partly why we're here. I wanted to show you the little camping stove we have in the back shed. You can use it, if you like, until it comes back on."

"I'll get in some more wood for the fire," added Tom.

"Can I do anything to help?" asked Dan, not taking his eyes from Flora.

"Why don't you sit and keep Flora company?" giggled Annie.

Doris was as happy as a cricket to have a place to cook something, even though it was just two tiny gas rings on an old battered stove. Soon she was brewing up hot coffee and cocoa.

Tom had built the fire up, and we all gathered around.

Annie tapped Dan on the hand. "How on earth did you find us?"

"After you all left, I went back to work with

Ian on the project car. I was having real trouble keeping my mind on my work." His eyes found Flora's. "I was concerned that the repairs were holding out okay."

Sure, I thought, he was worried about "the car."

"Then, when I woke up at the lake house the following day, I turned on the news. They talked about the unexpected snowstorm that had blown in and that a landslide had blocked the pass. I knew you might be trapped in your car on this side of the mountain. So I borrowed Ian's truck and hightailed it after you. I called into the bait store to see if they'd seen you. I'm glad to see you're all okay."

Once again, his eyes found Flora's. Beaming, she sat down next to him and slipped her hand into his.

"I have personally been taking care of these ladies myself," said Ronald with an uppity air. "And I am pleased to report that they are all in one piece."

"The only thing you've taken care of is polishing off our food supplies," snapped Doris sarcastically.

Tom finished adding the extra wood to the fire, saying, "We'd better get back. The plows are already out, so we should be able to get you safely off the mountain tomorrow, and they cleared the landslide late last night before the storm hit."

Suddenly, as if to herald this good news, the power flicked back on.

"There you go," said Doris. "At least now we can all have a nice hot breakfast in the morning. I take it you will be staying with us, Dan?"

"If that's okay," he asked coyly.

"Of course it's okay," said Annie, squeezing his arm.

Annie brought out some extra bedding so Dan could sleep on the sofa. Ronald settled himself down for the night, curling up on a bunch of cushions on the floor in front of the fire.

Dan and Flora disappeared into the kitchen to spend some time alone together, and Doris saw Tom and Joe out. Ethel yawned, and I realized I was exhausted too. Even though it was only 8:00 p.m., I decided to turn in.

The next morning, a weak winter sun greeted me through the bedroom window. I was feeling more optimistic than I had in days. All going well, we would be in San Francisco by the end of the day, and I was looking forward to seeing my daughter.

I dressed and made my way into the main room. Everyone was already up and moving around, everyone except Ronald. He was still asleep in the same position he'd been in the night before. He lay there, snoring like a large shaggy dog. Annie sat on the edge of the sofa, finishing a second sock. In the kitchen, Doris and Ethel already had breakfast going.

I grabbed a cup of coffee and looked out the

window, noticing that Dan and Flora were out in front of the cabin. They were huddled up together on a little porch swing, talking.

As soon as the food was ready, Ronald appeared. He was like a food magnet. Doris called out to everyone else, and we all gathered in the kitchen. We were a happy group as we started to eat. Toward the end of the meal, Ronald lifted his glass.

"To you all. Thanks for feeding me," he said as he nodded at Doris.

"Another two days with you, and you would have eaten us out of house and home," sniffed Doris.

I saved him a reply by raising my glass as well. "Just a few more hours and we'll be there, and I can't wait."

Everyone added his or her own agreements. Just before we left, I went back into the bedroom and removed the sheet from the moose. "I wish I could say it's been lovely meeting you," I said out loud. "But it wasn't. It would have been nice to have met you when you still had the rest of your body."

Outside, everyone was already in the cars. Dan planned to follow us all the way to San Francisco. He told me he would drive Ian's truck slowly down the mountain in front of me, and he'd already put chains on my tires.

Flora slipped in beside Dan, and Ronald asked if he could get a lift. We set off, slowly, inching our way down the mountain until we got onto the road. The sun had started to melt the snow, but it wasn't too slippery yet.

Soon we were back outside the bait shop. I slipped some money for the extra night through the letter slot with a thank-you note. We continued on to the garage, now that the rockslide was cleared. Ronald got out and, cinching his scruffy clothes tightly around himself, he walked, head down, away from the car without even a good-bye. Annie jumped out and raced after him. She handed him his brand-new pair of socks and some muffins Doris had wrapped up from breakfast. He took them as if they were a prized possession. But it was when he looked inside the socks that we saw that broad gummy smile, as we'd stuffed dollar bills in them.

"Payment for the storyteller," I yelled from my window.

He looked over at us and then gave us this big, overstated wave, as if we were miles out to sea. Then, with a skip in his step, he headed off toward the coffee shop next to the garage.

Dan and Flora had stopped to get gas with us, when Annie yelled out, "I've got a signal."

We all instinctively grabbed Doris's hand.

Annie quickly pushed the buttons on the iPad and a little ringing sound rang out. The picture on the screen came to life, and Lottie's face swirled into view.

"Hello," she said, sounding more subdued than she usually did, "who is this?"

As our picture flashed to life too, Lottie's voice changed to relief.

"Oh, thank the Lord. It's the girls calling, Lavinia," she shouted back over her shoulder.

Lavinia's face appeared on the screen too, and I noticed they both looked tired and worn, which was very unusual for the twins.

"We've been trying to get hold of you for two days," said Lavinia, the concern obvious in her tone. "Is everything okay?"

"Yes," said Doris, finding her inner strength. "We've been stuck in an old lodge in the mountains with no signal. Is everything alright there with Momma?"

The twins shared a look between themselves that informed us right away that something was wrong.

Lottie started. "Now, Doris, honey, I don't want you to go and worry yourself, but your momma has had a little turn."

"She's okay now," added Lavinia quickly. "The doctor has seen her, and she's resting, but she gave us quite a scare there for a while, that's for sure."

"What happened?" asked Doris somberly.

Once again, the twins shared a glance.

Lavinia spoke. "I think this whole thing might have been my fault," she said soberly.

"Now, Lavinia," rebuked Lottie, "no one was to know. The thing is, Doris, we were having a little get-together of our rejected ladies, and my sister found an old story journal in your attic."

Lavinia looked sheepish.

"I asked your momma if I could bring it down to read. She seemed fine with that. She said it belonged to her sister, who had loved to write stories. I had no idea, of course . . ." Lavinia's voice trailed off.

Lottie picked up the thread. "No one was to know. It had lots of sweet stories about goblins and fairies, and then there was this one story set during World War Two."

We all looked around at one another, knowing instinctively where this was going.

Lavinia searched for the right words. "Well, I started to read the story out to the group, and suddenly your momma let out a scream. I looked over at her, and she had gone ashen-white, and her whole body was shaking . . ."

"Ruby rushed to get her a glass of water, and I dropped straight to my knees to pray," Lottie interjected.

"Which was a good thing," added Lavinia, "because your momma suddenly jumped to her feet and then went down like a sack of oranges. If Lottie hadn't been there on her knees to break her fall, the doctor said we could have been dealing with broken bones."

"Prayer always helps," said Lottie wistfully, "in one way or another."

Lavinia picked up the thread. "Anyhow, her blood pressure was a mite low, but they released her as there was no reason to keep her as her health seems fine; it's just that this has hit her hard emotionally."

Lottie sighed. "She seems to be preoccupied with that story in the journal, saying over and over, 'How could she do it? How could she do this to me?'"

Lavinia jumped in. "We've tried to take her mind off it, but she's very sad and just won't get out of bed. I feel terrible about all this. You know the last thing in the world I would want to do is hurt your momma. This whole mess is just my fault, as usual."

"No," said Doris, "it's my fault. I should have destroyed that journal when I found it. Now it appears that we've uncovered something about Momma's past that she wanted to keep buried."

"We can burn it if you think it will help," said Lottie wistfully, "and then this whole thing can be put behind us."

"Not quite," said Doris softly. "Unfortunately, I added details of that story into the manuscript that's now at the publisher."

The twins drew in their breath together as if it were rehearsed. All of us instinctively reached out to Doris again.

"Oh my," said Lottie, "you need to get that back and destroy it as soon as you can. I don't want to even think about how that news would affect your momma."

"That is exactly what we're going to do," said Annie. "By tomorrow there will be no trace of this story, and we'll make sure of that."

The twins nodded their heads in approval.

Lavinia added, "In the meantime, we'll try to buoy your momma's spirits the best we can. I'm going to try and coax her out for one of her fairy teas in town. She can wear her sparkles, and I'm sure Ruby has something appropriate I can borrow."

"We'll be back soon," said Doris.

"I know this is difficult," added Lottie. "I'm praying for you all. Just know your momma is in good hands. Her health is fine. She's just very sad, but we'll do our best."

Doris nodded, and we all said our good-byes.

Once the twins were gone, we looked around at each other despondently.

Surprisingly, it was Ethel who broke the silence. "Looks like we have a job to do for Gracie's sake, so I think we had better get on and do it, don't you?"

I didn't know whether it was her words or that she had actually spoken a whole sentence that rallied us, but whatever it was, it was just the encouragement we needed. Doris nodded at me, and I started the car with renewed determination.

Chapter Fifteen

THE IVORY PALACE OF
THE ICE QUEEN

With Flora and Dan following behind us in the truck, we headed toward San Francisco and settled into our usual routine. Doris issued instructions from map-reading headquarters, Ethel stared out the window, and Annie caught up on two days of her missed soap.

A lot had happened since we'd been stuck in the snow. The doctor had been shot, his wife was arrested for the hit, and the secretary had given birth to her alien baby that had now also been abducted.

Phew, things sure happened fast on that show.

The sights changed again as we entered California; we left behind the stately cedars of the Northwest and traded them for the majestic splendor of the redwood trees. We stopped briefly in Redding for a coffee, but with the end in sight, we didn't stop for lunch but opted to eat the last of Doris's baked bread. Doris had made a ton of sandwiches to get us all the way through until we saw the Golden Gate Bridge, which was just before 6:00 p.m.

As we came up and over the brow of a long slow

hill the sun was just starting to set as the bridge appeared in our view, its vivid red framing glistening in the waning sun, an impressive and welcoming host beckoning us into the city.

"We're going to be staying at my cousin John's place in the north," Doris informed me, giving me the exact directions.

"Did you let him know you'd be arriving today?"

Doris looked at me as if I'd just dropped off Mars. "My cousin never goes anywhere," she snapped.

But when we turned up at his little brick house, there didn't seem to be anyone there, no matter how hard Doris banged on the door.

"Fishing!" shouted a neighbor as he was getting into his car. "If you're looking for John, he's gone fishing. He won't be back until the day after tomorrow."

Doris shuffled back despondently.

"Look, why don't you come over to Stacy's house? You could have some dinner and then call a motel from there."

"Okay," she muttered, but I could tell she wasn't very happy about it.

When we arrived at my daughter's clean, sprawling suburban house, we all sat in the car for a minute and looked around. She lived in one of those buttoned-up neighborhoods where everything was just a little too perfect to feel comfortable. It was a place that seemed to say,

"Welcome to our version of the American Dream. Now stay the hell off our pansies."

Walking up her whiter-than-white driveway, I passed the koi pond and lollipop-sculptured bushes and trees. The garden, manicured to death, gave the aura of being afraid to let a twig grow out of place.

The girls stared at me through the car window.

I rang Stacy's doorbell and an odd melodic chiming pattern rang out as I waited. There was no reply, so I rang once more, and she pulled open the door in a manner as if she were going to hit me. Then her expression changed.

"Mom, at last!"

Enveloping me in an enormous bear hug, she started to sob on my shoulder. I almost pulled her off to say, "Who are you and what did you do with my daughter?"

Wow, this was going to be a fascinating visit to the hormone amusement park.

She was on her third full sob when she noticed the girls all staring at her from the car. She stopped crying abruptly, as if she were doing it on cue, saying indignantly, "Who are they?"

"They're the women I was on the road with," I answered matter-of-factly.

"What are they doing here?" she spat out, as if I'd just brought her a gang of terrorists.

"The guy they were supposed to be staying with wasn't home. I was hoping they could come in here and use your telephone, maybe get a cup of coffee . . . or something?"

It felt as if I were asking my mom's permission.

"I suppose they could come in for a short while." She furrowed her brow, obviously not too hot on the idea. "Just make sure they remove their shoes!"

We all skulked into Stacy's foyer, dutifully doing as we were told. I shivered. Her house always felt more like a mausoleum than a home to me; its stolid reverence couldn't help but encourage an atmosphere of whispering and tiptoeing. Her walls, sparse and dark, were counterbalanced with lots of heavy white marble. All about the house, expensive art pieces balanced precariously on lofty, spotlighted plinths.

A long hour later, we sat lined up on the couch in our stocking feet, a group of nuns under a vow of silence. One person would attempt to start a conversation, and everyone else just appeared to be afraid to respond. Even Doris seemed subdued. Stacy's intense demeanor always seemed to have that effect on people. It was as if we'd been invited to tea with a stern old spinster aunt. Only Dan, who was seated on the other side of the room, seemed to be making comfortable inroads with her. Unbelievably, Ethel thawed the ice.

"I'm getting hungry," she said, not unlike a five-year-old child.

I realized I was hungry as well. We hadn't eaten anything since Doris's sandwiches on the road, hours before.

"I don't have a thing in the house. No point. I just honk it up anyway."

"Would you mind if I used your kitchen to cook something?" inquired Doris, a glimmer of hope in her eyes.

"No, of course not," responded Stacy in a tone that gave the impression that was the last thing she wanted them to do.

Doris, Flora, Ethel, and even Annie exited toward the kitchen as if someone had just yelled, "Fire," leaving me and Dan to entertain Stacy.

As I finished my second cup of coffee, Doris poked her head into the room, and boomed. Apparently, she also seemed unaware that any sudden vibrations might knock the exotic backlit crystal from its delicate pedestals. "I think we're going to need some supplies."

"I'll go," I whispered back, sounding a little more excited than I'd intended.

"Can I come?" inquired Dan in his regular tone as I was putting on my coat. He didn't seem the least bit perturbed by the precariously balanced décor.

When we got back an hour later, I found Annie curled up on the sofa next to Stacy. They were both giggling and talking about soaps. It was nice to see Stacy connecting at last.

As we were clearing the dinner plates later, my phone rang. It was Martin.

"Hey there, I hadn't heard from you for a couple of days, so I thought I'd give you a call." His voice was a calming sea. "How's it going?"

"It's going," I joked in our familiar banter.

I stepped outside into Stacy's bleached backyard to talk to him. I knew he was really inquiring about Stacy.

"Actually, it *is* going well. We had a crazy day yesterday, but I arrived at Stacy's a couple of hours ago, and it's slowly starting to thaw here."

And he knew I wasn't talking about the weather.

"I see," he said in a knowing tone.

Then he wanted to know all about the snowstorm and landslide in detail, so we chatted for a good while before I eventually hung up the phone.

When I stepped back into the house about thirty minutes later, there was a party atmosphere. Stacy had put on some sixties music and was singing along as she helped the other girls wash up in the kitchen. Grabbing a dishtowel too, I watched in a curious awe as Annie jigged and sang along at Stacy's side, like they were best buddies.

Suddenly, Stacy announced we were all going to play charades. I nearly dropped the exquisite swan-shaped gravy boat I'd been carefully drying.

So there we were, one hour later, armed with popcorn and a bottle of wine, trying to figure out why Doris was pretending to be a chicken and pointing and pulling at one leg of her pantyhose.

"*Chicken Run!*" shouted Stacy at the top of her voice, jumping to her feet, and bouncing up and down like an excited child.

If only my husband could have been there to see it. Swept up in the fun of the evening, Stacy had insisted everyone stay at her house overnight, so Doris never bothered to call the motel, and we all settled down into our museum-like rooms. It took all my might just to get the cardboard sheets to let go of the underside of the mattress, but I finally managed to sleep.

The next morning I wandered into the kitchen and found Doris at the breakfast table, strategizing. Everyone else was gathered around her like a pack of obedient puppies. Doris pointed her pen at each member of the group, one by one.

"Each of you will have a job to do. I'll be our main speaker and make sure we get in to see this editor. Janet, we may need you for strategic planning if this attempt fails," she informed me over her shoulder as I prepared my morning coffee.

I nodded absently, though I hadn't the foggiest what that really meant.

"Annie, you are to help Ethel chain herself to the toilet if we need it, and, Ethel, have you got what we need for plan B?"

Ethel nodded and went off toward the bedroom.

Dan appeared to be highly amused by all of this. "What's my job?" His eyes blazed excitedly, though his tongue appeared firmly in his cheek.

"Well, young man," said Doris, sucking in her cheeks as if she were thinking of exactly where to place him, "I think we may need you if things get ugly. Not bad to have a little muscle on our side."

Dan nearly spat out his coffee, and Flora's face registered horror.

Ethel arrived back, ceremoniously dumping nto the table a bag of chains and a leather bustier.

"Flora, if we have to go to plan B, I have this outfit for you. Your job is to use all of that youthful, sexual energy to wow him to our way of thinking."

Flora swallowed hard as another flash of amusement crossed Dan's face.

Doris slammed her hand down on the table. "We're ready," she announced in her best team player voice.

The plan was I would drop them all off at the office building and then come back to pick up Stacy and take her to her conference.

Within an hour, the whole group was sandwiched into my car in a determined mood as we trundled into downtown San Francisco. It was as if we were part of an episode of some old seventies TV show. All we needed was a flashy van and a theme song. I thought, not for the first time, that I was so glad I was just the getaway driver.

Chapter Sixteen

A BAG OF CHAINS &
A FANCY-PANTS SETUP

When we arrived downtown, however, the group's buoyant mood disappeared faster than a ten-pound note dropped by mistake on a Scotsman's table. Even I felt intimidated by the enormous shiny office building with the words "Welcome to the World of Publishing" etched in black on a brushed stainless steel sign. Behind me, I heard Flora draw a breath.

Doris took control as I circled the block to find somewhere to park.

"Don't be thrown off by this fancy-pants setup," she reminded them. "Remember, we're here for our group, not to mention getting this manuscript back for Momma's sake."

That was all the pep talk her cohorts needed. As I slid into a parking space, they all bounded out like ninjas—well-aged ninjas or the mothers of ninjas, perhaps, but there was a definite clip in their steps as they bounded toward the building.

Only Doris hung back and motioned for me to lower the window. "Can you wait here for a while? If things go well, we should be back soon. If not, I'm planning a media-encouraged sit-in. So if you see helicopters, you know it's going to be a long night."

I nodded absently as I watched her join the others striding defiantly toward the building.

I took a moment to call Martin. It took him a while to answer. When he did, I could tell he was in the middle of something.

"Can I call you back?" his tone was strained. "I'm at the doctor's."

"At the doctor's? Are you okay?"

There was a pause. He was hiding something.

"Honey, what did you do?"

"Nothing," he bounced back with the speed of a child being caught with his hand in the cookie jar. "I just needed to get a . . . rabies shot."

"Rabies shot!" I shrieked so loud that someone who was passing the car looked in at me with concern.

"Yeah," he murmured humbly. "One of the dang raccoons bit me!"

This was why I never went away.

"The doctor's here. Have to go. Talk to you later."

Hanging up the phone, I sighed. I already needed more coffee.

It was as I got out of the car that I noticed it: Doris's bag, complete with chains and a leather bustier, waving at me from an unzipped corner. I sighed again. I had the feeling it was going to be another sighing day. Staring at it for a long, hard moment, I considered the alternatives. Doris would want that bag, but taking it to them could risk association with the loony brigade inside, and I didn't really want to be on the local six o'clock news. But not taking it to them meant the wrath of Doris. The choice was easy.

Grabbing the bag and locking the car, I headed into the gleaming gray-stone building with the black-tinted windows. Entering the foyer, I felt totally underdressed in my gray tracksuit and sneakers. Bustling, coiffed people sidestepped around me, going on their businesslike way.

The publisher Doris had mentioned was on the eighth floor. I hurried to the elevator, arriving just in time to watch the slick, onyx-colored doors close, buttoning in its heaving mass. I stepped back and pushed the "Up" button. The building had another three elevators, and with a quick scan, I noticed one was exceedingly high up in the building. The third had an "Out of Order" sign, and the last one had a woman—the slowest cleaner in the world—mopping the floor inside. She was obviously paid by the hour.

Frustrated, I hit the button again, and out of the corner of my eye, I caught the cleaner shaking her head at me as she continued to drag her mop around on its snaillike crawl. Pacing back and forth, I made a decision and headed toward a sign for the stairs. After all, it was only eight floors, and I thought of myself as pretty fit.

Or I had.

It was as I rounded the stairwell on the sixth floor that I collapsed into a heap on the top step and tried to catch my breath. The thick leisure suit I had put on, feeling cold that morning, now felt as if it were strangling my hormone-flashing body. Breathing in long, deep waves, I pulled aggressively at the collar and mopped beads of sweat from my forehead. As I sat looking around the bleak, dark stairwell, I asked myself for the umpteenth time why I was doing this.

After a short break, I pulled myself back up. That bag now felt heavier than ever. Holding on to the handrail, I literally hauled myself up the last two flights, dragging the bag behind me. It bounced melodically off each step as the heavy chains clashed together, the sound ricocheting off the concrete walls in stereo.

Eventually, I reached the eighth floor and fell through the door into the quietest office on the planet. It would have made our library manager proud.

Gathering my composure and my breath, I closed the door quietly behind me. As I turned, I observed the office was full of people, and every eye fell curiously upon the bag now dumped at my feet. I realized they had no doubt heard me dragging it up every one of those last two flights of stairs. Pulling back my shoulders and wiping a new bead of sweat from my forehead, I tried to gracefully traverse the immense room toward a waiting secretary aloft in a marble tower. She eyed me all the way, a disapproving look already on her face as she fixed her eyes keenly upon the bulging mass I was now dragging toward her. Beyond her, I could see Dan and the group all seated together in a row, as if they were waiting for a bus. Even from a great distance, I could tell that Doris did not look happy to see me.

As I neared the desk, the secretary stepped out from behind it, and taking her eyes from my bag to me, she slowly looked me up and down. She was a gray, homely woman with an expression like a dried-up old teacher. Her face tightened.

"Can I help you?"

I tried to speak, but my voice was dry and rasping. I coughed to clear it. "I'm with my friends." I absently pointed at Doris in between gulps of air. "One of them forgot her purse."

I lifted the weighted bag and dropped it onto a nearby coffee table. As it hit the smoked glass, the chains clanged together in a mangled cacophony. The weight inside threw the bag over onto its side, forcing the zipper open and spewing the chains and bustier onto the floor. I didn't dare look down and just fixed my gaze upon the secretary. Doris swore behind me as Flora scrambled to help, stuffing the contents back inside.

Eyeing the mangled heap with disgust, she said, "This group is for you!" in the direction of a thin mouselike woman who practically fell through a side door, scattering a pile of folders everywhere. Then she tripped and fell against a table, and Annie caught her by the hand to steady her. The poor creature pushed her enormous spectacles back up her nose, muttering, "Oh my, not again!"

We all sprang into action to gather up her scattered papers and steady her. The schoolteacher-secretary appeared again and harrumphed.

"All these people are here to see Mr. Gilbert?" mouse-lady asked as she double-blinked nervously.

"Yes, ma'am. Please remove them. They are clogging up our foyer," the secretary demanded as she marched back to guard her granite castle. She made us sound as if we were a hairball in her sink.

With that, mouse-lady tried to choke back tears and ushered us toward an office. She opened a door etched on the front with the name Mark Gilbert.

We all followed, and Annie gave our grief-stricken maiden a flowery handkerchief. She motioned for us to sit down. "Forgive me. It's already been a terrible day. I'm Andrea, Mark's assistant," she finally managed to say as she blew her nose.

As we waited for her to pull herself together, I looked around the sparsely decorated office. It had that new-furniture smell and was a mass of leather, black chrome, and glass, a retro eighties theme with a modern twist. Smooth and sleek, but dang uncomfortable to sit or be in. The sort of office you could comfortably fire people in. There were only two leather-and-chrome seats in front of an imposing smoked-glass desk and a tight black leather chaise lounge below a window. The only other adornments were odd modern art pictures and a smooth, black marble shelf with a single white orchid placed meticulously in a pink cut-glass vase.

Doris opted for one of the chairs, which, honestly, didn't accommodate her bulk. It had high chrome armrests. As she sat down, some of her made it into the chair. The rest of her squished out under the arms. We were going to need WD-40 to get her back out, I thought to myself. Annie took the other chair and automatically settled down to knit. Dan wandered around the room, looking at the abstract art, which left Flora, Ethel, and me with the chaise lounge.

We all eyed it carefully, but when we turned to look at Andrea, she motioned for the rest of us to sit. So, like the three stooges, we all plopped down in unison, accompanied by an over-whelming squelch of tight black leather.

Andrea appeared to be getting her second wind and blew her nose again with determination. "Sorry," she said, placing the files she was carrying on a table. "Where are my manners? Can I offer you some refreshments? Tea, coffee, juice?"

"No, we're all fine," said Doris before the rest

of us could speak, oblivious to the fact some of us might need something after dragging a bag of chains up eight flights of stairs.

"I need a coffee," Andrea said and then busied herself making one.

As she prepared it, she poured out her story without taking a breath.

She'd been working at this job for three months. She'd always wanted to work in publishing. Her boss was a dear, but often gone, leaving her to deal daily with the gray schoolteacher, who'd been trying to get her fired since the day she'd arrived.

She took a sip of her coffee, and Doris took the opportunity to speak.

"As you know, we're here to see your boss, Mr. Gilbert," said Doris.

Andrea swallowed nervously. "That's impossible. There's absolutely no way you can see him."

Doris appeared to be about to say something brisk in response when a phone started ringing in a side office.

Andrea raised her hand apologetically. "Excuse me for a minute," she said and went to answer it.

Doris jumped into action. Well, not jumped, exactly. She de-sandwiched herself from the chair, then snapped in a hushed tone, "Looks as if it's going to be harder than we thought. We're going to have to go straight to plan B." Doris reached into the bulging bag, ferreted around, and threw the black bustier toward Flora. "Flora, go and put on the leather outfit. Ethel, to the toilet. And, Annie, you help her with the chains. We're not leaving until we see Mr. Gilbert."

Ethel jumped up like a jack-in-the-box and tried in vain to pick up the bag of chains, but it didn't budge from where it was planted on the floor. In the end, Annie came to her rescue, and between the two of them, they dragged it out the glass door and down the hall to the bathrooms. Flora clung to the bustier like a scared rabbit. All the color had drained from her face. Dan, who'd wandered over to Mr. Gilbert's desk, started to laugh.

"What's so funny?" snarled Doris under her breath.

"There's no way Flora is going to put on that leather gear."

Doris's face tightened like a drum. "Oh yes she will! Everyone must play his or her part, and she is our femme fatale. It is her job to wow him with her seductive charm."

"It will never work," said Dan, continuing to grin.

"Never work!" said Doris indignantly. "Let me tell you, the art of seduction is the oldest and most trusted trick a woman has up her sleeve."

"It will never work, because if anyone should put on the leather gear, it should be me."

"You! You're a man!" said Doris, incredulously. "Besides, the bustier would never fit you!"

"It should be me, because Mr. Gilbert's persuasions appear to go in a different direction."

Dan then held up a picture from the publisher's desk. It was of two men holding hands, staring lovingly into each other's eyes. Doris took the photo from Dan, and all the blood seemed to drain from her face. However, all the blood seemed to return to Flora's. I heard her let out a breath next to me. Dan took the bustier from Flora and held it up against his body. We all burst out laughing, even Doris.

Once we had all finished and wiped our eyes, there was a comfortable after-laugh silence as we collected ourselves again. Just then, Andrea walked back in.

"Andrea, it is imperative that we see Mr. Gilbert and see him today! We have come all the way from Washington State, and we are not going anywhere until we meet with him," said Doris.

Annie arrived back, breathless, and gave Doris a thumbs-up. Doris nodded and then turned her attention back to Andrea, who was wringing the hankie Annie had given her.

"That is most unfortunate. But you see, you can't see him because he is not here at the office for the next couple of days. He's at the San-Bay Writers Conference. He's the keynote speaker."

San-Bay, San-Bay. That name meant something to me. What was it? Somewhere in the far reaches of my mind, I knew that name.

"Well, how do we get to it?"

"Get to it? You can't. They won't let you in. That conference has been sold out for months."

Doris looked bereft.

"And unfortunately, Mr. Gilbert leaves for a vacation right after the conference. You should make an appointment to talk to him after he gets back."

"That's impossible. We're only here for a short time, then we're driving back home."

All at once, it came to me.

"San-Bay," I said, jumping up. "That's where I'm going to drop Stacy this afternoon. That's the conference she's going to."

"I thought your daughter worked in advertising?" said Flora, speaking for the first time since the bustier incident.

"She does, but she was talking last night about this new publishing account her firm is taking on. She's meeting with them this afternoon. Maybe she can get you in there that way?"

"What time is she going to leave?" Doris asked, her manner almost chirpy.

"One o'clock."

"Great. That gives us some time to come up with a plan. Let's go. We have no time to lose."

I thanked Andrea for her time, and as she moved to see us out, she managed to knock over another stack of manuscripts that were tottering in a high pile on the corner of her desk.

"Oh my," she said, blinking like a five-year-old. "Not again."

I felt sorry for her, but she really was the clumsiest person I'd ever met.

As we got back in the elevator, Doris started barking orders.

"I was wondering," asked Dan thoughtfully, "as you no longer need Flora as your femme fatale, if I could spend some time with her this afternoon?"

"I would love that," said Flora, her eyes brimming. "I've never been to San Francisco before."

"There's lots to see." He gazed lovingly down at her.

As the elevator doors opened on the ground floor and we stepped out into the lobby, Doris considered it. "It's probably going to be easier to get fewer of us into this conference. So, I think that will be okay. If that's what you really want to do?" Doris said it in a tone that implied, "I can't think why that could be better than getting a rejection letter."

But both Dan and Flora seemed oblivious to Doris's disapproving tone as they stared lovingly at each other. He took her hand.

"Great. Let's walk to the waterfront."

Then off they went, giggling.

Chapter Seventeen

UNCHAINING ETHEL
FROM THE TOILET

The car seemed empty without Flora and Dan as we started our drive back, just Annie, Doris, and me.

We were almost back at my daughter's before Annie dropped her knitting and shouted, "Ethel!"

I screeched the car to a halt. The realization hit all of us at once. Ethel was still chained to the toilet back at the publisher's office. How could we have forgotten her? I wheeled the car around and started back. Unfortunately, the traffic was terrible in the opposite direction. I gnawed on my bottom lip as I tried to steer the car through the traffic, weaving back and forth.

My telephone rang. It was my husband.

"I'm back from the doctor's, and I thought I would check in," he said, as bright as a button.

"I can't talk now," I barked back. "We have to rescue Ethel. She's chained to a toilet."

"I was just going to ask you if your day was interesting. Looks as if you've just answered my question. Call me back after you've finished with whatever it is you're doing."

As we arrived back at the building, a couple of

fire trucks pulled up behind us. I gave Doris a sideways glance. She looked annoyed. We hurried into the building and up to the eighth floor, but having to wait for the elevator meant the fire service made it up there before us.

We hurried to the bathroom, but a police officer stepped in front of us.

"Sorry, ladies, you need to find another bathroom. We have a crazy woman in there chained to the toilet."

"Stand aside, young man," snapped Doris. "That just happens to be *our* crazy woman!"

Once we got inside the bathroom, it was a chaotic scene. Staff, a few medics, and Andrea fretting. One woman was quietly talking to Ethel through the locked door as if she were a small child.

"Now come on, dear, why don't you come out? We can talk all about your letter once you've unlocked the door."

Doris spoke abruptly. "Ethel, plan B is canceled. We now have a plan C. Unlock the door at once."

Everyone in the bathroom stopped and stared at Doris. There was a long pause.

Then, Ethel's strained voice floated back. "I've lost the key."

Twenty minutes and a hacksaw later, we all stood sheepishly in the foyer while the same policeman gave us a talking-to. He made it clear that if we agreed to leave the building quietly and not attempt anything like it again, the publishing house would not press charges.

We shuffled back into the car. It was like a tomb.

Annie broke the silence. "Best road trip I've ever been on!"

And that was it. We all burst into laughter. We arrived back at my daughter's house. She was standing in her doorway, waiting for us, and marched toward the car when she saw us. The look on her face was enough to sober us to silence.

"I've been waiting, Mom!" she said, scowling. "I have to be there by one, and it's already after twelve."

"I know. We had"—I coughed—"an emergency."

With that, everybody burst out laughing again.

Stacy looked from one to another in bewilderment and then stomped off to fetch her jacket. When she got in the car, I noticed she was pretty pale. "Are you okay?" I asked gently.

"No, actually, I don't feel very well today."

"If you're going to barf, do it out the window," was Doris's sympathetic comment from the driver's seat.

I felt irritated by Doris's insensitivity.

"I have a bag!" said Stacy defiantly. "I already threw up three times. I don't think there's anything left to come up."

Annie stopped knitting for a moment to tap

Stacy on the knee. "I bet it's a boy. They're the most trouble to carry," she giggled as she hooked a new row.

"How was your meeting?" asked Stacy absently, trying to change the subject.

I looked around the car. Everyone was smirking.

"Interesting," Annie snickered.

"Where are you all going now? Sightseeing?"

There was a sudden silence.

"Well," I said, clearing my throat. "We actually have something to ask you."

Stacy's brows furrowed.

Annie picked up the thread. "You see, dear, the man we wanted to see wasn't available at his office because he was . . . gone today."

"Gone?" said Stacy, distracted as she straightened her skirt.

"Yes," said Doris, "at your conference. We want you to find a way to get us all in."

Stacy collected herself for a moment, taking in the information. "My conference? Do you mean the San-Bay Writers Conference?"

"Yes, dear," said Annie, trying to soften Doris's forthrightness. "Do you think it would be possible to go in with you?"

Stacy sniffed. "The conference has been sold out for months. I'm only going because my company is handling one of the publisher's advertising. I don't see how I could get away with taking in four of you."

"You'll just have to," said Doris, reverting to her bullying tactics.

But if ever Doris had met her match, it was in Stacy.

"No, I don't," said Stacy. "I don't have to do anything. You should have bought tickets like everyone else."

Doris's face reddened. She wasn't used to anyone standing up to her.

I quickly changed tack.

"Could you get *one* of them in?" I asked quietly.

"No," snapped back Stacy, now defiant. Then as an afterthought she said, "I *had* mentioned to my boss that you might be with me as my support, but that's all."

Doris's face brightened a little. I could tell she was thinking.

"Okay," she said breezily. "Sorry to have asked."

I looked at her, bewildered. It wasn't like Doris to back down so quickly.

"I do think your mom should go in with you, though, especially as you're not feeling well." Doris's tone was sweeter than honey. She obviously had a new plan.

After a thankfully uneventful drive, we pulled up to the building, and Stacy got out and walked off.

I sighed and started to get out when Doris grabbed my arm. "Once you're inside, you have to find a way to get us in an exit door or something—

anything. It's all up to you. Our whole rejection group is counting on you. Don't let us down."

I looked out the car window to where Stacy was standing by the entrance, waiting for me, her face set in stone. She was not happy to be kept waiting. Looking back at Doris, I wasn't sure whom I was more afraid of. My head seemed to nod by itself as I got out of the car and hurried toward my daughter, who was now tapping her foot.

Doris rolled down the window and shouted, "Come out in about fifteen minutes once you've scouted the land and let us know our plan of attack."

She then roared off in a cloud of dust as she headed toward the parking lot. Plan of attack. Oh no. She was in war mode again.

Once Stacy and I got inside, the atmosphere seemed almost festive, as they were just breaking from the morning session. At the entrance, we were issued nametags for the conference. Stacy found her peers, and I was chopped liver. So off I went to scout the building for Operation Rejected Writers' Book Club.

There seemed to be only one entrance, and there were a lot of volunteers buzzing about. It was going to be hard. I felt like a teenager trying to sneak my friends into the movie theater. I made my way to the bathroom, and when I got there, I found the answer I was looking for. The bathroom windows opened out to the parking lot, and the windows were a fair size. I surmised Ethel and Annie would possibly fit through them. However, Doris was another matter. Giggling to myself, I shook my head. This was so ridiculous.

Chapter Eighteen

GATE-CRASHING THE LADIES' BATHROOM

Hurrying to the front entrance again, I stepped outside. The girls were already waiting there, as if they were a bunch of groupies.

"Well?" asked Doris.

Informing them about the bathroom window, I tried, as tactfully as possible, to tell Doris about the size.

"We'll make it work," she said. "Synchronize your watches, and we'll meet you around the back in five minutes."

Rushing back in, I was halfway through the foyer when a hand grabbed my arm. It was Stacy. She looked gray.

"I'm going to be sick," she managed to say as she gulped for air.

"This way." I took her arm.

We made it into the bathroom with seconds to spare, and even though there was a line, it cleared pretty fast for the heaving pregnant woman.

Waiting for Stacy, I studied the windows in detail. They were at the far end of the room, but I noted they could be seen easily as you entered the bathroom. It was going to be tricky getting the girls in undetected. As I stood there listening to my heaving daughter, three faces appeared at the window.

The glass was beveled for privacy, so their faces were distorted, but still it was obvious to me who they were.

A woman entered the bathroom, and I did my best to distract her by making light banter about pregnancy while I steered her gaze away from the windows and toward the décor of the ladies' room. As soon as a cubicle became free, she made a pretty sharp exit into the toilet, obviously feeling the need to get away from the crazy lady talking about all the different types of soap dispensers she had encountered in her life.

As soon as she was safely in her stall, I made a beeline for the windows. They were high, so I climbed onto a vanity chair to reach them. Cracking the window, I hissed at the girls to get out of sight.

"I'll let you know when the way is clear."

I just managed to get those words out before one of the stalls opened. Stacy emerged, bedraggled and worn.

"What are you doing?"

"Oh, I was just admiring these . . . uh . . . lovely windows," I lied, getting down from the chair and placing it back in front of a mirrored dressing table.

She gave me an odd look and then made her

way over to me. In front of the windows was a plush pink velour couch that she collapsed into, saying, "I think I need to rest for a minute."

"Okay," I said tightly, wondering how long Curly, Larry, and Moe could loiter outside a women's bathroom window without being arrested.

Stacy started rambling on about her job, how it was all going to change now that she was pregnant and just how unhappy she was. I only half-listened, as I was suddenly aware of the window opening above her. Doris was obviously becoming impatient, and I could feel her eyes boring down on me from above. Stacy seemed oblivious to anything as she complained about her life. I flicked at my hair, trying to conceal the fact I was signaling to Doris to get out of sight. Even without looking at her directly, I sensed she wasn't happy.

Finally, Stacy got up, saying she was ready to join the others.

"We have to sit with my client for lunch," she informed me. "You'll stay close by, won't you, Mom?"

The last comment was said in her little-girl voice, and suddenly she was ten years old again and vulnerable.

"Of course."

She started for the door before she realized I wasn't following.

"Are you coming?" she asked, reverting to impatient Stacy.

"Umm . . ." I stalled. "In a minute. I just need to powder my nose."

She knitted her brow and moved toward the door. "Okay. But don't be long. I'll save you a place at our table."

She left, and luckily the bathroom appeared to be empty for a moment. Quickly I opened the window as far as I could. "Come on," I hissed through the gap.

What followed was nothing short of a comedy skit. Annie and Doris hoisted up Ethel and practically threw her headfirst through the open window. Fortunately, I was there to catch her as she landed on the sofa, bouncing like a teddy bear. I couldn't believe it had been so easy. I started to laugh as Annie's head appeared. Not quite as petite as Ethel, she was going to be a little more difficult. Doris hoisted her up as best she could, and she started to squeeze herself, huffing and puffing, through the window.

Suddenly, one of the toilets flushed. We all gave each other one of those looks as the stall door opened. We just had enough time to shove Annie back out through the window and for Ethel and I to look nonchalant as the occupant gave us a quick look and made her way to the sinks. I'd obviously missed the fact that she hadn't exited. There was a muffled noise coming from outside the window, which I was pretty sure was Doris swearing.

Once the woman had left the room, we started

again. This time, with much pulling and pushing, the baby was born right onto that pink velour couch. We all laughed with relief.

Doris stuck her head in through the window.

"There's no way I'm going to get in this little bitty thing since I have a full, womanly figure. I'll just have to find another way. You need to locate that publisher guy, so when I get in I can start talking to him. Now go on, and remember, the fate of our Rejected Writers' Book Club lies in all your hands."

Like the anthill mob, we all bundled out of the bathroom on our mission. We had to find . . . we had to find . . . I had a senior moment. I couldn't remember his name or his publishing company. Lot of good I was. From the blank look I got back from the girls when I asked them, it was obvious they didn't remember either.

As we reached the main entrance, we saw that the conference volunteers had just finished setting up for lunch. We decided to split up and see if any of the names on the name badges around people's necks rang a bell. I started loitering around the room, staring at people's chests. Stacy found me.

"Where have you been?" she demanded.

"I got hung up in the bathroom."

She shot me a scowl. "Remember, I need you to sit with me. You can make excuses for me if I suddenly have to leave. I have to listen to our client talk about his book."

She turned from me then and waved to a bespectacled, awkward-looking man in an expensive suit, who joined her. By his side was a tall blond who looked as if he'd been cut out of cheese, just too good-looking, not a hair out of place. There was something oddly familiar about him. They made an unusual pair.

Stacy introduced them both to me, the tall blond was Brian Smith. His name didn't ring a bell, but I was sure I knew him. Suddenly, I remembered. He was in the picture on the desk back at the publisher's, but the name wasn't familiar. This must be Mr. Gilbert's partner. All at once, I remembered the publisher's name.

"Mark Gilbert!" I blurted out, excitedly.

Brian and Stacy stopped talking.

"Do you know my partner?" he inquired, appearing a little bemused by my sudden Tourette-style outburst.

"Sort of, yes," I said smiling sweetly as I delicately retrieved an hors d'oeuvre from a passing waiter with a silver tray.

"He's here somewhere," he noted, looking around. "He's always so popular. I suppose I'd better go and find him and a place to sit. We have friends here somewhere. We were hoping to catch up with them."

"Won't you and Mark sit with us?" I blurted out, totally inappropriately.

Stacy gave me one of those "Mother!" looks.

Mark Gilbert appeared at his partner's side. He looked a little harried. Thrusting out my hand, I introduced myself. Mark looked a little bemused as I added, "As you know, I'm such a great admirer of your work."

He peered at me as if he were trying to remember me.

"We would love it if you and Brian could join us at our table. You could tell me all about the books you're publishing right now."

Brian looked bewildered and attempted to work them out of the noose I was stringing up for them.

"Aren't we sitting with Chad?" inquired Brian.

"Yes, I thought so," responded Mark, obviously still trying to place me. "But I can't find him."

His interest was piqued, I could tell, and he even appeared to be close to sitting down with us just to find out who I was. I didn't waste a second.

"I haven't been over to your office since you had it renovated."

Stacy looked at me as if I had gone mad.

"How did the black leather chaise work out?"

Now I had his attention. It was obvious by the way his face lit up that decorating was his passion. He started to go into a whole stream of details about how hard it had been to find just the right choice of furniture and where to place it in his office. He took a drink from a tray and sat down next to me at the table. Doris would be proud. I listened intently as he rambled on and pretended to be interested in all the intricate details of his redecoration. Ethel and Annie saw me sit and wandered over to the table. While he was reaching over to encourage his partner to sit down, I gestured to them that he was the one.

Brian attempted to join us, but before he could get close, the girls sat down next to Mark, forcing him to sit on the other side of Annie. Brian looked bewildered at this sudden onslaught of old ladies but settled himself down with a glass of white wine. My daughter seemed mortified to see Ethel and Annie as she and her client prepared to sit with us at the same table.

"How did they get in?" she hissed into my ear as Mark Gilbert was taking a swig of water in between telling me about the dangers of decorating with camel fur and the side effects of using lead-based paints.

"This is the guy we need to speak to," I whispered, not moving my lips.

Ethel, for some odd reason, sat smiling up at him. It was extremely disconcerting. I'd never seen her smile before. She looked like an odd little ventriloquist dummy. Annie, on the other hand, seemed oblivious to her mission and was enjoying helping herself to a bread roll. It occurred to me that without Doris we were adrift, a ship without an anchor of hope.

I was wondering if I should try to find her when the most bizarre thing happened. A waitress appeared at our table to add water to our glasses. I turned to thank her, and it was Doris herself. She winked at me, asking Stacy if she would like some water. Stacy looked up, and when she saw Doris in her little white apron, she practically choked on the bread she was nibbling to curb her nausea.

"We're overrun by them," she spat at me.

I blinked innocently. "Overrun by what, dear?"

"Your little old lady friends!" she snapped back.

I noticed Doris was filling Mark Gilbert's glass and gesturing with her head for me to follow her. Waiting a second or two, I then excused myself from the table. As I got up, I overheard Annie talking to Brian about the different knitting patterns she liked best and the challenge of knitting sweaters for dogs. By the look of bemusement on Brian's face, I could see this wasn't going to be a luncheon he would forget in a hurry.

I followed Doris toward the back of the room to a little serving station when she beckoned me closer as she picked up another full water jug.

"How did you get in?" I asked.

"As I walked around the building, I noticed a group of ladies filing into the kitchen being checked in by a supervisor. Listening, I overheard one of the women saying that Antonia wouldn't be here, as she was sick. The supervisor seemed

291

agitated and commented that they wouldn't have time to contact the agency to get a replacement. That's when I stepped forward and said Antonia had sent me to cover her shift.

"The supervisor didn't seem particularly convinced, saying about the proper regulations and so forth, but I could see she was desperate for another body. She then asked me about my experience, so I told her I'd worked at the Little Red Wagon. Remember? The place we stopped off in Oregon, for lunch? She told me to go and put on a uniform and that she would check my references. As soon as she was gone, I found a phone and called Betty. She was more than happy to help and gave me a glowing reference, saying I'd worked for them for years.

"Now," she said, moving away with her water jug, "this is the plan. Make sure he has a really good time and drinks plenty of wine during the meal. Once you've got him all liquored up, I'll come in for the kill and get my manuscript back and a rejection letter out of him."

Walking back to the table, all I wanted to do was walk straight out of the front door, get in my car, drive all the way home, and crawl into my bed. But instead, I found my feet walking me to the table, and I sat down, ready to play my part.

As the salads were served, I plunged in.

"Tell me about the publishing business," I asked as I heaped a forkful of salad into my mouth.

Mark Gilbert launched into a spiel he obviously rehearsed for gatherings such as this. I tried to listen attentively, all about statistics and pie charts. Doris arrived at our table and started taking away the salad plates so slowly that I was amazed it wasn't obvious to everyone else at the table.

"So," I asked, trying to be tactful, "it must be very difficult to decide on the books you're going to publish?"

Doris was at his shoulder like a soldier with a tower of salad plates. He didn't seem to notice her, but I was starting to sweat. He launched into another long speech about the number of manuscripts he has to read. He finished with, "There are only a select few that we can put our energy behind, and we work hard for those authors."

With those words, Doris sprung to life and grabbed at his plate before he'd even finished his salad and left him sitting there, holding his fork.

"Poor devils," she spat out without lowering her tone, and marched off.

He knitted his brow, trying to figure out Doris's comment. She was back again soon, filling up his glass of wine almost to the top and giving me a wink.

I tried my best to continue. "It must be difficult sorting through them all and having to write to them to let them know if you've accepted them or not."

With that comment, Doris slammed a plate of

lemon chicken in front of him. He looked at her, a little surprised, but continued talking as Doris very slowly made her way around the rest of the table, serving food.

"Oh yes, I have an assistant to do that. But between you and me, she is utterly hopeless."

"She sends out your letters?"

"Yes. I just couldn't possibly do them all myself."

One of the other occupants of the table turned to Doris and asked if he could get a refill of his water glass. She brushed him off coldly. "In a minute," she grunted as she continued to eavesdrop on our conversation.

It was as dessert was being served that the final straw came for Doris.

"Sometimes we have to send out thirty or forty rejection letters a week. I do have to read the most appalling stuff."

That was it. Doris snapped as she slammed down the crème brûlée in front of him.

"Why couldn't you just send one to us? We're at four hundred and seventy-five, for goodness' sake! We were a few months away from our rejection celebration, and the money was going to forgotten children. You could have easily put one in an envelope."

The whole table became silent at Doris's outburst.

"My dear," said Mark Gilbert, obviously used

to dealing with stroppy authors, "have I done something to offend you?"

"Yes, you have." She pulled me out of my chair and took the seat next to him. "You've accepted my manuscript and want to make a book out of it!"

He looked confused.

"How terrible of me. Let me offer my sincere regret at wanting to give you some money and get your life's work out to the masses."

"Exactly. As if anyone in their right mind wants that."

He started to laugh. "So why, exactly, did you send it to me if you didn't want it published?"

"All I wanted was number four hundred and seventy-six," she snapped back.

"Sorry? You've lost me."

"All I wanted was a rejection letter for my group, the Rejected Writers' Book Club of Island County!"

He raised his eyebrows and seemed to be enjoying this lively banter. "The who?"

"My rejection group. We collect rejection letters from publishers and keep them in a scrapbook. We're at nearly five hundred," added Doris proudly.

"Well, forgive me for liking it," he said, pouting and taking a sip of his wine. "What is the name of your masterpiece?"

"*Love in the Forest.*"

"*Love in the Forest*?" He screwed up his eyes as if he were trying to remember. "I don't think I know of that book."

"Yes, you do!" said Doris as she pulled out the acceptance letter and slammed it down on the table.

He pulled out a pair of Armani reading glasses and started to look over it. "Oh dear," he muttered as he finished it.

"Exactly. Isn't that the most depressing letter you've ever read?"

"Well, not normally for a writer, but that's not why I'm saying it. I'm saying it, my dear, because there has been the most awful mix-up."

Together they both said, "Andrea!"

He removed his glasses and sighed. "I'm hoping to publish a book called *Love of the Forest*. It's all about nature and trees. I adore trees."

Brian added, "He's a wildlife enthusiast."

"I don't understand," said Doris, now looking confused.

"What was your book about?" inquired Mark Gilbert.

"Jane Austen. She was abducted by aliens, time travels, and then goes back to the eighteenth century with a dishwasher."

He couldn't contain himself. He burst out laughing. "Oh, yes, I remember that one," he said, trying to regain his composure. "If you don't mind me saying, my dear, I think it needs a lot of work to find an audience."

"It's terrible!"

"I couldn't have put it better myself. I rejected that one a few weeks ago. How did you get this?" Then, suddenly, he slammed down his glasses. "If you got the acceptance letter, then what did the *Love of the Forest* author get?"

"My rejection letter, I bet," said Doris triumphantly.

"Oh dear," he said. "Excuse me. I must make a phone call." He threw down his napkin and started to leave the table.

Doris grabbed his arm. "I've got to get that version of my manuscript back. It's important. And could you promise me a rejection letter, please?" pleaded Doris, who appeared unable to let go of him.

He patted her hand, as if appeasing a small child. "It will be my greatest pleasure," he said, unpeeling her fingers one by one.

Doris was like a child with its first gift at Christmas. She was so excited that she knocked back the glass of wine she'd just poured for Brian, slammed it down on the table, and whooped.

Everyone at the table jumped. All at once, Doris's supervisor was behind her. Doris stood up and started collecting plates with a new skip in her step.

"I don't know about you," said Stacy's client,

"but I'm having the most wonderful time. Normally these conventions are pretty dull. But with all this entertainment . . ."

Stacy smiled awkwardly.

"Do introduce me to your guests," he said, gesturing at us.

Stacy begrudgingly introduced us all.

"My name is Dennis," he said with the excitement of someone joining a new group. "Tell me more about your rejection club." He took a sip of his white wine and listened intently as we related the details of the club and how it had started.

Just then, Mark Gilbert returned to his seat. He listened to the tail end of our conversation and commented, "There is a book in there, somewhere." Then he added, "Though I don't suggest you get your fearless leader to write it."

"Absolutely not," said Ethel, like a little terrier with a bone. The word "book" was a swear word for members of the Rejection Club.

Doris was now back, happy as a cricket and filling up our coffee cups.

Mark had a thought. "You know, if you want rejection letters, you should stay this afternoon for the pitching session. There are going to be literally hundreds of publishers here just waiting to reject your book."

Doris stopped in her tracks and almost dropped the coffee pot she was holding. She hoisted me out of my seat again; I was up and down like a whore's drawers.

"Tell me more," said Doris, as if she were a child engrossed in a bedtime story.

"This afternoon is the pitching part of the conference. Authors come from all over the country to pitch their stories." I think he actually had a soft spot for Doris. He seemed to enjoy her rough, forthright manner.

"Could I pitch mine and see if they hate it enough to reject it?" She was practically salivating.

"I can't see why not. It stinks!" He was obviously enjoying this fun turn of the tables when dealing with an author. "Do you have a copy of it with you? You could have them read the first page. That should be enough."

"I don't travel anywhere without it. You just never know when you might meet someone who might hate it. What time is the pitching session?"

"In about an hour. You'll have about five minutes with each to pitch."

"Right. I'm off to get ready."

Chapter Nineteen

A FISTFUL OF REJECTIONS

Doris was back five minutes later, out of breath, grasping an instruction sheet.

"We have work to do," she barked. "We need to find a photocopier to print out four copies of my first chapter and a stack of prewritten rejection letters for them to sign."

"There's a print shop just down the street," said Dennis, getting into the act.

"Janet and Annie, you get on that."

"Won't I need a badge to get back in?" asked Annie, putting away her knitting.

"Here, take mine," said Dennis. "I'm excited to help the cause."

Doris nodded gratefully. "Ethel and I will start spying out the land—you know, buying tickets and making a list of the publishers we can hit and mark all the ones we've already hit."

She made us sound like the mob.

She clapped her hands. "Come on, let's get going! We only have an hour!"

So, off we all went, like the Scooby-Doo gang.

We made our way to the print shop. From the counter I was greeted—"greeted" being a loose term; grunted at would be a better description—by a guy with a pin attached by a chain to his lip. The chain then moved up through a nostril until it ended up firmly anchored in his left eyebrow. On his neck, in blue ink, was the word "Whatever."

He blinked at me as if I were crazy as I dictated the rejection letter for the publishers to sign. Even when I tried to tell him about the club back home and our town party, he just looked at me, bewildered. It wasn't until I said I was from Washington State that something seemed to register.

"That's up in Alaska, right?" he said, gazing past me, all-knowing, now seeming to understand why I appeared so weird.

Starting back to the conference with Annie, I couldn't help but feel a sense of excitement. As crazy as all this was, I felt such a part of it all. Somewhere between being snowed in with Ronald the homeless billionaire and bouncing Ethel through a bathroom window, I'd actually started to bond with this group, and I was having too much fun.

Arriving back from the print shop exactly forty-five minutes later, armed with updated manuscript copies and rejection letters, Annie and I burst through the doors, out of breath. We ran smack into a familiar face, scattering papers like confetti around the foyer. As we stooped to pick them up, Andrea joined us on her knees.

"I'm so sorry!" blurted out Andrea, gathering up

papers with the speed of someone who did this sort of thing twelve times a day.

"I might have known it would be you," sniffed Doris as she sorted the papers into order.

"Oh! It's you ladies. I'm so glad to see some friendly faces here." She beamed as if we were old friends. "Nice to see you all again."

"Well," said Doris, her feathers appearing to be well and truly ruffled, "you wouldn't be looking into our friendly faces if it hadn't been for your mistake!"

Andrea flushed red as she climbed to her feet. "What on earth do you mean?"

"I mean, I am the author of *Love in the Forest*, the book you mixed up with *Love of the Forest!*"

Then Doris swept her up into a massive bear hug. It was disconcerting for all of us to watch. Maybe Doris was so upset that she was trying to squeeze the life out of her. But when she finally released the bewildered Andrea, Doris had a smile on her face.

"Thank you so much! Not only does your publisher hate it, but we also have a whole room full of publishers that are also going to hate it. We couldn't be happier."

She had no idea what Doris was talking about, but she pulled a manuscript from a pile in her arms, saying, "Mr. Gilbert asked me to return this to you. I didn't expect to do so in person, but here you go."

Doris yelled and hugged her again. Then, right there in the foyer, she started to rip the manuscript up into a million pieces, saying, "For Momma." Ripping a full manuscript was no easy feat, and it took a little time. All the while, Andrea giggled as writers all around the room gasped in horror.

"Now," said Doris as she finished, "battle stations. We need a quick powwow. Ethel and I have come up with a game plan."

She flagged us all over to a coffee stand, and we gathered around a table.

All about us in the foyer were people wearing blue nametags with the word "writer" on them. Each one was clutching bags and folders, waiting eagerly for the doors to open. I doubted any of them was gunning for a rejection letter, but that's what we were there pursuing.

Doris handed us all numbered tickets. "This is the plan. Behind those doors are literally dozens of rejections waiting for us. The goal is twenty-five. I want to go back to the club with all the rejection letters we could ever need."

Everyone at the table became animated. No one had thought about the potential of the conference. This could be a rejection jackpot for us.

"Everyone gets ten pitches. Here are the tickets. We'll all break off and scatter and try and get as many rejections as we can."

I was standing with my nose practically touching the door, holding a precious ticket, as if Willy

Wonka would be there any moment to collect it, when Stacy appeared again. I hated to admit it, but I'd almost forgotten about her.

"Mom, Dennis and I are going to get a coffee and talk through some of these layouts, okay?"

"Okay. I'm sure I can amuse myself."

I'd barely finished my sentence when the doors swung open and excited writers with bulging bags raced into the room. Swept up by the crowd, I felt a sense of excitement.

Rushing in, I found my assigned desk. As I caught my breath, I realized that I knew virtually nothing about Doris's book, the one I was supposed to now pitch to a publishing professional.

A sweet blonde girl with round apple cheeks and a businesslike expression extended her hand to me. Sitting down, I felt like a fraud. The expectancy in her eyes was palpable. I shuffled papers to play for time as she patiently asked, "So, what do you have for me?"

"Oh. It's a novel." I put down the first chapter in front of her. "In fact, it's a historical novel about Jane Austen."

She smiled and nodded as she started to read it.

"About her time traveling"—I struggled to get the rest of the words out—"being abducted by aliens, and . . . a . . . a . . . dish . . . washer."

That's when I lost her. Her eyes literally glazed over, with a "so it's going to be one of those days" expression.

My cheeks were starting to tingle with the beginnings of a hot flash. I pulled at my tracksuit collar aggressively as the feeling escalated. More than anything, I wanted to rip that darn thing off and sit there in my bra.

I stiffened, trying to gather a businesslike composure. "I realize it's not everybody's cup of tea."

"Yes," she nodded, rescuing me from my embarrassing monologue. "It definitely isn't mine. I publish recipe books!"

I laughed, an awkward "get me out of here" kind of a laugh.

"Thank goodness," I said, surprising both of us. "I have a letter here saying that you're not interested. Would you mind signing it so I can keep a check of all the publishers I've been to?"

She wrinkled up her nose and looked at the letter. "That's highly irregular. Normally I just say no."

"Yes . . . but I'm middle-aged and forgetful and . . ."

I was falling down a mountain into a cavern with no way of knowing how to stop myself.

She didn't look convinced by my explanation, I could tell, but she read the letter and signed it reluctantly. Then it was back to that professional smile.

"Good luck with your book," she said with an obvious lack of enthusiasm. And then she was looking over my shoulder for the next victim—er, writer.

As I headed for the main door, my knees were weak. I felt my heart beating out of my chest, and I was flashing like it was going out of fashion.

I headed to get a glass of water. As I downed it, I marveled at what was in my other hand. I was now an official rejected lady—with my very own letter. I started to get my second wind.

I saw Annie, Ethel, and Doris all smiling and waving their own letters. This was going to be a breeze.

Taking another ticket, I got back in line for another go-around. I was more confident now.

This time I found myself in front of a huge man with a bushy beard and a mass of unkempt, tangled brown curls. As I sat down, he beamed, revealing a huge gap between his teeth.

It gave him a rueful look.

"Hello there. Now, you look like a woman on a mission. Peter is my name. I hate these events, and I hate people pitching at me. So, why don't you tell me about yourself, and we can have a nice chat. Because, you see, even if you had the best book since *Harry Potter*, if I don't think we're going to get along, what's the point?" Then he let out an enormous belly laugh. "So, what's your name?"

Before I knew it, I was telling him the whole

story, all about the Rejection Club and the letters.

His eyes grew and his head nodded. "Sounds as if you've been on quite an adventure. Could be a book in there somewhere."

We chatted like old friends, and I ended up telling him all about my raccoons. He interrupted me.

"Peppermint oil," he stated with conviction.

"Sorry?" I asked, not quite following.

"Peppermint oil! Critters hate the smell of it and stay away. You can put it everywhere. And it smells lovely. And they hate it."

"Great," I said excitedly.

"We've just published a book about organic ways to keep away garden pests, and that peppermint oil works on almost all of them except carpenter ants—then you want cinnamon."

"Thank you."

"No problem. Now, where is that rejection letter you want me to sign? I hate your book, whatever it is."

He winked at me and flashed that gappy smile again. As I was leaving, he handed me his card.

"If ever you want to write something based on your swashbuckling adventures, I think we would get on just fine! So keep me in mind as your publisher."

"Thanks. I will." And with a skip in my step, I exited the room.

Chapter Twenty

AN EMERGENCY DASH

When I got back to the foyer, Stacy was waiting.

"Are you okay?"

"No, actually, I'm not." She looked weak.

I got her some water as she sat down.

"Maybe we should get you home. After all, this is your first day out, and you've done an awful lot. You don't want to overdo it."

"Dennis and I are nearly finished. We have a couple of more layouts to go over. He's here all the way from New York, so I want to make sure I give him all my time."

"Okay, but as soon as you're done, I think we should leave. I can always come back for the girls later."

She brushed me off as Dennis reappeared, and they left together. I joined the line again, but something about the way she seemed had concerned me. Her color wasn't right; she was really pale. I managed to go through the line another five times before she finally arrived back. She had gone from white to ashen.

"I think you're right, and I should go."

Something tightened in my stomach. "Okay. Let me find Doris."

Doris was at a table counting rejection letters. I handed mine to her, and she whooped with joy. "Twenty-eight," she screamed. "That's way over five hundred. The group will be so excited, and what a story we'll have to share."

Stacy appeared again. "Mom," she said, grabbing at my arm.

I looked at her face, and the blood drained from mine. She was sweating.

"I think I need to see my doctor. I've started cramping again."

We all froze. Everyone pedaled into action, everyone except me. I was frozen to the spot, terrified.

Doris took the lead. "I'll get the car," she announced, and she was off in the direction of the door.

Annie put her own sweater around Stacy's shoulders, and Ethel just stared at her.

Helping Stacy, slowly we made our way outside as Doris screeched the car to the front of the building. I climbed into the back with Stacy and squeezed her hand. As we started to drive away, Stacy let out a cry of pain. She never screamed out, even when she'd fallen off her swing set as a child and had to have six stitches in her head.

"Hurry," I said to Doris, who didn't need another word on the matter.

As she pulled the car onto the freeway, Stacy started shaking.

"Straight to the hospital," I said firmly over Doris's shoulder.

Doris eyed us both intently in the mirror and then nodded. Stacy tried to protest, but as she opened her mouth, she screamed instead. Annie encouraged her to take deep breaths. Stacy did as she was told. As she perched awkwardly on the end of the seat, she kept grabbing at the handrail for strength.

"Quickly, Doris!"

I felt the car speed up as Doris put her foot down harder. She pulled the car out into the fast lane. Out of the corner of my eye, I saw a flash of red, then heard the screech of brakes. There was the sound of metal crunching and a high-pitched whining, and then I was up in the air, like I was on a trampoline—a sudden feeling of weightlessness. Then everything went black.

When I came to, someone was taking my vitals, and I ached all over. Paramedics quickly whisked Stacy to the hospital first. Even though they couldn't let me travel in the ambulance with her, they assured me they would take good care of her.

Shaken but thankful to be alive, the rest of us rode in another ambulance to be assessed at the ER. I had a broken arm and a potential concussion, Doris had scrapes and bruises and a twisted ankle, Annie had bruised ribs and a gash in her leg, and

Ethel looked as if she hadn't been in a crash at all. She hadn't a scrape or a bruise on her anywhere. And with Stacy . . . we were still waiting to hear.

Flora and Dan suddenly appeared in the ER.

I was surprised to see them. "How did you know?"

"We were on our way back to Stacy's when we passed the scene of an accident and saw your car," remarked Dan with concern.

"We knew it couldn't be good, so we came straight here," added Flora.

We managed to piece together the information about the accident from a state trooper in the waiting room who'd taken statements from the crash. Apparently, somebody in a red sports car had pulled out sharply in front of Doris, causing her to brake to avoid hitting it.

"You then scraped the side of a cement block. I'm afraid your car is not looking good," added the state trooper.

Because of my concussion, the doctor wanted me to stay in overnight. Later that evening, Martin arrived on a late flight. I was so glad to see him.

"I still haven't heard any news on Stacy and the babies," I told him as soon as he came in. "I'm beside myself." He reassured me that he would find out and left me to rest. He came back later to tell me Stacy's contractions had stopped, and she was now sleeping. Relieved, I collapsed into a fitful sleep.

· · ·

The next morning, the doctor visited me to check on me.

"Hello there, Janet."

He was a balding guy with quick brown eyes, stylish glasses, and a bright, snazzy tie. He wouldn't have been out of place as a stand-up comedian.

"Hello, doctor."

"How are you feeling?"

"A little like my head is stuffed with cotton," I joked halfheartedly.

"I'm not surprised. You took quite a bump to your head. And your arm was broken in several places."

The doctor examined me and told me I was making considerable progress and that I would be able to take a walk down the ward to see Stacy later, but for now I was just to rest.

No such luck. I had barely closed my eyes when the walking wounded arrived. I actually heard them before they came in, clamoring and arguing out in the corridor. The door burst open and in came a wheelchair, with Doris lounging in it like the Queen of the North. She had pillows and blankets, a cane, and her leg up in a stirrup. She barked directions and orders to a sweaty Ethel, who was trying to guide the wheelchair. Right behind was Annie in another wheelchair pushed by Flora. It was like a day out for the infirm.

"Good, you're awake," said Doris, gesturing to Ethel to get her closer to the bed. "We have already checked on Stacy, and she is fine. We have so much to tell you."

I wondered if I closed my eyes, if they might think I was unconscious, though the minute I closed them, I felt a jab in my side. It was Doris's walking cane.

"I think you should try and stay awake now. I brought the cards. We can play gin!"

One hour, several hands of cards, and a round of Jell-O later, Doris eventually drew breath as she recounted her version of the accident and the paramedics, especially the cute one whom she said had taken a shine to her.

"It's my animal magnetism," she quipped. "I've always had trouble with it."

Ethel just blinked as I nearly choked on my second helping of Jell-O.

Doris went on to complain about the food, the hospital, the bed, and the view . . . What was she expecting from a hospital window? The beach?

I was so glad when Martin, who'd been out talking to Dan about the car, turned up to rescue me. Martin would get it towed back to the garage in Portland, where Dan said he could work on it. Then he could at least get it into some sort of shape to drive it home. I laughed weakly when he inquired, "So, how are you enjoying your road trip so far?"

"Oh, it's been an experience."

After my next visit with the doctor, I was given the okay to take a walk to visit Stacy. I made my way slowly and stiffly to her room. When I arrived, I opened the door to find her already sitting up in bed, and by her side, knitting, was Annie. They were giggling about something, Annie sniggering carefully because of her bruised bones. Stacy looked amazing. Radiant was more the word.

"Wow, Mom! You're up."

I nodded as Annie got up from her wheelchair, saying, "I'm off to check on the others."

"I couldn't come and see you. They won't let me get out of bed," Stacy grumbled. "I'm on complete bed rest for a week. It's very frustrating because I feel fine now."

I made my way to the bed and hugged her gently. "I'm so glad to see you looking so well."

Unexpected tears sprang to my eyes. Seeing them, she also started to mist up. My husband looked from one of us to the other and then said, "I'll leave you girls to it. I'm going to see what the café has for breakfast this morning."

Stacy reached out toward him.

"Thanks for everything, Dad. You have been great. I was so glad you were here to take care of me."

Martin looked choked up at her sincere grate-fulness and covered up his brimming emotion by coughing and nodding. Then he patted her leg and made his way out the door.

Once he'd left, I settled next to Stacy in a chair and took her hand. It didn't look that much different than when she'd been a child—a simple, white, youthful hand.

"What did the doctors say?" I asked, smiling.

I couldn't stop looking at her and thinking about how incredible she looked. I felt a wave of guilt as the tears started again. It had been me who'd told Doris to drive faster. What if I'd lost her or the babies?

"They say everything is fine now," she said, reading my expression as concern. "It was a little scary there for a while, and those first eight hours were terrible."

"I'm so sorry I wasn't there for you."

She squeezed my hand back tightly.

"Dad was here within a short time, and honestly, Annie has been amazing. She's really been taking care of me since I arrived."

"And the babies are fine?"

She started to tear up again. "Yes, they are. But something weird happened, Mom. As I lay here, hooked up to a monitor, listening to their little heartbeats and willing the contractions to stop, I realized I wanted those babies to live more than anything in the world. Up until now, all I could think about was how this pregnancy was going to change my perfect life for the worse. But suddenly it occurred to me that with all that fear, I hadn't once thought about the joy they were going to bring me. Annie and I have spent the last hour or so talking about all the wonderful things I have to look forward to. I just can't believe how selfish I was being before."

The tears were flowing freely now down both of our faces, and I couldn't resist hugging her. It was as we started sobbing that the door flew open. Standing in the doorway was her very disheveled, unshaven husband, Chris, carrying his suitcase. His face was ashen and grave. Seeing us both crying, his face registered fear.

Stacy reached out to him with her voice. "Everything is fine, Chris. The contractions have stopped, and the babies and I, we're all fine."

He came to her side and held her in his arms. I could see tears of relief in his eyes too.

"I'm going to see if I can find your father before he eats his way through the cafeteria," I said, excusing myself.

I wasn't sure if they heard me as I quietly exited the room. It felt like a new day.

Chapter Twenty-One

A PIÑATA HOMECOMING
ON CHILLY STREET

When we were released the next day, Stacy insisted that we stay at her house, as Chris was spending the majority of his time at the hospital anyway. Doris responded by sneaking bowls of home-cooked food in her large wicker basket when we went to visit. Annie spent her time knitting for the babies and chatting with Stacy at the hospital. Doris's only purpose in being there seemed to be to exasperate the nursing staff, with Ethel pushing her here and there in her wheelchair.

Stacy would be released the next day and was ordered home to total bed rest.

My husband had arranged airline tickets for us all to fly back to Seattle the next day. I knew Stacy would be ready for us to leave by then. And now Chris was home, so I knew he would take good care of her. I understood and really couldn't have done another three-day journey on the road, but once again, my fear of flying took a hold of me whenever I had a minute to think about it.

We had just one more night's stay in San Francisco, and we wanted to go to a hotel, but when we went to pick up Stacy, she once again insisted we all stay overnight at her house.

"I need the company," she confessed, more vulnerable than I had ever seen her.

I mused about her openness as I looked out on the streets of San Francisco. Their pastel-colored art deco neighborhoods were a cheerful and pleasing site. It showed some promise, her confession of needing companionship. Maybe there was some common ground where we could both plant a flag and hoist a tent. The chance for real connection, an impossible feat while she was still brushing me off or pushing me away under the guise of independence and detachment, was here. Maybe this visit would actually turn out well for a change.

As we pulled into Stacy's starched-white street, we were making small talk when she stopped mid-sentence. Her eyes widened, and she whispered what seemed to be a profanity. I followed her gaze. Even from the very end of her road, her house stood out like a pork chop at a bar mitzvah. It looked as if a six-year-old's birthday party had thrown up in her yard, with a multicolored explosion of balloons, streamers, and a large hand-painted banner that read "Welcome home!" I drew in my breath and girded myself for Stacy to explode. Instead, she burst into tears.

As the car pulled up in front of the house, Doris

and the girls gathered around like clucking hens to get Stacy's reaction. Before I could warn them, Annie pulled open the door, and they all shouted, "Surprise!" Everyone, that is, except Ethel. She just let off a party popper. I supposed that was instead of having to strain her face to look happy!

I waited for the eruption but was entirely thrown off guard when Stacy squealed, "How wonderful! Thank you all so much."

I thought for a minute I was hearing things. The girl who hated surprise parties and had once called balloons "of the devil" was happy! She climbed out of the car. I looked at my husband, whose jaw was also hanging open. I shrugged, shook my head, and followed the heaving mass into the house.

Once we were inside, Martin helped Chris put up a folding bed in the living room so Stacy could be a part of our conversation.

Doris and Ethel busied themselves in the kitchen, and I dropped off my things in my room. When I came back, everyone was occupied. Dan and my husband were chatting about the car; Annie, Stacy, and Flora were discussing baby names; and Ethel and Doris were cooking up a storm in the kitchen.

Suddenly feeling the urge for fresh air, I stepped out into Stacy's garden. It was delightful to breathe in fresh air and take in the late-afternoon scent. I was aching to get home once I heard Chris had been able to get time off work to take care of Stacy. Then, once again, I remembered I was going to have to fly the next day. Gulping, I started to feel a little lightheaded, so I sat down on a garden bench and closed my eyes, breathing deeply.

There was a gentle hand on my shoulder. It was Martin.

"How are you? I bet you're ready to go home."

"Oh yeah."

He smiled. "And home is ready to have you back."

"I'm just nervous. You know, about flying tomorrow."

He patted my hand. "I know. You could take one of those sedatives the doctor has given you to relax. I'm sure they'll help."

We sat on the bench together in a companionable silence. There was something so comfortable about that when you had been married as long as we had.

"Peppermint," I said, almost to myself.

He looked at me. "What?"

"Raccoons hate the scent. You sprinkle it around, and they leave you alone. One of the publishers I talked to just published a book about natural garden pest deterrents."

"Really?"

"Yes. I told you I would find a way. That's one

of the reasons I ended up at Doris's in the first place, and look, she led me to the answer."

We both started to laugh.

"There are easier ways of finding out answers." He slipped his arm around my shoulders. "Come on," he said, tapping me. "I don't want you to get cold out here. Let's go inside."

"Just give me one more minute to collect myself."

"Okay."

Getting up, he started to walk away. "I'll go and put the kettle on. So, we'll try peppermint, then. I hope that works. I've been worried about them eating our cat."

The words hovered over me for just a minute before I realized what he had said.

"Cat? We don't have a cat." At least not one I agreed to having, I thought.

He looked over his shoulder with a mischievous grin as he walked into the house. "You're going to love her!"

I didn't sleep particularly well that night. The cast on my arm was uncomfortable, and the thought of flying was really overwhelming me. So when I tiptoed out of bed at 5:00 a.m., leaving my husband still sleeping soundly, I expected to find myself alone in the kitchen. But Doris was there, her hair wound up in a large pink scarf, hobbling around the kitchen with a cane and one fluffy blue slipper on her good foot. She seemed startled when I opened the door.

"What are you doing creeping around at this time?"

"I could say the same to you," I joked back.

"I'm raising cinnamon rolls for breakfast," she said, obviously put out that her integrity was on trial.

As if to emphasize the seriousness of raising bread buns, Ethel thumped the ball of dough she was molding.

"I have to get started on them before everyone gets up so they'll be ready in time," Doris said, wagging a spatula at me.

Before she had even finished her sentence, Dan poked his head into the room.

"And what do you want?" she asked Dan, pointing her spatula at him.

He put his hands up in mock submission. "Don't shoot! Just a cup of coffee, and I'm out of here!"

It was obvious Doris did not like being caught in her nightwear with her buns half-baked. She sighed and banged dishes about while Dan and I made the quickest drinks ever, then returned to the safety of our rooms.

Lying in bed, watching the sun start to come up, I thought about the day ahead. Dan, Flora, and Martin were going to set out early and try to make it to Medford that day. The car would arrive later on via tow truck. The rest of us would be on a plane in about six hours. I shuddered at the thought.

A couple of hours later, Doris sent Ethel to knock on our doors. She informed me that breakfast would be ready in ten minutes and, as we all had an early start, we had better get a move on.

My husband was in the little en-suite bathroom, shaving. As I closed the door, he poked his head out.

"That Doris sure runs a slick ship."

"Tell me about it," I said. "She should have been in the marines."

As we sat down to breakfast, there was a buzz around the table. All Doris could talk about was how she was going to surprise the group when we got back with the announcement of the rejection letters. She was also a little chipper, as she had just spoken to Lavinia, and Gracie had perked up a little and had even summoned the strength to go out for one of her fairy teas. For the rest of us, even though we had only been away for just over a week, I think we were just excited to get home. To think I would be sleeping in my own bed tonight. That was a thought of sheer joy.

After breakfast was over, we all went to our rooms to pack. As Martin hugged me good-bye, he reminded me to take a sedative if I needed to. "The last thing you need is to be worrying."

As I waved them off, a monstrous tow truck trundled up into Stacy's clean, tidy neighborhood, like a blemish. A scruffy-looking guy with a day's growth of beard poked his head out the window and waved. He opened the door and was wearing a grubby T-shirt with the words "Whatsup" above an exposed, hairy belly that seemed to be desperately trying to fight its way out of the top of his jeans.

"Hey," he said loudly. "I'm your man. What have we got?"

I took him toward the car, and he whistled. "Wow, that's a mess. Who was driving? Evel Knievel?"

"I was, young man," said Doris, as she hobbled out with a cane.

"Wow, Grandma. Seems like you know how to party!"

Chapter Twenty-Two

SAUCEPANS, DRUGS, &
DORIS'S "SMALLS"

Doris had refused to part with any of her kitchen equipment and insisted on squeezing as much as she could in her main luggage, forcing us to distribute the rest between our bags. She packed her favorite pots and pans in her carry-on luggage and had Ethel take all her "smalls," as she called them. Though I was guessing the items in question were far from "small" in any form.

We climbed into Chris's truck, each clanging like a one-man band. The other thing that Doris guarded with her life was that bundle of rejection letters. Judging from the odd shape of her breasts, I was pretty sure that she had stuffed a couple down her bra that morning.

As we got all the paraphernalia in the car, I popped back inside to say good-bye to Stacy. I could tell she had been crying again. This was becoming a regular occurrence. I held her tightly and felt her body relax into mine. She spoke in a small voice that was barely above a whisper. "I'm scared."

"I know, but you're going to be fine. You're going to be a wonderful mother. Those babies have already proven their intention to stick around, so all you need to do is take really good care of yourself. No more high-powered work-related stress. And let Chris take care of you."

Then I said something I never thought I would ever say. "Want me to stay?"

She dried her eyes. "No, Mom, you need to go home and be with Dad. Chris has already talked to the lady who cleans for me. She has a college-aged daughter who's studying childcare, and she wants to come help."

I raised my eyebrows. "Wow, that's great!" Inside I was shocked. Letting someone into her world and home was a big deal.

"And, of course, I have Chris. You've been great too, Mom. Annie really speaks so highly of you, and seeing you through her eyes has made me view you differently. I always just saw you as my mother, the person doing her best to control my life. But as I've talked to Annie and heard her talk about how great you've been with all the ladies, I'm really proud to call you my mom."

You could have knocked me over with a feather. First, to hear Stacy talk this way and to know Annie thought so highly of me. I almost got teary myself.

Fortunately, Doris saved us. "Got any room in your case for my crockpot?" she asked, poking her head in the front door. "It's just broken Annie's zipper!"

Stacy and I burst out laughing, and she blew her nose.

I gathered myself up and kissed her on the forehead, just like I used to when she was a little girl. "See you soon."

The traveling, rattling circus set off. Doris placed herself up front to help Chris navigate, never mind the fact that he'd lived in San Francisco his whole life.

I took my medication; two tablets to be on the safe side. As they started to take hold, I found myself in a happy place.

We arrived at the airport and clanked in, making our way to the check-in desk. Doris pulled her suitcase onto the scales.

"Ma'am, you're going to have to redistribute. This is way too heavy."

Doris's face reddened. She was steamed. She pulled all of our suitcases onto the floor, and she conducted what could only be described as a three-ring circus. We were her performing animals. The comedy show was only made more entertaining as we helped each other with only half of our limbs in working order. The staff watched with amazement as she pulled out various pots and pans and cooking utensils and instructed us to redistribute them one by one into different suitcases, then demanded we weigh each one until they all eventually came under the weight. As she placed the last one on the scales after at least ten passes, the baggage handlers couldn't contain themselves and burst into spontaneous applause.

Doris huffed and gave the ticket handler her "don't you dare ask me to do anything else" stare.

The ticket handler responded with a plastic smile, saying, "Thank you for traveling with us today." Then he handed us our tickets.

If we thought that was the end of our problems, we were totally wrong.

We made our way to the x-ray machine. Fifteen minutes later, we were all lined up without our shoes, coats, belts, or dignity, waiting for a hulking guy with the name "Al" printed on his name badge to wave us all through the x-ray machine. As our bags passed through, I heard one of the x-ray people whistle and call out a code word to Al, who jumped into action. This was hard to watch, as Al was about four hundred pounds of wobbling mass. I didn't think he'd jumped since kindergarten. All at once, an alarm with a flashing light was activated. I thought maybe we were their millionth customers and would get free packets of airline nuts for life or something.

No such luck. The four of us were rushed off into a side bay faster than our little stocking feet could carry us. We were asked politely but firmly to identify our luggage. Then we were lined up in front of a table while Al and his sidekick, Betty—a skinny, scrappy blonde with too much red lipstick—asked if we were all together. We nodded, obviously. Standing there, I became aware that everything around me was spinning and moving unusually slowly. The drugs were clearly starting to kick in.

Doris spoke. "Young man, we have a plane to catch. I hope this isn't going to take long."

This obviously wasn't the right thing to say to Al. His eyes blazed as he answered her, "Ma'am, I can keep you here till doomsday if I want to."

"Oh, you wouldn't want Doris for that long," I said before I could stop myself.

I slammed my hand over my mouth, realizing I'd actually spoken my thoughts out loud.

Al thundered again. "Pardon, ma'am?" he asked, putting one hand on his hip.

"Don't pay any attention to her," said Doris. "She's all drugged up!"

He looked at us, and Betty looked like the cat that got the canary. We were probably the most exciting thing to happen to her in her scrappy blonde life.

"Open your cases," Al barked. His look lingered on me with intense interest.

We did what he said, and I managed to stop myself saluting him sarcastically, just in time.

These drugs were making me into a perfect floozy.

We opened our cases, and Betty and Al got to work. They started with Doris's and pulled out a rying pan, a spatula, and a corkscrew. Al placed them on the table in front of her and asked in an accusing tone, "So, exactly what are you planning to do with those?"

Doris looked at him incredulously. She straightened up, matching him in weight and stature. "What do you mean?"

"I mean, what were you planning to do with them?"

Doris snapped back, "What do you think I was planning to do with a frying pan and a spatula? Cook, of course! That's my best onion pan!"

"Likely story," sneered Al.

"What, exactly, are you insinuating?" asked Doris, her eyes squinting.

"I think you were planning to hit some poor, defenseless stewardess over the head with it and try to highjack the plane."

"And why would I want to do that? I want to get home, and I don't know how to drive a 777. Plus, you might have noticed my spatula isn't loaded!"

I couldn't help myself. I burst out laughing.

Al scowled at me, then said, "And as for you, hashhead, what goodies do you have in your bag?"

He pulled out a bag of various spices and powders, nodding his head in a knowing way, then pulled out half a bag of flour that just wouldn't fit in the main luggage.

"Aha! What do we have here?"

"Flour," I said, bursting out laughing again. I just couldn't seem to stop myself.

"Right," he said in a sarcastic tone and handed it all to Betty, who took it away to check it for explosives.

Then he opened Annie's case and pulled out fourteen balls of wool and three sets of knitting needles. He shook his head. Ultimately, he opened up Ethel's bag. The first thing he pulled out were Doris's "smalls." Let's just say they were very far from small. In fact, Ethel could have gone hang-gliding with them. Ethel blinked nervously as Al held them up, looking at the size of Doris's underwear and the size of Ethel. He whistled. "You ladies are a piece of work."

It took another thirty minutes, and a lot more explaining, but eventually it was evident, even to Al, no terrorist organization would be foolish enough to hire us. However, we did have to bag up Doris's kitchen utensils and put them in the luggage hold, much to her chagrin. The whole event meant that we had to run as fast as we could to our gate to catch our plane. Not a pretty sight at the best of times, we were now a tangled herd of gray hair, wobbling fat, and polyester hobbling toward the gate. With the drugs, I felt as if I were running in a bubble of pink gummy happiness. We arrived just as they were about to shut the gate, and it looked as if the ground staff was about to tell us we were too late when they saw the hardened expression on our faces and waved us through.

Once on the plane, we panted down the aisle, looking for our seats. We were on one row of four. When we got there, a balding, elderly man was sitting on the end of our row. Doris scowled at him.

"Young man," said Doris, who was way past nice as much as he was undoubtedly way past young, "I believe you are in our seat."

He looked up at her and blinked, then beamed.

"I probably am," he said in a perfect British accent, squinting at his ticket. "I always have a problem reading these numbers."

Ethel huffed and took the ticket off him, saying, "You're there." She pointed at the seat behind hers.

"Oh. So sorry to take the seat of such a lovely lady."

I heard Ethel make an inner grinding sound that was like catching her breath and snarling at the same time.

Annie giggled. "Why don't you sit in my seat?" she said, obviously enjoying the fun of the whole thing. "I'll take yours."

Ethel about had a kitten, and if looks could kill, Annie would have slumped over that chair right there and then.

He smiled. "Well, that would be lovely," he said. "I couldn't think of a nicer thing than to have

the opportunity to converse with such lov
ladies."

"I want the window seat," demanded Doris, lik
a small child.

I looked at my ticket and realized I had that seat.

"I don't like slopping out into the aisle," stated Doris indignantly, "and someone with my womanly figure would slop right out, and it's just not ladylike!"

What could you say to that? I handed over my ticket like a dutiful child and sat between Doris and Ethel. Doris started huffing, puffing, and fighting like a two-year-old in the middle of a tantrum with her safety belt when another stewardess with the same plastic smile arrived to do her cabin check.

"I need you to take your seat and buckle up, ma'am," she said in a singsong way to Doris.

Doris snapped back, "I would, but I seem to have some sort of child's safety belt. Do you have one that fits a real woman? I am not one of those anorexic supermodels that you're usually accustomed to have traveling on your airplanes!"

The flight attendant blinked twice and smiled again. Then, without a second's hesitation, she said, "Let me get you an extender." And *whoosh,* she was gone.

Even with the drugs, this flight was the longest I'd ever taken in my life. I dug my fingernails into the armrest on takeoff and never really relaxed whole way, which wasn't helped by Doris's ᵇed to bounce up and down all the time. Also, ᵗhough she wasn't slopping into the aisle, she was slopping into me. Ethel, who was sitting on the other side of me, kept gravitating toward me like a scared rabbit to get away from the English guy sitting on the end. He kept chatting to her and showing her pictures of his family and especially his wife. He explained that she had passed away a few years before and then added with a smile that she had looked just like Ethel.

It was on Doris's next bounce up that I felt extremely overwhelmed. It was hard enough for me to fly to begin with, without all this bouncing around. "I need to check out their kitchen facilities," she said, noticing my annoyance. "I might want one of those stale sandwiches I hear they always serve now on airplanes. I want to see if they need some help to prepare them and if their kitchen is clean. I like my sandwich to come from a very meticulous environment."

I huffed and got up for what felt like the thirtieth time. Then off she went, squeezing her bulk down the narrow aisle, taking wayward small children and anything not nailed down with her. She was like a snowplow; nothing stood a chance in her wake.

I was so happy to get to Seattle. I could see the relief in the flight attendants' faces too when we left the plane. We all boarded a shuttle bus from the airport back to the island, and Doris insisted on sitting up front in case the bus driver, who had been doing the trip three times a day for ten years, needed any help navigating. I knew how long he had been doing the route because he announced it more than once to Doris on our journey home.

Soon we were there. Lavinia was waiting in her midnight-blue Cadillac to pick us up from the shuttle. She whistled as she watched us getting off the bus with our casts and canes.

"My goodness, you girls sure know how to party." We clambered into her car as she added, "I need to make sure I come on the next road trip."

"You can take my seat," I whispered to her sarcastically.

"How's Momma?" asked Doris.

"She's okay," said Lavinia quietly. "She's resting right now, and Lottie's with her. This thing sure knocked the wind out of her sails, that's for sure."

Lavinia dropped off the other ladies, and we said our good-byes and then made our way to my house. I was so happy to see my little cottage. Lavinia helped me into the house with my bags, and I looked around with joy. It had that "my husband's been living alone" look. It wasn't that it wasn't tidy, just not cozy. I would enjoy spending the next day or so making my house my home again.

I was just surveying my kitchen when something brushed up against my leg. I screamed.

Lavinia came to my rescue. "It's a cat," she said laughing. "I didn't know you had one."

"I don't," I said, picking it up. Instantly, the cat snuggled down in my arms and started to purr contentedly.

"I think you do now," Lavinia said, ruffling the fur on the top of its head.

Chapter Twenty-Three

GRACIE'S STORY

As I lay in the rapturous comfort of my own bed a week later, I found myself feeling nothing but grateful. Grateful for my cottage, my family, and all the gifts I'd been blessed with in my life. It was Saturday morning, and I had absolutely nowhere to be.

Our cat, Raccoon (short for "Raccoon Bait"), jumped up onto the bed and nestled in close to me as the smell of strong coffee being brewed found its way up the stairs and swirled around my senses. I was home.

Martin was whistling in the kitchen, preparing a drink, and I enjoyed the simple pleasure of listening to him until the telephone ringing jarred me from my sweet reverie. I leaned up on one elbow, wondering if it was Stacy again. She had called nearly every day this week to update me on her progress; she really seemed to be enjoying her pregnancy now. It was wonderful that she seemed to want to include us in it.

Martin picked it up, and I heard him have a muffled conversation before he came into the bedroom and looked in on me.

"It's Doris. Do you want to speak to her? I could tell her you're still asleep."

"No, it's okay," I said as I yawned myself awake. "I'm coming."

As I pulled the covers from the side of the bed, I noticed that I didn't feel the usual sense of dread. In fact, when I looked back at the road trip now, it was with fondness. This group was much different than the world I'd known before in my prepackaged life in California. Days that had been filled with "doing lunch" and cocktail parties had been replaced by desperate phone calls on a Saturday morning, but there was something endearing about it all.

I pushed my feet into my slippers and pulled on my robe, saying to my husband as I passed him in the hallway, "I wonder what the crisis is today."

I picked up the phone and was greeted on the other end by a very calm and subdued Doris with none of her usual brashness.

"Janet, it's me. I have something very important I need to ask you."

Doris's dogs greeted me with their usual excitement, but this time I was prepared. I had on my full beach-walking coat that covered me completely and was washable. Ruffling their soft heads and stroking their sweet ears, I made my way up to the door.

Ethel opened it and just huffed when she saw it

was me. Putting my hand in my pocket, I pulled out a gift-wrapped package and handed it to her. She looked taken aback.

"It's for you, to say thank you for all your help with the group."

She blinked twice and then opened it. It was a little pin I'd made for her. It said "Rejected Writers' Book Club Helper."

She didn't say anything, but I could tell she was touched because she didn't flank me up the hallway as usual. She just took the pin and pinned it onto her scarf.

Once inside the living room, I noticed all the other ladies were there, and the atmosphere was hushed and expectant, not unlike the final minutes before a theater show is about to start, a feeling of anticipated excitement. The cake of the day was apparently carrot, but before Doris could push me down into a chair, I curled up in the orange bucket chair next to Lavinia, who greeted me like a long-lost friend.

"Oh my, Janet," she said, gingerly touching my arm. "How are you holding up, honey?"

I smiled. "It's not too bad. At least I can drive. How's Gracie doing?"

Lavinia smiled. "Better, much better. This is the best thing that could have happened to her. She's been holding all this in way too long."

Doris handed us both a piece of carrot cake, and I placed mine next to Lavinia's on the side table.

Everybody was now seated, except Gracie and Lottie.

Doris started the meeting. "As you know, this is a special meeting of the Rejected Writers' Book Club. Thank you all for coming. Because of the circumstances, I would like us to keep other business till the end and get straight to the reason we're here."

Everybody nodded in agreement.

"This has been hard for Momma, but since she decided to do this, there has been a lightness in her that I haven't seen in days. So let's begin. Ethel, could you go and tell Lottie that we're ready?"

Ethel disappeared, and two minutes later Gracie came into the room on Lottie's arm.

"I'm okay," she said buoyantly. "This is the best day of my life."

Her eyes shone with tears of relief, and it was hard not to tear up myself. Soft, rippled laughter filtered through the group, more of relief than joy.

"I'll take my usual place," she said, pointing her finger toward her wicker chair. "But I would be so happy, Lottie dear, if you might sit right here in case I need the support." She sat down and patted the empty chair next to her.

"That's exactly where I was planning to sit," said Lottie, finding her spot.

Gracie settled herself between the twins as they both took a hand and squeezed it. As if she had been strengthened by that one small gesture, she straightened up in her chair like a tiny teacher about to tell her class something very important. She cleared her throat and started to speak.

"Thank you all for coming. What I am about to tell you is a true story, a story about me. It has taken me seventy-one years to have the courage to tell it, so I plan to tell this only once, and I would appreciate it if it never, ever leaves this room."

Everyone nodded their heads in agreement that that would be the case.

"You can count on us, honey," cooed Lavinia.

"Lips are sealed," echoed Ruby.

Gracie took in a deep breath, letting it out slowly. "This is the story I have always wanted to tell in my memoirs ever since I started writing them down, but I never had the courage. But now, because the sordid details of my sister's story have come to light, I feel I need to set the record straight. And in doing so, I will honor someone, someone who meant a great deal to me, someone I should have honored a long time ago before now."

A single tear found its way down one of her porcelain cheeks. Lottie offered her a lacy hankie as tears seemed to find their way to all of us.

She giggled then and shook her head. "No, I'm not going to cry, because this is not a sad story. It's a very happy one. And it starts when I was just a little girl.

"I was born and grew up in a small village in England, which, in a lot of ways, wasn't that much different from Southlea Bay. Tucked in a hamlet on the south coast, I lived with my sister and my mother and father, who ran the local post office. It was the 1930s, and life was so much simpler then. My days were filled with climbing trees and catching sticklebacks in the stream. Books didn't come on computers, and food didn't make you sick. We worked hard, and we respected our elders.

"Our little village was so tiny that my school was located in one large room in the back of our local church. There were a set of desks for each of the years, and there were no more than five or six pupils for each of those."

She started to giggle again.

"So that gives you an idea of how big our little town was. Our school had a heavy oak door and thick, smooth slabs of polished gray limestone that made up the walls and floor. It was a drafty old place, but I loved it. I loved the history of it; I loved walking up the hill at the far end of our village just to get to it every day. I was always fascinated by all the figures depicted in the tall, arched stained-glass windows. Back then, I believed they had all been painted there just to welcome me to school every day. Walking into the building, I would feel delighted by the smell of wax and dust that greeted me in the morning.

Every Wednesday, the local choir rehearsed in the front of the church, and their angelic sounds would find their way back to us in our schoolroom. I would often close my eyes and listen to them as I worked on a story or my sums, believing that the filtered voices drifting from the sanctuary were singing just for me. But I have to admit, my most favorite part of my church/school was the steeple. My desk was positioned right underneath it, and if I looked straight up, I could just catch a glimpse into the bell tower.

"I would gaze up there and constantly fantasize about coming to school early one day when no one was about. Then I would race up the stone spiral staircase that sloped all the way to the top and ring the bells with all my might. I think I would still do that if I got the chance," she added with a mischievous twinkle and then took a deep, easy breath.

"Well, it was the summer of 1933, and I'd just turned twelve years old. My mum had made me a new blue cotton dress for my birthday, and I was in love with it. It was such a treat to have new clothes, and normally I kept them only for best. Sundays and special occasions, Mum would say. But I loved the blue of this dress so much that, once she'd finished making it, I carried on something terrible. I pleaded with her to let me wear it, just this once to school, and eventually, exasperated, she'd given in.

"The day this story starts, I was staring down at this dress when the big wooden door with its heavy iron latch into the church opened, and he arrived . . . Douglas . . ."

She said his name slowly, savoring it, as if she liked the sound of it, as if she'd wanted to say that name for a very long time.

"Now, I didn't see him come in because I was looking at that dress, and I didn't even know he was there until he sat down next to me. My best friend, Mary, was sick that day and that was normally her seat, so I do remember that when he sat down, I felt angry that someone was now sitting in Mary's place. But the teacher told him to sit there, so he did.

"The first thing I noticed about him was his hair. He had the blackest hair I'd ever seen. Not mousey-brown like so many of the other boys, but thick and black, like a raven. I watched him curiously as he settled himself at his desk. He was strange to me. We didn't get many new people in our village, and so he fascinated me. He pulled his pencil case out of his satchel and looked around the classroom. As he looked up, he had the most striking blue eyes. They reminded me of a marble I'd once owned that had come all the way from Germany for one of my birthdays from a distant relative. I was thinking about that marble when the teacher introduced him to the class. 'This is Douglas McKenna. He said he has come from a long way away in Scotland, so we will treat him kindly, as he is new and doesn't know anyone here.' When the teacher spoke Douglas's name, his face reddened, and his quick blue eyes flashed around the classroom, as if he was trying to figure out whom he could trust.

"The teacher then went on to say that one of us would be assigned to take care of Douglas for the day and show him where to go for lunch and help him find the playground. Then, before anyone could even volunteer, our teacher was saying my name and saying I would have to take care of him. I remember thinking I didn't want to take care of a boy, not one that was sitting in Mary's seat and was going to want to follow me around all day. I didn't know any boy games, and I didn't want to start playing them.

"I got up from my desk then, as we had to go out on the field for recess, and he followed me. Turning to him, I said, 'I've got you, and I wish I didn't, but I've got you all the same.'

"The minute I said it, I regretted it because I saw the hurt in those lovely blue eyes, and I realized I was just angry because he'd taken Mary's seat. So after that I tried to be nicer to him and showed him the bathroom and the playground and the place we went to for lunch. He hardly spoke, but when he did, he would just say, 'Thank you, Gracie,' in his thick Scottish accent, and I found I liked the way that he said my name. It sounded so different to me. I wanted to tell him that my name was really just 'Grace,' but I found I liked the way he rolled the *r* and over-pronounced the *e*. It made my name sound exotic somehow, as if I was a person you would read about in a book, so I never corrected him.

"Eventually, he found a group of lads to play with, and when Mary came back, the teacher moved him to a different spot. I was glad to have Mary where she belonged, next to me. And that was that for a while.

"Then, as we all grew up, there were so few of us our age in the village that we would often all do things together as a group, like play table tennis or watch a movie. Sometimes Douglas would hang around with us. He had a hearing problem, so you had to look straight at him to talk, but he never let it hold him back. He was fun and charming, always kidding around and boisterous. He was very dashing too, and Mary liked him a lot.

"One day the guys had wanted to go out on little boats that were moored up at the village pond. Silly, really. We were about sixteen, maybe seventeen, and we had one of those mad adolescent moments. We all just grabbed a boat and jumped in. Mary and I found one, and she pulled Douglas into ours to be our rower. He obliged, and we all had a merry time playing around. That was, until Mary stood up and for fun started rocking the boat. It turned over and in we all went.

"The pond wasn't very large, but it was deep, so Mary just swam to the bank. But I couldn't swim and I hadn't wanted to tell anybody, as I was too embarrassed to admit it. So when the boat tipped, I panicked, trying desperately to keep my head above the water. I went under a couple of times. I thought no one had seen me and that I was going to drown right there and then, when suddenly I felt an arm around me, an arm around my waist, pulling me up toward the surface. And then I could see the light again. I was so grateful that I clung to my hero as hard as I could. It was Douglas. He lifted my head above the water with his hand under my chin, saying, 'Don't worry, Gracie, I've got you.' Then he added with a chuckle, 'And I wish I didn't, but I've got you all the same.' I didn't really think about it till later, but when I did, I felt ashamed because those were the first words I'd said to him all those years ago when we'd first met.

"So, he swam with me to the bank, which could have only taken a few minutes, but it felt like an eternity to me. Probably because I was so scared. My face was so close to him, I could hear him breathing as he swam. His thick black hair was like a mop floating in the water next to me. I remember thinking, even though I was petrified, that I wanted to reach out and just touch that hair just once while I was so close . . ."

Gracie giggled then, saying, "But I didn't. He got me to the bank, and someone put a coat around me, but I did get a cold and had to stay in for a couple of days.

"One day after that, Douglas came to visit me. I remember how shocked I was when I saw him at the door. I'd been sitting by the fire in an old cardy, as my mum always called them. My nose was running and my eyes were red, and I was feeling pretty miserable. When I heard the knock on the door, I thought it was the baker, who was due to drop off bread that day, so I opened it without even thinking, and there on the doorstep was Douglas.

"Well, I wanted to die," added Gracie, looking straight at Lavinia.

"Absolutely," added Lavinia. "No lady wants to be caught in her cardy."

The group laughed then, and I noticed Gracie was becoming more and more buoyant as the story went on, as if in telling it she were being released from the power of the past.

Doris topped up our tea, and I actually took a bite of the carrot cake.

"Anyhow, I didn't let him in. It wasn't the done thing when a girl was alone at home, but he said he'd just come to check on me, and I was so touched. Something was ignited in me that day. I found that whenever we were out as a group, I would find myself looking for him, trying to get closer to him whenever we were together.

"One day, we all went to a village dance together for a lark. Mary had been dancing with Douglas, and I had taken a turn around the dance floor a couple of times with some of the other local boys. When Mary and Douglas returned to the table, he was raucous, and she was exhausted.

"He was saying, 'Is that all you have in you, Mary? I could go another two or three at least.' Mary was laughing and said, 'Not with me, you won't. Why don't you take Grace around instead?' I felt my heart leap in my chest.

"Mary pushed me to my feet, and before I knew what was happening, I was in Douglas's arms, and we were on the dance floor. At first, we were both a little tongue-tied. I know my face was beet-red, but he eased me by telling me he would try not to step on my feet, and we laughed. But as my body got closer to his, there was an electric energy between us, one I can't even explain to this day, a merging of our souls that can't be expressed in words. As our bodies circled around the dance floor, it was as if on each turn, we were becoming closer and closer to becoming one person. I know he felt it too. I could hear his heart pounding in his chest. It was as if a magnetic force was willing us together.

"We didn't dance again, but in my mind, that was the beginning for Douglas and me. Something had awakened, something that was a little fearful for both of us, I believe.

"At the end of the night, we all walked home. Mary wasn't feeling well, so Douglas and I walked her home first to make sure she got back okay. I also think secretly I'd wanted to be with Douglas alone. Once Mary went in, we looked at one another on the doorstep, and he said, 'I should walk you home,' and I nodded. We talked as we walked, and normally when we were together with the group it would have been all fun and light, but this was different, more careful, purposeful. Just a short distance from my house, I lost my footing on some broken stones, and he grabbed me again saying, 'I've got you.' I responded, laughing, 'Don't tell me, you wish you didn't?' His blue eyes met mine, and we both said together, 'But I've got you all the same.' And we laughed.

"He held my hand then and didn't let it go, and we didn't speak for a minute. Then he said, 'Gracie, there's something I want to ask you.' My heart was pounding through my chest, and I didn't want him to keep speaking, but he did. We paused under a large oak tree that grew on the edge of our town. I remember thinking that it was all so romantic."

She giggled once again, as she added, "Then he said, 'Gracie, I would like to kiss you.' I almost laughed then. He said it in such a proper way." Gracie repeated the words again, this time matching them with a perfect Scottish accent. " 'Why don't you, then?' I said, and he reached

down and gently stroked my face, looking into m
eyes as if he wanted to remember that momen
forever. Then he kissed me. And it was lovely,"
said Gracie, her voice becoming dry with
emotion. "I think I need a minute," she said,
clutching her hankie to her chest.

"I think we all do," said Lavinia. "I'm perspiring
like a racehorse."

"Let's take a short break," said Doris.

As we got back together ten minutes later, the
mood in the room was so much lighter. The door
was now open, and Gracie seemed to be enjoying
herself. After we'd all had another cup of tea and
finished our cake, Gracie returned to full storytelling mode.

"Where was I?" she said, getting comfortable in
her favorite chair.

"In my favorite place, the throes of passion,"
joked Lavinia.

"Oh yes. Well, when I got home I realized that it
was a big mistake, and I knew that Mary was
totally smitten with him. So I decided to put him
out of my head. The next time I saw him, we were
both embarrassed and agreed that we'd just got
swept up by the moment. I think we both knew it
wasn't the case, but neither of us had the heart to
hurt Mary.

"Then the war started, and everything changed.
Most of our young men went off to fight, but
because of Douglas's hearing problems, he had to

ay behind. So he worked for the home guard and used his own tiny fishing boat to ferry soldiers to and from France whenever they needed him. He and Mary decided to get engaged, and I remember my feelings were mixed. I was so happy for them both but still felt a yearning. There was something unsatisfied in me.

"Then the GIs came to town, and our world turned upside down. I remember the feeling of excitement as they arrived. Strong and full of confidence, they lifted our spirits, and we were all a little in awe of them. And that's when I met Doris's father, the dashing William Jonathon Miller, whom everyone called Will. He told me later that he'd wanted to marry me the very first day we met. I'd been helping Mum in the post office when he came in to post a letter home. He'd been so brazen and charming, refusing to leave the post office until I agreed to go out with him to a dance they were having in town to welcome the GIs. He was larger-than-life and a hoot to be around, and before I knew it, I was having so much fun with him. It had been such a long few years, and we had been working so hard for the war effort, it was nice to take a break and enjoy a breath of fresh air.

"Then, in a moment of craziness, he proposed to me, and I found myself saying yes, as I loved being around him. He made me laugh all the time. Then he was shipped out. I remember how devastated I was when he left, frightened that I might never see him again. We wrote to each other constantly. Then, when he was listed missing in action, I took to my bed for a week. My mum would try and tempt me with all sorts of treats, but I was heartbroken. I just kept the letters he had written under my pillow. I convinced myself he was dead. Somehow, it was easier that way, because if he was still alive, I believed he would have found me to tell me. So instead I decided he wasn't coming back—so many didn't—and to hold out hope just hurt somehow.

"One day I decided to take a walk out and found myself at that little duck pond I'd almost drowned in. As I sat staring into the water, I became aware of a familiar presence next to me on the bench. It was Douglas. I was thrilled to see him; with the busyness of the war, I hadn't seen him for months. 'Not thinking of throwing yourself in, I hope,' he said mischievously, 'because I'm not wearing the best clothes to save you today.' We both laughed.

"He'd been busy ferrying soldiers back and forth to France. Mary had also been busy volunteering at the local hospital, and I hadn't even seen her for about six weeks either. It was then that he told me he and Mary weren't together anymore; apparently, she'd met someone in the hospital who won her heart. The Florence Nightingale effect, I believe they call it now.

"Douglas and I were now both alone, and we

needed someone. The constant loss of war was all around us, and it made you want to hold on to anything that was good and safe. We started to see each other, just as friends at first. We would go to the pictures or out to eat. However, whenever we would get close, that same electricity was still there. We carefully chose to keep our distance, as we were both still in a lot of pain. Then, one day, something happened.

"We'd got caught in a downpour and had to run to a bus shelter to get out of the rain. He'd taken off his raincoat to put around my shoulders, and as he did, I looked up into his dripping wet face and found, more than anything, that I wanted to kiss him. His eyes were full of fear, as if maybe he felt the same way and didn't know what to do about it. He was about to back away when I said, 'Douglas, there's something I want to ask you.'

"'What?' I remember his tone was serious as he looked down at me.

"I gazed back up at him, saying, 'I would like to kiss you.' He'd smiled back, remembering that day, years before. He appeared to hesitate for just a minute before his lips were upon mine. Both of us were so hungry for love, both of us hurt and lonely; it was inevitable, I suppose. So much loss and hurt all around us."

Gracie stopped, lost deep in her thoughts, and then she added in a quiet, gentle voice, "It was one of the most passionate times in my life,

and we couldn't get enough of each other, b
contrary to my sister's lies, he was the perfec
gentleman and never took advantage of me."
Gracie took a sip of her tea thoughtfully before
saying, "He asked me to marry him over and
over again, but I was still engaged to William and
felt a sense of obligation. Until there was the
final letter telling me he was officially dead, it
just didn't seem proper."

She giggled then.

"Funny, there I was having a passionate relationship with Douglas, and it didn't seem proper to
give up on an engagement my heart had already
let go of. We were so full of ideals back then and
making sure we all did the proper thing. That time
with Douglas was a wonderful time, a window of
joy in a time of so much sadness."

She took a sip of water and then her eyes
clouded over as she added, "Until the day Douglas
went away from me. He'd been in the post office
that morning and was trying to talk me into going
out with him that evening to see a movie. I needed
to stay at home, as my mother was sick. As we
bantered playfully, the post arrived, and there
was something in it for me from America. I was
surprised, as, apart from Will, I didn't know
anyone in the United States. It was from Will's
mother. He was alive, and she'd been trying to
locate me to let me know he'd only just been
transported from a French field hospital.

"I couldn't believe it. It was with such mixed feelings I received the news. I was overjoyed that he was alive but not sure how I felt about Will anymore. Douglas, however, was not so overjoyed, and we quarreled. He wanted me to choose between them, and I couldn't. I loved both men in different ways.

"Douglas left the post office that day, and that night the D-Day invasions began. Douglas was called to collect soldiers all night from the beaches in Normandy. On his last run, his boat was attacked, and he was badly injured. He was sent to the hospital that Mary worked at, and she told me right away.

"I raced that night to his side. I didn't think he was going to wake up, and I really needed him to wake up. I wanted to say how sorry I was and to tell him that I'd chosen him and that I loved him. I waited all day and all night for him to open his eyes. I waited until I finally fell asleep across his bed.

"Late that night there was an air raid, and the whole hospital was rocked. I jumped up when a bomb dropped nearby, nearly knocking me off my feet. Then I felt a hand take my arm, and I heard Douglas say, 'I have you, Gracie. Don't worry, I have you.' I was so glad to see his eyes open that, even with the air raid going on all around us, I sobbed and pulled him close and kissed him all over his face. 'Don't leave,' I shouted through the noise. 'I love you and I'm sorry.' He nodded and smiled before his eyes closed for the final time.

"William arrived the next day to the same hospital that Douglas died in that night. He was so glad to see me, and in a way, I was so glad to see him. As I held him, I thought how the grief of losing Will had thrown me into Douglas's arms and now the loss of Douglas had thrown me into the arms of Will. It made me wonder if there is much difference in our hearts between love and grief. They both have a yearning that seems unable to be satisfied. When I eventually married Will, I never regretted it. He gave me Doris, and he made me very happy. He was a wonderful, warm, larger-than-life human being, and I felt lucky to have found not one, but two amazing men to love in my life.

"I went to Douglas's funeral a week after he died. As I was leaving the church, the same church we'd met at all those years ago, I put my hands on his coffin, and I whispered to it, 'I have you, Douglas. I wish I didn't, because it hurts so much, but I've got you all the same.'"

Gracie stopped then as the raw emotion swept through the whole room. She pulled her little lace hankie into her chest, saying, "And I do have him, till this day. I have him right here."

We all wept together in quiet companionship, taking in this amazing story. Then, slowly, Lavinia took my hand. I knew instinctively what she was doing, and I took Ruby's, and slowly the whole circle of ladies followed suit. Then Lavinia started very slowly and everyone joined in,

"Selected for rejection
We reach for true connection
Choosing a path of celebration
As we bond . . ."

We all paused then. I think the words caught in our throats as we finished the promise,

"With true affection."

We stayed at Doris's awhile longer. We laughed, we hugged, we ate cake, and we went home.

"How was the crazies'?" asked my husband, not looking up from the newspaper as I walked in that evening.

I couldn't answer, and he finally looked up and noticed my red, puffy eyes.

"What?"

"I love them," I said, bursting into tears again.

He looked bemused as I fell into his arms, sobbing.

He pulled me in close and shook his head, saying, "Yep, never a dull moment living with you, Janet Johnson, that's for sure."

EPILOGUE

The invitation came in the mail one week later in a crisp, white envelope. I knew who'd sent it before I'd even opened it because Doris had written a note on the back in black marker which read: "Don't forget, you MUST REPLY!!!!" Then, under that, in pencil, Mrs. Barber, the post lady, had drawn a little arrow toward it and scribbled the words, "Sorry about this. I'm going to talk to Doris about defacing her envelopes. However, she sounds serious, so I would respond if I were you!"

I shook my head. That was a small town for you, all watching out for each other while also butting in. Raccoon nuzzled up against my legs as I opened the letter. It was indeed Doris's official invitation to the Rejectathon. She had been boiling up the town about it all month. She wanted it to be a big, flashy affair. It read:

> The Rejected Writers' Book Club of Island County requests the pleasure of your company at the Reflection and Connection in aid of the Rejected Children's Fund of Island County.
> Place: Southlea Bay library
> Day: Saturday, December 3
> at 6:00 p.m. (sharp)

Please bring your partners and all your gifts of rejection. There will be a home-made trophy for the most Rejected Super Star of Southlea Bay.

Please RSVP (soon, I need to know the numbers!)

Kind regards, Doris Newberry

PS: This is a very fancy affair, as I have a hand in the catering, so make sure you all get dressed up.

Then she'd added a note to my letter, also in black marker:

Janet, don't even think about wearing those gray pants you're so fond of!

PPS: Remember, respond soon, like now.

So why are you still reading?

I found myself jumping up to get a pen to write straight back to her. I couldn't believe she could still boss me around through a letter.

I waved the invitation at my husband as he came in from closing up the chickens.

"I have news."

"Me too!" he answered, all excited. "Day sixteen of Raccoon Watch and not a sign of them. That peppermint oil is working great!"

"Good, but that's not as exciting as mine. We've been invited to a party."

"Oh," he said, mildly impressed. "Who's doing the honors?"

"Doris Newberry."

"Oh," he responded, his tone audibly dropping to disappointment. Then he added, petulantly, like a small child, "Do I have to go?"

I gave him the "yes, you have to go" look, and he sighed, walked into the kitchen, and made himself a cup of coffee.

"Okay," he said meekly, giving in. "Can I wear my jeans?"

"Of course, if you're interested in Doris Newberry rearranging various parts of your body! Apparently the food she wants to make is very fancy-schmancy."

He smirked and took the invitation from me.

"Then I guess I'd better get out my party suit."

The week of the big event, the party had been the talk of the town, and the thrift store was completely out of glad rags and evening bags, according to Mrs. Barber at the post office. "They've made a whopping profit over in that Second Glance store," she'd informed me as I was buying stamps one day.

On the evening of the event, we drove early into town, and even though it was dark, a full, luminous moon highlighted the tips of the waves as they jostled jovially in its beams. We passed the florist and Ruby-Skye's Knitting Emporium. I noted that the Crabapple Diner was unusually quiet. Apparently, Doris had talked the owners into hosting the after-event refreshments. It was rumored that she had wanted all her own recipes cooked for the party and had driven the staff batty all week running in and out of the kitchen, testing dishes and barking her orders.

As we made our way up the hill, the library building was a glowing, welcoming sight and already a bustling hive of activity.

As soon as we were in the door, Doris put us to work. Martin blew up balloons while I checked in the rejection contestants. They all had ten minutes of stage time to dazzle the judges—Ethel and Doris—with their feats of failures. The biggest reject of the night would be presented with a homemade trophy from the worst artist in our community.

The competition was a lot of small-town fun at its best, and we raised over six hundred dollars for the Children's Fund. Over the two-hour event, many odd, disheveled, and frightful things were paraded out. Blackened sunken cakes, curtains with huge puckers, uneven homemade woodwork projects, and even waitress Gladys was there with a menagerie of crispy, black houseplants that apparently couldn't survive more than two days in her house before they curled up their roots and died.

The winner was Mr. Fritz, a one-legged German landscape painter with a white beard and an overextended laugh. He stole the night by dancing the worst polka ever with more gusto than people who weren't sporting one leg made of wood.

Once we finished the library event, we all paraded over to the Crab to eat. After a very pleasant meal, Doris got to her feet and banged a gavel on her table.

"I just have a couple of things to say. Firstly, I want to say how proud of you all I am and how this dinner and the bond we share wouldn't have been possible if it wasn't for the fact that we've all failed so miserably!"

There was a ripple of laughter around the room.

"But there are also some people I feel I need to acknowledge at this time. When my own group of rejects was in trouble, they helped me keep it going. Those are the ladies of the Rejected Writers' Book Club. Also, Flora's new beau, Dan, who helped us out."

Everyone clapped, and Flora beamed at Dan, who had come to Southlea Bay for the occasion. Stacy had also hinted that she had wanted to be here, but the doctors wouldn't let her travel. The good news was that her babies were thriving, and she had felt them move for the first time that morning.

"And lastly," continued Doris as the hubbub died down, "I want to thank a lady who isn't even member of our Rejected Writers' Book Club, but e couldn't have achieved this success without her help. Our local Southlea Bay librarian, Janet Johnson."

Everybody cheered and clapped in my direction.

"In fact," Doris added, "we have also decided to bestow a very special honor on Janet to say thank you for all she has done for us. So, even though Janet has never been rejected, we would like to make her an honorary member of our group so she will be able to meet with us all every month."

"Oh no," I said through gritted teeth to my husband as I nodded my thanks.

"So, Janet," Doris continued with gusto, "if you would like to come up here, we have something special we would like to give you."

My husband pushed me to my feet with utter glee at my displeasure. He was having way too much fun at my expense. "Off you go to join your tribe, newest member of the Rejected Writers' Book Club."

I kicked him playfully as I got to my feet and walked to the front of the table. As I approached her, Doris picked up a huge homemade pin from the table, which she proceeded to pin to my dress. It read: "Honorary Rejected Lady." Everyone clapped and cheered again.

"I don't know what to say. I'm speechless."

"Don't worry, dear," Doris whispered in my ear

while squeezing my arm. "We'll have plenty of time to talk next Friday when we see you at your first official meeting of the Rejected Writers' Book Club. I bet you can't wait."

"I can't," I admitted honestly, as I looked around at all those happy, smiling people, including one who was shaking his head and laughing.

ACKNOWLEDGMENTS

When I started writing my first novel, I was under some strange illusion that just one person created a book. As I have come to realize in the four years it has taken me to bring this book to fruition, writing a novel is nothing akin to giving birth sideways, and you just couldn't achieve it without a village of people, a village not unlike Southlea Bay. I want to thank all my cheerleaders, editors, and readers, which include Audrey Mackaman, Eric Mulholland, Melinda Mack, Shauna Buchet, Tina Joselyn, Tracy Huffman, K. J. Waters, Susan Hanzelka, Susan Jenson, Rowena Williamson, Dana Linn, and Susannah Rose Woods. My fabulous original book cover team from Blondie's Custom Book Covers, K. J. Waters and Jody Smyers of Jody Smyers Photography. My amazing models drove through a red dust storm to get to the photo shoot for the original cover; thank you so much for your time and enthusiasm, Mary Johnson, Kate Delevan, Taylor Boudreau, Sandy James, Marjan Wilkins, and Ann Thompson. Also, special thanks to Andrea Hurst of Andrea Hurst Literary Agency, who encouraged me to keep going when I had actually given up on the book because "it just wasn't funny." All my amazing family and friends on this coast and in the UK have always been incredible cheering team. My husband, Matthe and son, Christopher, supported me even when was getting up at five o'clock in the morning and going to bed at eleven o'clock at night just to get it finished, and believe me, I wasn't very funny then either. And to all of you, thank you for buying this book. My hope is you will find your own version of Southlea Bay in whatever form that is for you, a community of loving, caring souls with just enough small-town mentality to be wonderful and infuriating all at the same time.

ABOUT THE AUTHOR

Suzanne Kelman is the author of the Southlea Bay series and an award-winning screenwriter. Born in Scotland and raised in the United Kingdom, she now lives in the United States in her own version of Southlea Bay, Washington, with her husband, Matthew; her son, Christopher; and a menagerie of rescued animals. She enjoys tap dancing, theater, and high teas, and she can sing the first verse of "Puff, the Magic Dragon" backward.

Center Point Large Print
600 Brooks Road / PO Box 1
Thorndike, ME 04986-0001 USA

(207) 568-3717

US & Canada:
1 800 929-9108
www.centerpointlargeprint.com